The Adventures of Gurudeva
and other stories

The Adventures of Gurudeva

AND OTHER STORIES

Seepersad Naipaul

With a Foreword by V. S. NAIPAUL

ANDRE DEUTSCH

First published 1976 by
André Deutsch Limited
105 Great Russell Street London WCI

Printed in Great Britain by
Cox & Wyman Limited
London, Fakenham and Reading

ISBN 0 233 96758 3

Contents

Foreword

My father, Seepersad Naipaul, who was a journalist on the *Trinidad Guardian* for most of his working life, published a small collection of his short stories in Trinidad in 1943. He was thirty-six; he had been a journalist off and on for fourteen years and had been writing stories for five. The booklet he put together, some seventy pages long, was called *Gurudeva and other Indian Tales*; and it was my introduction to book-making. The printing was done, slowly, by the Guardian Commercial Printery; my father brought the proofs home bit by bit in his jacket pocket; and I shared his hysteria when the linotypists, falling into everyday ways, set – permanently, as it turned out – two of the stories in narrow newspaper-style columns.

The book, when it was published, drew one or two letters of abuse from people who thought that my father had written damagingly of our Indian community. There also came a letter many pages long, closely written in inks of different colours, the handwriting sloping this way and that, from a religion-crazed Muslim. This man later bought space in the *Trinidad Guardian* to print his photograph, with the query: *Who is this* [here he gave his name] ? And so, at the age of eleven, with the publication of my father's book, I was given the beginnings of the main character of my own first novel.

Financially, the publication of *Gurudeva and other Indian Tales* was a success. A thousand copies were printed and they sold at a dollar, four shillings, high for Trinidad in those days. But the copies went. Of the thousand copies – which at one time seemed so many, occupying so much space in a bedroom – only three or four now survive, in libraries; even my mother has no copy.

Shortly after the publication of *Gurudeva* my father left the *Guardian* for a government job that paid almost twice as well; and during the four or five years he worked for the government he wrote little for himself. He was, at first, 'surveying' rural conditions for a government report. He was, therefore, surveying what he knew, his own background, the background of his early stories. But as a social surveyor compiling facts and figures and tables, no longer a writer concerned with the rituals and manners and what he had seen as the romantic essence of his community, my father was unsettled by what he saw. Out of this unsettlement, and with no thought of publication, he wrote a sketch, 'In the Village', a personal response to the dereliction and despair by which we were surrounded and which we had all – even my father, in his early stories – taken for granted.

Later, out of a similar deep emotion, perhaps grief for his mother, who had died in great, Trinidad poverty in 1942, he wrote an autobiographical piece – the first part of 'They Named Him Mohun'. It was the only piece of autobiography my father permitted himself, if autobiography can be used of a story which more or less ends with the birth of the writer. But my father was obsessed by the circumstances of his birth and the cruelty of his father. I remember the passion that preceded the writing; I heard again and again the forty-year-old stories of meanness and of the expulsion of his pregnant mother from his father's house; and I remember taking down, at my father's dictation, a page or two of a version of this sketch.

A version: there were several versions of everything my father wrote. He always began to write suddenly, after a day or two of silence. He wrote very slowly; and there always came a moment when the emotion with which he had started seemed to have worked itself out and to my surprise – because I felt I had been landed with his emotion – something like literary mischief took over.

'They Named Him Mohun' was read, long after it had been written, to a Port of Spain literary group which included Edgar Mittelholzer and, I believe, the young George Lamming. There was objection to the biblical language and especially to the use of 'ere' for 'before'; but my father ignored the objection and I, who was very much under the spell of the story, supported him. 'In the Village' was printed in a Jamaican magazine edited by Philip Sherlock.

A reading to a small group, publication in a magazine soon lost to view: writing in Trinidad was an amateur activity, and this was all the encouragement a writer could expect. There were no magazines that paid; there were no established magazines; there was only the *Guardian*. A writer like Alfred Mendes, who in the 1930s had had two novels published by Duckworth in London (one with an introduction by Aldous Huxley and a blurb by Anthony Powell), was said to get as much as twenty dollars, four guineas, for a story in the *Guardian* Sunday supplement; my father only got five dollars, a guinea. My father was a purely local writer, and writers like that ran the risk of ridicule; one of the criticisms of my father's book that I heard at school was that it had been done only for the money.

But attitudes were soon to change. It was local publication that brought Derek Walcott and his *Twenty-Five Poems* to our attention in 1949. In that year, too, the Hogarth Press published Edgar Mittelholzer's novel, *A Morning at the Office*; Mittelholzer had for some time been regarded as another local writer. And then there at last appeared a market. Henry Swanzy was editing *Caribbean Voices* for the BBC Caribbean Service. He had standards and enthusiasm. He took local writing seriously and lifted it above the local: he got Roy Fuller to review Derek Walcott's *Twenty-Five Poems*. And the BBC paid; not quite at their celebrated

guinea-a-minute rate, but sufficiently well – fifty dollars a
story, sixty dollars, eighty dollars – to spread a new idea of
the value of writing.

Henry Swanzy used two of my father's early stories on
Caribbean Voices. And from 1950, when he left the government to go back to the *Guardian*, to 1953, when he died, it
was for *Caribbean Voices* that my father wrote. In these
three years, in circumstances deteriorating month by month
to nightmare – the low *Guardian* pay, debt, a heart attack
and subsequent physical incapacity, the hopeless, wounded
longing to publish a real book and become in his own eyes a
writer – in these three years, with the stimulus of that weekly
radio programme from London, my father, I believe, found
his voice as a writer, developed his own comic gift, and wrote
what I think are his best stories: 'The Engagement', 'Gratuity', 'Ramdas and the Cow'.

I didn't participate in the writing of these stories: I didn't
watch them grow, or give advice, as I had done with the
others. In 1949 I had won a Trinidad government scholarship, and in 1950 I left home to come to England to take up
the scholarship. I left my father at the beginning of 'The
Engagement'; and it was two years before I read the finished
story.

My father wrote me once and sometimes twice a week. His
letters, like mine to him, were mainly about money and
writing. When Henry Swanzy, in his half-yearly review of
Caribbean Voices, praised 'The Engagement', my father, who
had never been praised like that before, wrote me: 'I am
beginning to feel I *could* have been a writer.' But we both
felt ourselves in our different ways stalled, he almost at the
end of his life, I at the beginning of mine; and our corres-
pondence, as time went on, as he became more broken, and
I became more separate from him and Trinidad, more adrift
in England, became one of half-despairing mutual encouragement. I had sent him some books by R. K. Narayan, the
Indian writer. In March 1952 he wrote: 'You were right
about R. K. Narayan. I like his short stories . . . he seems

gifted and has made a go of his talent, which in my own case I haven't even spotted.'

In that month he sent me two versions of 'My Uncle Dalloo'. He was uncertain about this story, which he thought long-winded, and wanted me to send what I thought was the better version to Henry Swanzy. I like the story now, for its detail and the drama of its detail; in a small space it creates and peoples a landscape, and the vision is personal. My father hadn't done anything like that before, anything with that amount of historical detail, and I can see the care with which the story is written. I can imagine how those details which he was worried about, and yet was unwilling to lose, were worked over. But at the time – I was nineteen – I took the quality of the vision for granted and saw only the incompleteness of the narrative: my father, working in isolation, had, it might be said, outgrown me.

Henry Swanzy didn't use 'My Uncle Dalloo'. But his judgment of my father's later work was sounder than mine, and he used nearly everything else my father sent him. In June 1953, four months before my father died, Henry Swanzy, at my father's request, asked me to read 'Ramdas and the Cow' for *Caribbean Voices*. The reading fee was four guineas. With the money I bought the Parker pen which I still have and with which I am writing this foreword.

2

Naipaul (or Naipal or Nypal, in earlier transliterations: the transliteration of Hindi names can seldom be exact) was the name of my father's father; birth certificates and other legal requirements have now made it our family name. He was brought to Trinidad as a baby from eastern Uttar Pradesh at some time in the 1880s, as I work it out.

He received no English education but, in the immemorial Hindu way, as though Trinidad was India, he was sent – as a brahmin boy of the Panday clan (or the Parray clan: again, the transliteration is difficult) – to the house of a brahmin to be trained as a pundit. This was what he became; he also, as I have heard, became a small dealer in those things needed for Hindu rituals. He married and had three children; but he died when he was still quite young and his family, unprotected, was soon destitute. My father once told me that at times there wasn't oil for a lamp.

There was some talk, among other branches of the family, of sending the mother and the children back to India; but that plan fell through, and the dependent family was scattered among various relations. My father's elder brother, still only a child, was sent out to work in the fields at fourpence a day; but it was decided that my father, as the youngest of the children, should be educated and perhaps made a pundit, like his father. And that family fracture shows to this day in their descendants. My father's brother, by immense labour, became a small cane-farmer. When I went to see him in 1972, not long before he died, I found him enraged, crying for his childhood and that fourpence a day. My father's sister made two unhappy marriages; she remained, as it were, dazed by Trinidad; until her death in 1972 – more cheerful than her brother, though in a house not her own – she spoke only Hindi and could hardly understand English.

My father received an elementary-school education; he learned English and Hindi. But the attempt to make him a pundit failed. Instead, he began doing odd jobs, attached to the household of a relative (later a millionaire) in that very village of El Dorado which he was to survey more than twenty years later for the government and write about in 'In the Village'.

I do not know how, in such a setting, in those circumstances of dependence and uncertainty, and with no example, the wish to be a writer came to my father. But I feel now, reading the stories after a long time and seeing so clearly (what was once hidden from me) the brahmin standpoint from which they are written, that it might have been the caste-sense, the Hindu reverence for learning and the word,

awakened by the beginnings of an English education and a
Hindu religious training. In one letter to me he seems to say
that he was trying to write when he was fourteen.

He was concerned from the start with Hinduism and the
practices of Hinduism. His acquaintance with pundits had
given him something of the puritan brahmin prejudice
against pundits, professional priests, stage-managers of ritual,
as 'tradesmen'. But he had also been given some knowledge
of Hindu thought, which he valued; and on this knowledge,
evident in the stories, he continued to build throughout his
life; as late as 1951 he was writing me ecstatically about
Aurobindo's commentaries on the Gita.

The Indian immigrants in Trinidad, and especially the
Hindus among them, belonged in the main to the peasantry
of the Gangetic plain. They were part of an old and perhaps
an ancient India. (It was entrancing to me, when I read
Fustel de Coulange's *The Ancient City*, to discover that many
of the customs, which with us in Trinidad, even in my childhood, were still like instincts, had survived from the pre-
classical world.) This peasantry, transported to Trinidad,
hadn't been touched by the great Indian reform movements
of the nineteenth century. Reform became an issue only with
the arrival of reformist missionaries from India in the 1920s,
at a time when in India itself religious reform was merging
into political rebellion.

In the great and sometimes violent debates that followed
in Trinidad – debates that remained unknown outside the
Indian community and are today forgotten by everybody –
my father was on the side of reform. The broad satire of the
latter part of 'Gurudeva' – written in the last year of his life,
but not sent to Henry Swanzy – shouldn't be misinterpre-
ted: there my father fights the old battles again, with the
passion that in the 1930s had made him spend scarce money
on a satirical reform pamphlet, *Religion and the Trinidad
East Indians*, one of the books of my childhood, but now
lost.

It was on Indian or Hindu topics that my father began

writing for the *Trinidad Guardian*, in 1929. The paper had
a new editor, Gault MacGowan. He had come from *The Times*
and in Trinidad was like a man unleashed. The *Trinidad
Guardian*, before MacGowan, was a half-dead colonial newspaper: a large border of advertisements on its front page, a
small central patch of closely printed cables. MacGowan's
brief was to modernize the *Guardian*. He scrapped that front
page. But his taste for drama went beyond the typographical
and he began to unsettle some people. Voodoo in backyards,
obeah, prisoners escaping from Devil's Island, vampire bats:
when the editor of the rival *Port of Spain Gazette* said that
MacGowan was killing the tourist trade, MacGowan sued
and won. But MacGowan was more than a sensationalist. He
was new to Trinidad, discovering Trinidad, and he took
nothing for granted. He saw stories everywhere; he could
make stories out of nothing; his paper was like a daily celebration of the varied life of the island. But sometimes his
wit could run away with him; and the end came when he
became involved in a lawsuit with his own employers (which
the *Trinidad Guardian*, MacGowan still the editor, reported
at length, day after day, so that, in a perfection of the kind
of journalism his employers were objecting to, the paper
became its own news).

My father had written to MacGowan; and MacGowan,
who had been to India and was interested in Indian matters,
thought that my father should be encouraged. My father's
iconoclastic views, and their journalistic possibilities, must
have appealed to him. He became my father's teacher –
beginning no doubt with English which, it must be remembered, was for my father an acquired language – and my
father never lost his admiration and affection for the man
who, as he often said, had taught him how to write. More than
twenty years later, in 1951, my father wrote me: 'And as to
a writer being hated or liked – I think it's the other way to
what you think: a man is doing his work well when people
begin *liking* him. I have never forgotten what Gault Mac-
Gowan told me years ago: "Write sympathetically"; and this,

I suppose, in no way prevents us from writing truthfully, even brightly.'

My father began on the *Guardian* as the freelance contributor of a 'controversial' weekly column. The column – in which I think MacGowan's improving hand can often be detected – was, provocatively, signed 'The Pundit'; and my father remembered the Pundit's words well enough to give blocks of them, years later, to Mr Sohun, the Presbyterian Indian schoolmaster, in the latter part of 'Gurudeva'. 'Gurudeva' has other echoes of my father's early journalism: Gurudeva's beating up of the drunken old stick-fighter must, I feel, have its origin in the news story my father, now a regular country correspondent for the *Guardian*, wrote in 1930: *Fight Challenge Accepted – Jerningham Junction 'Bully' Badly Injured – Six Men Arrested*. A country brawl dramatized, the personalities brought close to the reader, made more than names in a court report: this was MacGowan's style, and it became my father's.

It was through his journalism on MacGowan's *Guardian* that my father arrived at that vision of the countryside and its people which he later transferred to his stories. And the stories have something of the integrity of the journalism: they are written from within a community and seem to be addressed to that community: a Hindu community essentially, which, because the writer sees it as whole, he can at times make romantic and at other times satirize. There is reformist passion; but even when there is shock, as in 'In the Village', there is nothing of the protest – common in early colonial writing – that implies an outside audience; the barbs are all turned inwards. This is part of the distinctiveness of the stories. I stress it because this way of looking, from being my father's, became mine: my father's early stories created my background for me.

But it was a partial vision. A story like 'Panchayat', which reads like a pastoral romance, offers one side of the truth: the people in that story exist completely within a Hindu culture and recognize no other. The wronged wife does not take her husband to the alien law courts; she calls a panchayat against him. The respected village elders assemble; the wife and the husband state their cases without rancour; everyone is wise and dignified and acknowledges *dharma*, the Hindu right way, the way of piety, the old way. But Trinidad, and not India, is in the background. These people have been transported; old ways and old allegiances are being eroded fast. The setting, which is not described because it is taken for granted, is one of big estates, workers' barracks, huts. It is like the setting of 'In the Village'; but that vision of material and cultural dereliction comes later, and it is some time before it can be accommodated in the stories.

Romance simplified; but it was a way of looking. And it was more than a seeking out of the picturesque; it was also, as I have since grown to understand, a way of concealing personal pain. My father once wrote me: 'I have hardly written a story in which the principal characters have not been members of my own family.' And the wronged wife of 'Panchayat' – as I understood only the other day – was really my father's sister; the details in that story are all true. Her marriage to a Punjabi brahmin (a learned man, who could read Persian, as she told me with pride on her deathbed) was a disaster. My father suffered for her. In the story ritual blurs the pain and, fittingly, all ends well; in life the disaster continued. My father hated his father for his cruelty and meanness; yet when, in 'They Named Him Mohun', he came to write about his father, he wrote a tale of pure romance, in which again old ritual, lovingly described, can only lead to reconciliation. And my father, in spite of my encouragement, could never take that story any further.

He often spoke of doing an autobiographical novel. Sometimes he said it would be easy; but once he wrote that parts of it would be difficult; he would have trouble selecting the incidents. When in 1952 he sent me 'My Uncle Dalloo' – which he described in another letter, apologetically, as a sketch – he wrote: 'I'd like you to read it carefully, and if you think it good enough, send it to Mr Swanzy, with a note that it's from me; and that it is part of a chapter of a novel I'm doing. Indeed, this is what I aim to do with it. As soon as you can, get working on a novel. Write of things as they are happening now, be realistic, humorous when this comes in pat, but don't make it deliberately so. If you are at a loss for a theme, take me for it. Begin: "He sat before the little table writing down the animal counterparts of all his wife's family. He was very analytical about it. He wanted to be correct; went to work like a scientist. He wrote, 'The She-Fox,' then 'The Scorpion'; at the end of five minutes he produced a list which read as follows: . . ." All this is just a jest, but you can really do it.'

But for him it wasn't a jest. Once romance and its simplifications had been left behind, these little impulses of caricature (no more than impulses, and sometimes written out in letters to me), the opposite of MacGowan's 'Write sympathetically', were all he could manage when he came to consider himself and the course of his life. He wrote up the animal-counterparts episode himself (I am sure he was writing it when he wrote that letter to me) and made it part of 'Gurudeva', which had become his fictional hold-all. But even there the episode is sudden and out of character. There is something unresolved about it; the passion is raw and comes out, damagingly, as a piece of gratuitous cruelty on the part of the writer. My father was unhappy about the episode; but he could do no more with it. And this was in the last year of his life, when as a writer – but only looking away from himself – he could acknowledge some of the pain about his family he had once tried to hide, and was able to blend romance and the later vision of dereliction into a purer kind of comedy.

It is my father's sister – once the wronged wife of 'Panchayat', a figure of sorrow in a classical Hindu tableau – who ten years afterwards appears as the road-mender's wife in 'Gratuity' and acts as a kind of comic chorus: Sanyasi, the road-mender, was the man of lesser caste with whom she went to live after she had separated from her first husband, the Punjabi brahmin. Ramdas of 'Ramdas and the Cow' – the Hindu tormented by the possession of a sixty-dollar cow which turns out to be barren – is my father's elder brother in middle age; he appears again as the father of the boy in 'The Engagement'.

The comedy was for others. My father remained unwilling to look at his own life. All that material, which might have committed him to longer work and a longer view, remained locked up and unused. Certain things can never become material. My father never in his life reached that point of rest from which he could look back at his past. His last years, when he found his voice as a writer, were years of especial distress and anxiety; he was part of the dereliction he wrote about.

My father's elder brother, at the end of his life, was enraged, as I have said. This sturdy old man, whose life might have been judged a success, was broken by memories of his childhood; self-knowledge had come to him late. My father's own crisis had come at an earlier age; it had been hastened by his journalism. One day in 1934, when he was twenty-eight, five years after he had been writing for the *Guardian*, and some months after Gault MacGowan had left the paper and Trinidad, my father looked in the mirror and thought he couldn't see himself. It was the beginning of a long mental illness that caused him for a time to be unemployed, and as dependent as he had been in his childhood. It was after his recovery that he began writing stories and set himself the goal of the book.

3

Shortly before he died, in 1953, my father assembled all the stories he wanted to keep and sent them to me. He wanted me to get them published as a book. Publication for him, the real book, meant publication in London. But I did not think the stories publishable outside Trinidad, and I did nothing about them.

The stories, especially the early ones, in which I felt I had participated, never ceased to be important to me. But as the years passed – and although I cannibalized 'They Named Him Mohun' for the beginning of one of my own books – my attachment to the stories became sentimental. I valued them less for what they were (or the memory of what they were) than for what, long before, they had given me: a way of looking, an example of labour, a knowledge of the literary process, a sense of the order and special reality (at once simpler and sharper than life) that written words could be seen to create. I thought of them, as I thought of my father's letters, as a private possession.

But the memory of my father's 1943 booklet, *Gurudeva and other Indian Tales*, has never altogether died in Trinidad. Twelve years after his death, my father's stories were remembered by Henry Swanzy in a *New Statesman* issue on Commonwealth writing. In Trinidad itself the attitude to local writing has changed. And my own view has grown longer. I no longer look in the stories for what isn't there; and I see them now as a valuable part of the literature of the region.

They are a unique record of the life of the Indian or Hindu community in Trinidad in the first fifty years of the century. They move from a comprehension of the old India in which the community is at first embedded to an understanding of the colonial Trinidad which defines itself as their background, into which they then merge. To write about a community which has not been written about is not easy. To write about this community was especially difficult; it required unusual knowledge and an unusual breadth of sympathy.

And the writer himself was part of the process of change. This wasn't always clear to me. But I find it remarkable now that a writer, beginning in the old Hindu world, one isolated segment of it, where all the answers had been given and the rituals perfected, and where, apart from religious texts, the only writings known were the old epics of the Ramayana and the Mahabharat; leaving that to enter a new world and a new language; using simple, easily detectable models – Pearl Buck, O. Henry; I find it remarkable that such a writer, working always in isolation, should have gone so far. I don't think my father read Gogol; but these stories, at their best, have something of the quality of the Ukrainian stories Gogol wrote when he was a very young man. There is the same eye that lingers lovingly over what might at first seem nondescript. Landscape, dwellings, people: there is the same assembling of sharp detail. The drama lies in that; when what has been relished is recorded and fixed, the story is over.

Gogol at the beginning of his writing life, my father at the end of his: even if the comparison is just, it can mislead. After his young man's comedy and satire, after the discovery and exercise of his talent, Gogol had Russia to fall back on and claim. It was the other way with my father. From a vision of a whole Hindu society he moved, through reformist passion, which was an expression of his brahmin confidence, to a vision of disorder and destitution, of which he discovered himself to be part. At the end he had nothing to claim; it was out of this that he created comedy.

The process is illustrated by 'Gurudeva'. This story isn't satisfactory, especially in some of its later sections; and my father knew it. Part of the trouble is that the story was written in two stages. The early sections, which were written in 1941–2, tell of the beginnings of a village strongman. The character (based, remotely, on someone who had married into my mother's family but had then been expelled from it, the mention of his name forbidden) is not as negligible as he might appear now. He belongs to the early 1930s and, in those days of restricted franchise, he might have developed (as the original threatened to develop) into a district politician. Although in the story he is simplified, and his idea of manhood ridiculed as thuggery and a perversion of the caste instinct, Gurudeva is felt to be a figure. And in its selection of strong, brief incidents, its gradual peopling of an apparently self-contained Indian countryside (other communities are far away), this part of the story is like the beginning of a rural epic.

Ten years later, when my father returned to the story (and brought Gurudeva back from jail, where in 1942 he had sent him), the epic tone couldn't be sustained. Gurudeva's Indian world was not as stable as Gurudeva, or the writer, thought. The society had been undermined; its values had to compete with other values; the world outside the village could no longer be denied. As seen in 1950–2, Gurudeva, the caste bully of the 1930s, becomes an easy target. Too easy: the irony and awe with which he had been handled in the first part of the story turns to broad satire, and the satire defeats itself.

Mr Sohun the schoolmaster, the Presbyterian convert, holds himself up, and is held up by the writer, as a rational man, freed from Hindu prejudice and obscurantism. But Mr Sohun, whose words in the 1930s might have seemed wise, is himself now seen more clearly. It is hinted – he hints himself: my father makes him talk too much – that he is of low caste. His Presbyterianism is more than an escape from this: it is, as Gurudeva says with sly compassion, Mr Sohun's bread and butter, a condition of his employment as a teacher in the Canadian Mission school. Mr Sohun's son has the un-Indian name of Ellway. But the boy so defiantly named doesn't seem to have done much or to have much to do. When Gurudeva calls, Ellway is at home, noisily knocking up fowl-coops: the detail sticks out.

In fact, the erosion of the old society has exposed Mr Sohun, and the writer, as much as Gurudeva. The writer senses this; his attitude to Gurudeva changes. The story jumps from the 1930s to the late 1940s. Gurudeva, no longer a caste bully and a threat, becomes a figure of comedy; and, curiously, his stature grows. He is written into the story of 'Ramdas and the Cow' (originally an independent story);

turning satirist himself, he writes down the animal counterparts of his wife's family and begins to approximate to his
creator; at the end, abandoned by wife and girl friend and
left alone, he is a kind of brahmin, an upholder of what remains of old values, but powerless. He has travelled the way
of his baffled creator.

Writers need a source of strength other than that which
they find in their talent. Literary talent doesn't exist by
itself; it feeds on a society and depends for its development
on the nature of that society. What is true of my father is
true of other writers of the region; we all in different ways
discover that we stand nowhere. *We, being all islands in air*:
the words are from a poem in Derek Walcott's first, locally
published book. The writer begins with his talent, finds
confidence in his talent, but then discovers that it isn't
enough, that, in a society as deformed as ours, by the exercise
of his talent he has set himself adrift.

4

I have dropped two of the stories that appeared in the 1943
collection: 'Gopi', an early story of emotional deprivation,
which in his final typescript my father pruned away to almost
nothing, and 'Sonya's Luck', an earlier and more romantic
version of 'The Wedding Came'. I have not attempted to
change the idiosyncrasies of my father's English; I have
corrected only one or two obvious errors. In the later stories
(partly because he was writing for the radio) he wrote
phonetic dialogue. Phonetic dialogue – apart from its inevi-
table absurdities: *eggszactly* for 'exactly', *w'at* for 'what' –
falsifies the pace of speech, sets up false associations, is
meaningless to people who don't know the idiom and un-
necessary to those who do. The rhythm of broken language
is sufficiently indicated by the construction of a sentence. I
have toned down this phonetic dialogue, modelling myself on
my father's more instinctive and subtle rendering of speech

in *Gurudeva and other Indian Tales*; like my father in that
early booklet, I have not aimed at uniformity. 'Obeah' is
more or less as it appeared in 1943. Not having the original
version of 'In the Village', written before my father began
writing for the radio, I have left that sketch as my father
finally typed it out.

Since 'Gurudeva' was written over a period of ten years,
it has not been possible to put the stories in the order in
which they were written. I have therefore – after 'Gurudeva',
which moves into the early 1930s, jumps to the late 1940s,
then back again to the 1930s – put the stories in their historical sequence. The events of 'They Named Him Mohun' can
be dated 1906 (though some details in the second part of that
story suggest a much later period). 'My Uncle Dalloo' is a
memory of the early 1920s. 'The Wedding Came', 'Dookhani
and Mungal' and 'Panchayat' belong to the 1930s. 'Obeah' is
a war-time story. 'In the Village' comes from 1944. 'Gratuity'
and 'The Engagement' (like 'Ramdas and the Cow' from
'The Adventures of Gurudeva') belong to the very late 1940s.

My father dedicated his stories to me. But the style of
publication has changed; and I would like to extend this
dedication to the two men who stand at the beginning and
end of my father's writing career: to Gault MacGowan, to
whom I know my father wanted to dedicate *Gurudeva and
other Indian Tales* in 1943; and to Henry Swanzy.

June 1975   V. S. NAIPAUL

The Adventures of Gurudeva

1. *A School Inspection*

Gurudeva was only fourteen years old when he was taken away from the Mission School in the village in order to be married. He made no objections, and even if he had, it is doubtful whether Jaimungal, his father, would have let him off lightly. It is just possible that he would have put him out of the house as a *pukka badmash*, or at least given him a sound beating.

Old Jaimungal was regarded by everybody in the village as a staunch Hindu, and as such he could not of course tolerate marrying a son who had already grown a moustache. Moreover, he was sure – though he could not say exactly why, for he was not one who could read and write well enough to understand the subtleties of the Shastras – he was sure that marrying a son after that son had already crossed his teens was an odiously un-Hindu affair. And then, too, a *doolaha* or bridegroom looked so much the more picturesque in his flowing wedding gown and tall scintillating crown if his face behind the low-hanging tassels of the crown – colloquially called a wedding hat – was a boyish face; not one marred by whiskers. Otherwise even the most telling of regalias served only to emphasize the marrying one's hardness of features. A state of things compatible only with low-caste Hindus.

Gurudeva was actually in school giving up his lesson on tenses with a semicircle of boys at the headteacher's desk, when his father, accompanied by a heavy little man, came to show him off.

The little man was a portly person in dusty, unlaced shoes. He had a white skull-cap on his head and, unlike Jaimungal, who wore trousers and shirt, was clad in dhoti and *koortah*. His broad forehead was decorated with three horizontal lines of white sandal paste, and he carried a parasol on the crook of one arm. His features were rather vague, but he seemed well-fed and prosperous. Once he shifted the tight-fitting skull-cap and you saw that his hair was partly black and partly grey. He could not have been more than forty-five, or fifty, perhaps.

Immediately Gurudeva saw them he guessed the purpose of the visit. The knowledge made him partly proud and partly shy; but he tried to behave as though he had not seen them.

'Schoolmaster,' Jaimungal called, a shade obsequiously, 'good evening!' He took off his faded felt hat, and you saw that his hair too was streaked with grey. He was built on the large side and was tall and long-limbed.

Mr Sohun came up and shook hands cordially with both persons. He was a dapper little man.

'This is Pundit Sookhlal,' Jaimungal said, indicating his portly companion. 'He come to have a look at the boy, Schoolmaster.'

Pundit Sookhlal bowed, shifted the parasol from the one arm to the other.

'You see, Schoolmaster,' Jaimungal explained in an undertone, 'I think I goin' to get the boy married.'

Mr Sohun lifted his eyebrows.

'You know, Schoolmaster, how boys get out of hand these days?'

Mr Sohun was taken aback. He pursed his lips and threw out his chest. He had a broad chest.

'It's your affair, of course,' he said; 'but the boy is only in the third standard. Besides, he is absurdly young for marrying. I thought you would give at least this son of yours a chance. You are not a poor man, you know. You are one of the biggest cane-farmers this side of the colony, and you can afford giving the boy a good education – possibly a profession.'

Old man Jaimungal gave a half deprecating, half patronizing smile. It was a smile, in fact, that plainly told Mr Sohun that he didn't know better. 'This,' thought the old man, 'is what comes of sending one's children to school. Always they want you to conform to practices outside your religion.'

He waved the reminder with a short flourish of his hand. 'That is orright, Schoolmaster,' he said. 'He know 'nough. He could read. He could write a letter. He could even write a receipt. What mo' he want?'

Mr Sohun saw the futility of argument. He couldn't possibly put right all the wrong things in the world, but he could at least give a warning and wash his hands of the business.

'Very well, Jaimungal. Do as you please.' He bowed shortly and returned to his class. 'Go,' he said to Gurudeva; 'your father wants you.' And, as the boy turned to leave the class, Mr Sohun grinned and added, in a somewhat quizzical tone, 'Wedding for you, boy!'

There was a titter, and all the boys looked up perkily. Gurudeva wilted with shame. Then he went away and stood dutifully before his father. He did not look at the other man. He knew what the other man had come for and he was shy to look into his eyes.

'This is the boy, Punditji,' Gurudeva heard his father say proudly. 'He grow big for he age.'

Pundit Sookhlal looked the lad up and down most appraisingly and seemed to melt with pleasure. He patted Gurudeva lightly and affectionately on the shoulder. 'He will do,' he said in Hindi. 'He is just the match for my Ratni.'

A fortnight later Gurudeva was a married 'man'.

2. *Gurudeva as Husband*

Gurudeva himself could not say whether he loved or hated Ratni. She was twelve years old, small and plump and pretty with a full brown face. Her eyes were large and dark, her movement slow, and there was something in her attitude that suggested the significant casualness of the martyr. She hardly spoke and seldom smiled, and it was difficult to say when she had last laughed. Gurudeva himself would not let her laugh, because, he said, that was bad manners in a newly married girl; and if she sometimes forgot and did laugh out, he promptly silenced her with a look, if not with a slap. Indeed, the time came when Ratni often found herself in the very puzzling position of not knowing which was the worse – to laugh or to cry. If she laughed, there was Gurudeva to crush her with a glance or stun her with a slap; if she cried, Jhulani, her mother-in-law, let her know, in no mean tone, that she was a most sulky and trying person – the embodiment of ill-omen in the house.

But it was not always thus. When she first came everybody liked her – very much. Almost to suffocation. She was decidedly the pet of the house. They called her *doolahin*, bride, which was in itself a pet name. She reigned a queen, and like a queen she could do no wrong; and if she did happen on anything that seemed not right, everybody, but especially Jhulani, glorified the blunder. It was looked upon as the harmless, innocent prank of a child; something to be amused at, something to enjoy. Jhulani gave every evidence that she was both proud and fond of Ratni. Oh yes, Ratni herself could say that. Jhulani would put Ratni right in front of her, undo her hair and pick out every nit and every louse. And then she would say, 'Now, *doolahin*, come and pick *my* head.'

All very motherly, to be sure.

But the thing had not lasted. Three months – and she was no longer a novelty. She was hated. Everybody hated her –

even the old man, the old man who used to bring her 'swee-
ties' every so often. How it started – this business of hate and
apathy against her – she could not say. It was gradual, like
the subtle, insidious growth of a disease. The little blunders
that had hitherto called forth smiles and gay laughter were
now looked upon as wilful wickedness . . . Now the rice was
too soft-boiled; now the dahl had too much salt; now the
roti was burnt; now she had stood before old Jaimungal with
her *orhani*, veil, off her head . . . There was no end to
complaints.

Nevertheless, Ratni's coming in the house brought Gurudeva a definite prestige, and, automatically enough, he found
himself wanting to behave as a man. He was suddenly pon-
derously precocious. He discarded his short trousers for long
ones and tried by innuendoes as well as by a variety of subtle
and tangible ways to impress his wife that he was not one
to be trifled with; that, in fact, he was his own man – *her*
man at any rate – and that, in virtue of it, he could beat
her with impunity whenever he chose to do so. Which was
often.

Gurudeva became a prodigy at quarrelling – especially
with Ratni. As the conjurer produces a florin apparently from
nowhere, in some such manner he would evolve a quarrel out
of nothing. She might cast a timid glance at him, and he
would say in a voice as though he had seen a *mapepire* snake,
'Now, why the hell you lookin' at me like that for?' And she
would answer, 'Who lookin' at you? Me? Well, an' you must
be lookin' at me, too.' And that, Gurudeva would find, was
'too much back-answer'; and he would right away busy himself on her with fist or foot, or with almost anything he could
catch hold of.

Gurudeva was cruel, to be sure; but in his cruelty there
was no malice and little, if any, anger. Once he caught, back
of the house, a stray puppy sucking hen's eggs in a clump of
bush. Suddenly he pounced upon the dog and grabbed it by
the hind leg, and called out to Ratni to bring him a bag; and
when she brought it he put the puppy in it and gathered the

ends and lifted the bag with the dog in it. Then, with every step that he took forward, he bumped the bag on the ground; and every time that the creature yelped with the thud, Gurudeva laughed outright in sheer delight. But somehow one corner of the bag slipped down his fingers and out dashed the puppy.

'You bugger!' he exclaimed. 'You run, eh?'

He was not angry. He was just having a good joke. And, had the puppy not escaped, he would have put a steaming egg into its mouth. Not because he hated the creature; but just to break its habit of stealing eggs.

So, too, he beat Ratni; not from any overwhelming surge of anger, nor from any conscious wickedness, but because the privilege and prerogative of beating her was his, by virtue of his being her husband. He was not doing anything shameful. He was only beating his wife. It would be a fine world if a man could not beat his own wife!

And Ratni knew this, too, young as she was, and bore up under her travails without complaint and without murmur, as any good wife was expected to do. And her father and mother knew this likewise and were often sorrowful about the whole rotten affair, but would hardly put in a word of protest, old and knowing as they were.

3. *The Beating of Ratni*

It was in the fifth year of her marriage, when she was nearly seventeen, that Ratni got her worst mauling. That day Gurudeva was really angry. Ratni was in the kitchen, preparing the midday food, when he came rushing in.

'Ei!' he called. 'What about me food?' He jammed his hands against his waist, pressed his teeth on his lower lip and waited ominously for answer.

Ratni grew pale. She sensed trouble. She had not yet finished cooking the midday food.

'Come on, I waitin'!' thundered Gurudeva.

Long spoon in hand, Ratni turned from the pot and faced him, trembling in every limb. She said:

'I – I was washing clothes today. There was plenty to wash. I will give you food jus' now . . . Two minute . . . The *bharth* finish, the dahl finish too; the *bhaji* cookin'.'

'*Bhaji*! What *bhaji*?' roared Gurudeva.

'Pumpkin vine wid sal'fish.'

'Pumpkin vine! Who tell you to cook pumpkin vine?'

'But you always eat it. I thought . . .'

'Back-answer, eh!' spluttered Gurudeva. 'I will show you.'

And he pounced upon her, even as he had pounced upon the puppy, and bundled her out into the yard. Artfully he entwined her long hair around his fists and dragged her in a circle over the rough ground as though she were a sack of potatoes. And when she neither wailed nor wept, he disengaged his hands from her hair and cuffed her and kicked her fanatically. His large, taut neck grew tauter, and his dark face darker. He foamed at the mouth. He was terrifying . . .

'You wouldn't cry, eh? You playing you could take blows . . . Well, take blows . . .' And he chucked her off and undid his harness-leather belt and flogged her and flogged her with it till the belt became too short for further use, and she, instead of howling with mortal pain, suddenly laughed out long and loudly, like a creature gone stark mad; and in that hard, mad gladness she shouted out, 'Beat me today, kill me and bury me!'

Then he was suddenly alarmed at her frenzy, and not letting her know he was alarmed, he left her.

In a heap, there she sprawled on the ground, inert as though dead. And there it was that Mira and Dhira, her elder sisters-in-law, found her, when they returned from the rice-lands, drenched and dripping, two hours later. Trembling with the cold as much as because of what had been done to Ratni, they stooped either side of her and held her under the armpits and helped to get her on her feet. Groaning and sagging, Ratni stood up, and leaning against their shoulders, allowed herself to be carried and put upon her *khatiah*, the bed of hempen string, in the little room back of the house, which was hers and Gurudeva's.

Then, still in their wet clothes, Mira and Dhira went down the track that led to the saffron patch in the cane-field. They brought saffron. Mira set to grinding the saffron into a paste with coconut oil on the stone slab used for grinding massala; while Dhira tore up into strips an old *orhani* for bandage. Then together they laid the saffron paste thick upon the body of Ratni – on all the parts of her body that were blue and black and bruised with the kicking and cuffing and belt-ing of Gurudeva.

And a poignant sorrow assailed Mira and Dhira as they ministered unto the hapless Ratni, and they wept till the tears flooded their eyes too much and they quickly brushed them away so as to see where and how to apply the healing paste.

And thus they felt because they knew that such was their lot as well, and they wondered in a vague, resigned sort of way why the Deity had allowed them to be born at all. For they had ever heard it taught by their fathers, by the elders of the village, as well as by the pundits who often read the *Ramayana* on evenings, that the husband was to the wife God, lord and master – all in one – and that a woman's highest virtue lay in her absolute submission to her husband's will – be that will of whatever complexion.

'But you see,' Dhira told Mira in Hindi, 'it is all a very one-sided operation. They want us all to be like Sita – that is, to try as far as possible to be like her; but on the other hand, *they* are far from being like Rama, the incarnation of the great God Vishnu himself. They do not even try. It is not fair. But wipe your tears, little sister. It is our karma.'

And in the days that followed the healing of Ratni, Guru-deva hardly spoke to anybody in the house, but took his food from one or the other of his sisters-in-law in the morning and ate it squatting on the floor, silently and sullenly. Then he would leave the house, returning at the midday hour; and he would eat and leave the house once more and would not return till late evening. He would then eat again and go to sleep in the hammock in the long, open gallery, away from Ratni, sullen and morose as ever.

On the third evening his father came to him by the hammock. Quietly, almost timidly, in a tone half patronizing, half admonitory, the old man said to him in Hindi:

'Son, it is not good to be like this. Be not cast down. What is to be will be.'

And Gurudeva looked up quickly and questioningly, as though the old man should have expressed a less silly thought, and rapped out in Hindi:

'Well, I have no patience with her. She is rude and crude and gives me back-answers.'

The old man nodded understandingly and put one hand on the shoulder of his son and said sympathetically:

'I know that. But she is only a woman and will be ever foolish, no matter what you do; but *you* must keep your temper, for you can read and write, and know good from bad ... But she – well, to her letters are like dirt.'

Phulmati, Ratni's mother, was turning paddy on a bag-spread in the sun out in the yard when Jokhoo – tramp, story-teller, and matrimonial matchmaker – brought news of the beating of Ratni.

Wiping the sweat off his face with the hanging bit of his dingy turban – for it was midday and pelting hot – Jokhoo said:

'And thoroughly has Gurudeva done her in this time. With kick and cuff and belt he has laid her low. Aho! Aho!' And the old man slumped down against the earth wall and sighed as though it was he who had been beaten.

Phulmati stopped turning the paddy. 'They will kill my child,' she said with conviction. 'I know they will. The hard-hearts! Shame they have not got to beat a young girl like that!'

And she went down on her haunches and smote her forehead resoundingly with her palms and fell to weeping. Then, recollecting herself, she quickly dashed away her tears with a corner of her *orhani*, and said bravely and understandingly, 'Well, it is her karma; I gave her birth, but for her karma I was not responsible.'

'Now you are talking sense, woman,' said Pundit Sookhlal. One dhoti-clad leg crossed upon the other, he sat naked-back on the bamboo bench in the open trash-covered hut. He was trying to coax a smoke from a sweaty *cheelum*, an Indian smoking-pipe, which would not respond.

'Ari! Ari!' he said. 'The more I ponder over the sufferings of Ratni, the clearer I see – as in a mirror – that whatever befalls the girl – whether of woe or weal – it is neither the doings of Gurudeva, nor mine, nor anybody elses, but Ratni's herself. She is simply reaping what she had sown in her previous life; just as how I and you, and Jokhoo here, are each reaping whatever we had sown. Only a fool will try to stop the workings of karma.'

Pundit Sookhlal thoughtfully fingered the bowl of his *cheelum*. 'Yet, against all the dark, menacing clouds of her life,' he said, 'I see one gleaming thing that makes me almost happy – certainly proud: it is fine how Ratni is putting up with everything. Thank God for that. It says a lot for the exemplary upbringing I have bequeathed her.'

And the pundit once more drew heroically at the *cheelum*, which now seemed dead. 'Bring me another lump of fire,' he said. 'This stupid *cheelum* has gone cold again.'

4. *The Making of a Bad-John*

Gurudeva was ambitious. From boyhood he was obsessed with a craving for fame. Had other things been equal he might at least have risen to the distinction of a legislator; he might have been a doctor or a lawyer or an electrical engineer; for his father was wealthy as well as indulgent. But Gurudeva remained where we find him, not only because he was divorced from the Mission School when he had gone no

further than the third standard, but also because, as in boyhood, so in later life, he ever lacked a sense of selection and
went on mistaking notoriety for fame.

Now, at twenty-two, his whole ambition was to be noticed.
It was not enough that he had made his presence felt and
feared in the house. It was not enough that his father, his
mother, his two elder brothers and their wives stood in awe
of him. He wanted to be looked upon with awe by the whole
village. He hankered to be popular, but to be popular in a
spectacular way. He wanted people to point at him and
whisper, 'See that fellow going there? He is Gurudeva, the
bad-John!'

This fancy of Gurudeva was born mainly of the stories
that old Jaimungal often told on evenings of the dare-devil
exploits of dead and gone bad-Johns. He would squat out in
the open gallery, and the people living near his house – the
best and biggest in the village, since it was roofed with
galvanized iron and floored with board and had jalousies in
the doors and windows and was painted in red and blue and
yellow – the neighbours would come and squat before him
with their dhoti-clad haunches on the floor and their knees
going up to their chins; and they would listen entranced to
the stories he told.

And among them the most entranced listener would be
Gurudeva.

'Those were the days!' the old man would say exultantly.
'There was that fellow Khardukhan, for instance. Well, he
was a great one for a fighter! Could he play the *gatka*? On
Hosey Day especially he broke many heads. He was born to
fight. Policemen! He would break their heads too. Jail! He
used to say that jail was not made for dogs. There was none
to touch him. On Hosey Day, when all the competing hoseys
met at the junction before Lee Tung's long provision shop, he
would throw his stick into the ring and bravely give out his
challenge. "Ya, Hassan! Any man!" Ha! But few dared to tilt
stick with Khardukhan. And if any did – well, that one was
sure to retire with a broken head.

'Blood. That was what Khardukhan's stick drew.'

And the old man would pause significantly and say in a low tone, 'You see, his stick was mounted!' (With the rebellious spirit of a volatile Spaniard.) A far-away look would steal into his eyes . . . 'And so was Nanna. Nanna now . . .' And he would reel forth from the recesses of his memory the amazing exploits of another hero, and of yet another, until the night would be far gone, and the doleful cry of the poor-me-one, otherwise the zombie-bird, the croaking choruses of frogs, the menacing chant of the mosquitoes, and the midnight crowing of cocks would make him yawn and say it was time to sleep.

And hearing these tales, Gurudeva's blood boiled within him, and he vowed to become a bad-John too.

5. *Bhakhiranji*

It should be said for Gurudeva that once a fancy possessed his mind, he set about translating it into action for all he was worth. He told no one of this new consuming ambition of his. It was too sacred for words; but he absented himself more and more from the rice-lands, leaving his share of the work to his two brothers, Ramnath and Makhan, and their wives.

Making sticks for fighting purposes became his hobby. He spared himself no pains making them. He would take himself into the high woods up in Chickland, three miles away, and cut the pouis that flourished abundantly on the high lands, and gathering them into a bundle, he would tote them home.

Out in the yard he would make a blazing fire of dry leaves and bake the sticks in it and beat the barks off them on the ground. Then he would cut each stick into the desired length – from ground level to his lower ribs – and then with cutlass, with broken bottles with razor-sharp edges, and finally with sandpaper, he would impart to each stick the smoothness and uniformity of a ruler. Then he would go to the giant bamboo clump near by and bring forth a length of bamboo, stout and ripe and roomy in its hollowness, and an inch or two longer than his stick; and he would punch out all the compartments but the last, and order Ratni to make enough oil from coconuts and fill the bamboo vessel with it to the very top.

It would be done.

Into the bamboo he would immerse as many of his precious sticks as it could hold. Then he would stand the vessel in a corner of his room and would not bring out the sticks from it till ten days or a fortnight, when he would let off a whoop of joy. For the sticks would be found to have taken on a rich brown colour and almost twice the weight they had before their protracted bath.

And Gurudeva, in an ecstasy of pleasure, would in turn hold each stick and bring the ends forward until the stick formed a semicircle; and though he would not risk making the ends actually meet, for fear the stick would break, he would boast he could do it.

'It goin' take blows in a fight without breaking anyway,' he told his father on one occasion. 'For it would limber and not break or let off splinters.'

And the old man shook his head and marvelled at the wisdom and industry of the youth.

Gurudeva loved his sticks. They were the joy of his heart. He had them standing in a row against the wall at the head of his *khatiah*; and, deep in the night, in the light of the unshaded oil-lamp, he would find himself wide awake and flat on his belly. Chin in cupped hands, he would contemplate his sticks with the intensity of a miser gloating over his treasure.

And then Gurudeva's joy would desert him and he would turn on his back and begin to worry. 'There is no sense in having sticks without having them mounted,' he thought. 'An' it is jus' as foolish to want to become a bad-John without bein' a able stickman.'

He knew no one who mounted sticks and he knew not

even the rudiments of the art of the *gatka* or duel with sticks. He sought out his father one morning and begged him to help him out of his difficulties. 'Tell me, Bap,' he begged, 'wey I can find a good stick-mounter? I mean somebody who really know the job.'

The old man was squatting on his heels out in the yard, scraping his tongue with a split bit of twig as part of the morning ablutions. A glad gleam lit his eyes. His little sparrow was getting to be a hawk. He finished scraping his tongue, and said:

'A mounter? Why, there is no better man than Bhakhiran.' Jaimungal spoke in Hindi. 'He is old and shaky now, but he still retains his powers. Oh, yes. You will find him in his tapia hut in the next village.'

Gurudeva beamed. First he would see to getting his sticks mounted, then he would see about practising the *gatka*.

It didn't take Gurudeva long to locate Bhakhiran's hut. An old woman, possibly Bhakhiran's wife, sat on her haunches, scouring brass plates under a mango tree in the yard back of the hut. A big girl, possibly Bhakhiran's daughter, came in, hot and sweaty, with a bundle of cow's fodder on her head. She threw down the bundle upon a *matchan* next to a palm-thatched pen, wiped the sweat off her face duck-fashion against her shoulder, and, without a word, went back the way she had come.

Gurudeva, a burning cigarette between his fingers, gave a low cough. It was a discreet and respectful cough which conveyed at the same time a weighty salutation.

The crone, swathed in faded voluminous skirt and *jhoolah*, or bodice, craned her neck and saw Gurudeva. Interest lit her eyes.

'You want something?' she asked. Her words were mongrel Hindi, a sort of patois Hindi which, spoken elsewhere but in Trinidad, would be unmeaning gibberish.

Gurudeva said: 'Yes, yes. I want to see Bhakhiranji. It is important.'

'Wait a little.'

The old woman stood up and waddled into the hut. 'There is a man here. He says he wants to see you.'

She stood in the doorway and waited. From within came a gurgle, a croaking and then a voice that sounded like the breaking of a calabash. The old woman turned to Gurudeva.

'You may come in,' she said, and returned to her work.

Gurudeva was shocked. He found himself looking down, as it were, not so much at a man as at a huge morocoy. For Bhakhiranji was a crumpled, wheezy, sagging old man – more sick than old – and it seemed to Gurudeva that the derelict of a man did not have enough backbone to enable him to sit up.

He was all in a recumbent heap on a bed of stripped *bois-canot* overlaid with dry tapia grass and sugar-bags and floursacks. Only his head moved now and then, in the manner of a morocoy's.

His thin, merino-clad belly was pressing on his legs as on pillows, and his chin – a gnarled thing – was resting on one knee. His feet were drawn in under his lean shanks and he wore a length of mildewed, dirt-sodden cotton for dhoti, which was not so much a cover as an apology for one. Its scantiness, thinness and dirt made it an offence. His hair, mouse-grey, was thin and sparse. His eyes, large and bleary, were sunken in their sockets. His collar-bones suggested rusty iron rings held under taut elastic. His whole attitude was one long cry.

Gurudeva knew not what to do. He felt it would be brutal to burden the old man with the business he had come to have with him. And then, as though someone else were speaking for him, he heard himself saying in Hindi:

'Bhakhiranji, how are you? I hope you are feeling better.'

The old man croaked and jerked his head up morocoy-like and looked at him. The mounter of sticks made an effort to speak, but no words came; only a surge of racking cough. The convulsions held for about thirty seconds, but to Gurudeva those thirty seconds seemed more like thirty minutes. When the coughing subsided, he said:

'Bhakhiranji, I have come to you on a very important business.'

Bhakhiranji asked: 'First, who may you be? I cannot say I have known you before. You see, I have been tied down to this bed for years.'

'Oh, I am Gurudeva, son of Jaimungal.'

The old man seemed vastly relieved. 'Oh, sit down. There is the box,' he said.

Gurudeva sat down.

'I knew your father,' gurgled the old man. 'He was somewhat of a *gatka*-man in his time. But you do not know about that. You were too small; or maybe you were not yet born.'

'It is about stick-playing that I have come to you, Bhakhiranji. I want you to mount my sticks.'

Bhakhiranji was visited by another bout of coughing, and when the paroxysm was over, he asked: 'Can you play the *gatka*?'

'Not yet, but I will learn it. I will learn it, Bhakhiranji.'

The old man said: 'Yes, yes; to be sure you will. You have long limbs that will make for fine reaches. But you see, it is no use having mounted sticks without knowing the art of the *gatka*. Your stick will draw blood, to be sure; but you have to fend too. No stick will fend for you.'

Gurudeva wondered at the wisdom of the man.

'Bring your stick tomorrow,' said Bhakhiranji. 'I will mount it for you. Just because you are Jaimungal's son. It will cost you a cock – a big cock; a quart of rum – puncheon rum; some tobacco – good tobacco. And – well, yes – five dollars for labour. Just five dollars; because you are Jaimungal's son.'

He had another bout of coughing and when it gave him a chance, he said: 'That is all. But listen! Do not let anyone touch the mounted stick. It will want to draw blood. 'Panish, you know! All right. Bring your stick tomorrow – along with the material.'

Gurudeva was impressed – tremendously impressed. 'I will, I will,' he said ecstatically.

And he did.

In time Gurudeva had as many as half a dozen sticks mounted by the dare-devil spirit of Bhakhiranji's gore-thirsty Spaniard. And once, when Ratni at an unguarded moment observed that he had but two hands, and what would he do with so many sticks, Gurudeva promptly silenced her with a slap. 'Mind you' own business,' he said. 'Don' put goat-mouth.'

Every time he brought home a newly mounted stick he would warn Ratni in a hushed, mysterious tone, 'Take care now! Don' touch this stick. It is mounted. It will want to draw blood every time you touch it.'

And Ratni would open her large eyes larger yet, and let awe shine forth from them, but would not say a word again, lest she say the wrong thing.

It was not long before Gurudeva's father and his mother, as well as his brothers and their wives and – mysteriously enough – almost everybody in the village, knew that Gurudeva was a man who kept mounted sticks; and they respected and feared him for that as much as they respected and feared the sticks themselves.

Old Jaimungal especially looked up to Gurudeva at this time with pride. Gurudeva was a Brahmin by birth and a Kshatriya by valour. Like Arjuna, the renowned warrior prince of yore! As far as he knew – and he knew a lot – every real bad-John in Trinidad was the son of a Kshatriya, the princely and soldier caste in the Hindu social hierarchy. Well, it was in his blood. But to have the qualities of a Brahmin and those of a Kshatriya, too – well, that was a unique combination.

And when Gurudeva sought out an *oustard* or veteran stickman and at his guidance began practising on evenings at *gatka*, which they play at Hosey time; and at creole stick, which they play at Carnival time and in fighting mêlées generally, old Jaimungal positively began to boast. He did not give a jot that Gurudeva was contemptuous of all real work. Wasn't he the famed one in the family? If his elder brothers bothered him any too much about doing his share of the work in rice-land or cane-field, Guru was just the man to beat *them*, too, and put them in their place. But no; he must not let that happen. People would laugh.

And Gurudeva did not waste time. He rallied together most of the young fellows in the village and announced the formation of a *gatka* band. The meeting took place on the big bridge that spanned the river half a mile away from Gurudeva's house. The fellows sat on the whitewashed concrete rails with their legs dangling before them. It was late evening, but an argent moon gave forth all the light that was necessary for the occasion. Dinnoo was there, and Jairam and Ramlal and Birbal; and Hansraj, the veteran *gatka*-man, whom everybody called *Oustard*, which was the same thing like calling him the champion.

'The thing is,' Gurudeva said, speaking English now, 'that this is a dam slack village. Why, we ain't doing one thing for the name of the place. Better we was all in frocks instead of in pants.'

'It is the struth,' agreed Dinnoo, who was Gurudeva's best supporter. 'It is a shame and something mus' be done about it.'

The *Oustard* put in: 'You boys mus' form up a *gatka* band. That is what you have to do. Hosey is two months off an' you can show you'self then.'

'Exactly!' said Gurudeva. 'What you sayin', boys? *Oustard* here can teach we. Each of we can give 'im a shillin' in the fortnight. Twelve of we will make him get twelve shillings. And we will throw up an' buy we own pitchoil for flambeau. Come on, what you sayin'?'

'We ain't sayin' nothing,' said Jairam, who already knew some *gatka*. 'We ain't sayin' no.'

'I agree too,' Ramlal added.

'And I ain't sayin' no. We all agree. Is a *gatka* band we going to have.' This was Dinnoo, son of Birbal the thatcher.

The motion was adopted unanimously, and – let it be said – enthusiastically. It was planned that they must each be proficient to 'breaks' for himself on Hosey Day, when opposing *gatka*-men would meet in combat before Lee Tung's rumshop at the three-roads junction.

They practised assiduously and with gusto, but none more so than Gurudeva. An hour or so before practice time – for that took place in flambeau light – Gurudeva would take his stick and go and take his stand by the kerbstone at the crossroads. He would be hatless and he would contrive to let his hair stand wild and rebellious. He wanted to look reckless and bad. His short-sleeved shirt would be open all down his chest, and he would stand against the kerbstone with folded arms, his stick held conspicuously down one closed fist. Tall he had grown now and his shoulders had broadened and his chest become heavier and hairier; and he was quite aware of all this and let the people take notice.

Keeping at that tense pose, he would not smile. Not he! His whole attitude told the passer-by: 'You see me, I am not joking. Just say something funny and you will see!'

But like the monkey that is said to know instinctively which branch to swing upon, Gurudeva knew whom to trouble. He never provoked a real fighter or anyone who at all looked like a fighter. He would consort with such. He knew his limitations. He knew that in spite of his best efforts he could not very well strike and parry without sustaining blows. He lacked the sixth sense, the ingenuity, the nimbleness – and, above all, the innate recklessness that went to make the true bad-John and the expert *gatka*-man.

But he had tact, and it is to his credit that from the outset he became the leader of the village bad-John clique. His tallness and carriage invested him with a character and individuality that served him well. He was the leader. He brought about all the fights – at weddings, at Hosey time, at Carnival, on pay-day Saturdays – but in almost every case the others did the spade work.

Sometimes their exploits had their sequels in the police court, but Gurudeva would let everybody see that he didn't care a button. Once he went up to his father and said:

'Bap, the whole thing comin' out in court. Jairam, Ramlal,

Dinnoo, meself – all of we is in it. But, Bap, don' pay for me. I will take jail for it. I is a man!'

And old Jaimungal felt great and puffed out his chest in pride. In the end he paid not only for Gurudeva, but for all his colleagues involved in the fracas.

And that was one reason – in fact it was *the* reason – why Gurudeva remained the leader of the village bad men.

6. *Hosey!*

Gurudeva never became a good stickman. He even decided to build a hosey, but this he did mainly to keep up the spirits of the members of his clique. To his father, however, he confided that he was building a hosey because he had gone and made a vow to Hassan to do so. The old man, without questioning him, understood. Naturally, Gurudeva wanted to become the father of a man-child. So he had vowed that he would build hoseys in memory of Hassan and Hussein for five consecutive years.

'You will have to offer them a cock too,' said the old man. 'And *maleeda* – sweetmeat. Go ahead, boy; try you' luck.'

Gurudeva had no idea as to the real significance of Hosey. In some vague way – mainly from the plaintive songs that the women sang during Hosey days – he gathered that it had something to do with two brothers, Hassan and Hussein. Some said that they were the adopted grandsons of Mohammed the prophet. He didn't know. They had fought in a war, it seemed, some time in the dim past, at a place called Kerbala, and were treacherously killed – the one murdered, the other poisoned. They were great fighters who could back a crowd. Of this much he was certain; but as to what they fought for, or what the hoseys signified or stood for, he neither knew nor cared.

It was enough for him that it all culminated in a festival, a passion play with a semi-religious as well as a semi-carnival tang about it, and that it commemorated the fighting talent and subsequent martyrdom of the brothers, who, though purely Mohammedan, with Hosey itself an intrinsically Mohammedan affair, had somehow found themselves included in the vast, ever-accommodating Hindu pantheon, and occupied fairly prominent niches in the infinite Valhalla of the gods; who could grant boons, even as Shiva or Kali or Hanuman could grant boons.

But to his chums Gurudeva advanced an altogether different reason for building the hoseys. He reminded them that the honour of the village must be kept. In fact, the village had no honour, and honour must be given it. Meeting them on the bridge rendezvous, he let them know with brutal frankness that they each ought to be ashamed of himself; that, in fact, each of them ought to drown himself in a handful of water – if more water could not be had – for keeping the village in such disgraceful obscurity.

The young fellows agreed. They resolved that apart from a *gatka* band they must have a hosey; and they vowed that it must eclipse all the other hoseys ten miles around, in splendour and design. The hosey must be a replica of the Taj Mahal itself. Dinnoo had a picture of the Taj Mahal, and the hosey-maker could use that on which to pattern the bamboo framework of the two hoseys – Big Hosey and Little Hosey.

The deliberations closed, the members vacated the bridge rails. The next Sunday, bright and early, Gurudeva himself, accompanied by two of his comrades in arms – Jairam and Dinnoo – sallied forth on a collection tour. From house to house Gurudeva and his companions went. Few dared refuse them a contribution; and the few who did refuse, pleading 'hard up', were given such a look by Gurudeva that they changed their minds there and then, and promised to give their bits as soon as they got money next pay-day.

Within a fortnight sixty dollars was collected, and Gurudeva hired the best hosey-maker to build the hoseys – Big Hosey and Little Hosey.

They were grand creations – especially the Big Hosey. It towered above the crowd on parade day. Gurudeva himself was resplendent in his *gatka* panoply. He wore red satin shorts on which were fixed miniature mirrors and hung with bells around the knees; bells that jingled with every tremor and motion of his body. His shirt was specially decorated; it carried more mirrors than his pants. He had scarlet silk bound tightly round his wrists, from each of which a length of the silk flaunted for style. Magnificently he pranced and pirouetted to the rhythmic thunder of the drums, shouting, 'Ya, Ali! Any man!'

He brandished his stick with style and gusto. He really was impressive, and everybody said so, and he was mighty proud to hear it and shouted, 'Ya Ali!' yet the louder.

But he knew that he was among his own crowd and that no one would take him seriously.

The hour was about three-thirty. The day was hot. The gallery of the big shop at the junction was thronged with spectators – men, women and children. The crowd spilled out on the road.

Then the competing hoseys – three in number – came round the bend in the road a quarter of a mile away from the junction. Borne along in procession, the hoseys gleamed in the distance. They were wonderful creations of bamboo and coloured paper and tinfoil. Each represented the tomb of Hussein. Drums thundered on both sides. With the thunder of the drums blended the voices of women raised in song. Of the valour of Hassan and Hussein, of blood and battle, treachery and murder, of gleaming swords and flying scimitars they sang.

Determined young men, armed with sticks, represented incidents in the war of the Caliph's succession. Gurudeva's cries of 'Ya, Ali!' lessened in frequency. They also lessened in tone and sting. He did not want to get into any serious *gatka* clash. He could not bear the prospect of his sustaining a broken head. He wondered what it felt like when a fellow got a whack on the head with a *gatka* stick.

There were three hoseys coming to the junction. That meant there would be three *gatka* bands. Here at the big shop, when the hoseys met, fights could hardly be avoided. The fellows who were beaten last year would want to get even this year with the fellows who had beaten them. They would throw down their sticks and issue challenges. They would even call the names of the *gatka*-men they would want to get even with. It was terrible.

Suddenly Gurudeva turned to Dinnoo. 'Look here, Dinnoo boy,' he said. 'I have a hell of a headache; me teeth hurting me, too, and me wrist – me right wrist – look like it sprain. Len' me you' handkerchief.'

He took the handkerchief and bound it tightly round his head; he borrowed another and bound his jaw with it, twisting the ends of the cloth into a knot on the middle of his head. The projecting ends went up into two shoots that looked like short horns. With a third handkerchief he bound the wrist of his right hand on top of the silk bandage.

'You look,' Dinnoo told him with a laugh, 'as if you now from hospital. You look funny.'

Gurudeva shot the interlocutor a medusa glance. 'Mind what you saying!' he scowled. He jerked his chin towards the advancing procession of hoseys. 'It is lucky for them, though, that I get sick today. Odderwise I woulda show them,' he said.

7. 'Ya, Ali!'

The hoseys were within a stone's throw of the junction. The *gatka*-men seemed terribly serious. They moved with agility and precision, timing their steps with the rhythm of the drums. Their faces shone with sweat. Sweat drenched their costumes till the thin cloth stuck to their bodies like wet paper. It was not altogether a mimicry representing incidents in the Kerbala battle that had been fought thirteen hundred years ago. The spirits of Hassan and Hussein were the spirits of the *gatka-wallahs*. The women were Bibis and Fatimahs.

The hosey-bearers set down their hoseys. The crowd

swelled in volume. The heat grew more oppressive. The din became an uproar and a babel.

'Ya, Ali!'

Gurudeva was suddenly confronted by a *gatka*-man from one of the opposing camps. The colour left his face. The challenger thwacked his leathern shield on the left hand with his stick dramatically. 'Ya, Ali!' he challenged again.

Gurudeva strove for nonchalance and folded his arms. 'Look here,' he said, 'it is lucky for you I sick today.' He placed his hand on his jaw. 'Me teeth hurting me.'

'Ya, Ali!' roared the challenger, a tall and hefty fellow – as tall and as hefty as Gurudeva himself. 'Is you I want. You play *gatka* wid you' hand, not wid you' teeth. I hear plenty 'bout you. Come out!'

'Orright,' said Gurudeva. 'I won't dotty me stick on you. You is only a little sardine. I will put one of me boys before you. Dinnoo, play this man!'

'Ya, Ali!' cried Dinnoo, thwacking his shield. 'Any man!'

The challenger turned and faced him. 'Ya, Ali!'

They walked to each other and touched hands ceremoniously.

'That is the *salaami*,' Gurudeva explained to a Chinese man who stood near him. 'It is stickman against stickman. Leh them have it out.'

'What is chalami?' asked the Chinese, puzzled.

'It mean,' Gurudeva said impatiently, 'leh we make we peace before we start fighting, because after the fight is over, one or the other of us may not be alive!'

'Leh me lun pack in me parlour den,' said the Chinese. 'Awlight, chus now police going going hold dem.'

The Chinese hurried back to his eight by ten refreshment shack over the road drain.

Stick clattered on stick eloquently. Then Dinnoo made his first blow. The challenger parried it smartly and retaliated almost simultaneously. Dinnoo took it expertly on his shield. The crowd surged around the stickmen. They cheered. Gurudeva held his stick at the ends and pressed back the crowd. 'Give them room!' he kept on saying. 'This is village against village.'

The two men duelled briskly and expertly. Each seemed equally dexterous. Dinnoo shot his second blow. The challenger broke it on his stick. They duelled for about ten minutes. Neither of them could hit the other. Then they stopped. They walked to each other, smiled and shook hands.

'You good for yourself,' the challenger told Dinnoo.

'*You* good too,' answered Dinnoo.

A Donald Duck of a man began to jump and prance before Gurudeva. He was a grey-haired fellow, drunk and merry. He kept on challenging almost everybody to engage him in a *gatka* duel, but no one minded him. 'Sookhwa game today,' they said. 'He remembering he young days.'

Sookhwa was a *gatka*-man in his time, and now that his limbs were no longer lithe, he enjoyed himself on Hosey Day with rum and memories. He kept colliding with people. He could hardly carry himself.

'Ya, Ali!'

He was before Gurudeva now, and prodded him limply with his stick.

Gurudeva began to think fast. Here was an opportunity to redeem himself from the shame of returning home without drawing blood with his mounted stick; of returning home without a spot or two of blood on his gay costume.

He squared up before Sookhwa.

'Ya, Ali!' he cried, and struck the drunken fellow a whacking blow on the head. Sookhwa fell. Gurudeva brought down another blow on the fallen man's head. Blood.

'It is advantage,' someone shouted.

A dozen voices echoed the cry. A police constable came running up. In a flash Gurudeva remembered the boast of his father: Khardukhan would break policemen's heads too. Aiming a blow he struck the constable on the middle of the head. The policeman staggered. Aiming another blow on his head, Gurudeva knocked him down. Then Gurudeva could not move. Three policemen bore down upon him and held him down as in a vice. They wrested away his stick. He struggled but they quickly subdued him with their batons.

Next day, of course, Gurudeva was brought to the police court. The courthouse was packed with spectators. Most of them were Gurudeva's friends. His father and his mother, as well as his brothers with a number of his bosom chums, occupied the front bench. Ratni was there, too, sitting next to Jhulani. Gurudeva had at first objected to her coming; but on second thought had decided to let her come. Only Mira and Dhira remained at home.

Gurudeva had no lawyer. He told his father from the outset that he would plead guilty.

'I beat them and I going take me jail,' he said bravely.

He was accused of wilfully and feloniously wounding Sookhwa and of wilfully and feloniously wounding Police Constable Harker in the execution of his duty. The accusations were laid indictably, but on the consent on Gurudeva, the magistrate decided to take them summarily.

Electing to conduct his own defence, Gurudeva reminded the court that the incident had happened on Hosey Day. Stick-playing, he said, was part of the festival. People got wounded, it was true, but that was only part of the game.

The magistrate dipped his pen in the ink-well before him. 'There is no justification whatever for what you did. The man Sookhwa was drunk. You knew that fully well. Besides, he was an old man. The evidence is that you knocked him down with the first blow of your stick; then you struck him again on the head as he sprawled on the ground. As to your attack on the policeman . . .'

The magistrate turned to the prosecuting sergeant. 'Any previous conviction?'

The orderly looked into a long book and held down a page with his forefinger.

'Six for fighting, seven for disorderly behaviour, three for throwing missiles . . .'

The magistrate puckered up his eyebrows.

'And if I may remind your worship,' said the prosecuting

sergeant, 'in the last case the missiles in question happened to have been addled eggs. Gurudeva went up a tree and hurled the stinking things on a tentful of wedding guests at one of these Indian weddings.'

'I remember,' said the magistrate. 'It was I who dealt with him.' He looked at Gurudeva. 'You are a rotten egg yourself. You will do six months for wounding Sookhwa, and six months for wounding Police Constable Harker. In addition, I deem you a rogue and a vagabond.'

Gurudeva glared. 'Orright,' he said, 'wait until I come back.'

'Constable, take him away.'

Jhulani and Ratni burst into sobs, but a constable at the door quickly ordered them outside. All of Gurudeva's friends walked out in file. On the way to the prison motor-van Gurudeva saw his father. The old man's eyes were red and misty with tears, but he looked bravely and proudly at Gurudeva and said:

'Orright, Guru, break you' jail as a man, boy, an' show dem.'

Gurudeva waved his hand and gave out a quiet smile. 'Is orright, Bap, I is a man.'

8. *The Return of Gurudeva*

When Gurudeva returned from jail it was as though he had returned from the war. It was as though he had returned from the war bedecked with medals for bravery of one sort or another. He was buoyant. He made himself look buoyant. Except that he was slightly paler and a bit thinner, twelve months of prison life seemed to have left him looking as good as his old self. His whole attitude said: 'Look, jail means nothing to me; I am as gay and dashing as ever.'

He alighted on the station platform with an agility that did him credit. He was in grey flannel trousers and in a spectacular 'hot shirt'. It was plain he had these sent him specially for his home-coming. Old Jaimungal was the first to greet him; and here Gurudeva did a thing he had never done before: he stooped and reverently took the dust of his father's foot and carried it to his forehead, as any devoted, well-mannered son should. The old man, in a voice flurried with emotion, murmured: 'Live, son!' Then he embraced Gurudeva. A tear trickled down the old man's cheek.

'Don' cry, Bap,' said Gurudeva. 'I come back; and I come back like a man again.'

Both Ramnath and Makhan, Gurudeva's elder brothers, were there, too, and Gurudeva hurried to meet them. The brothers shook hands, then, before all the people, they kissed each other.

'So how?' asked Ramnath, in a quiet, affectionate undertone.

'Who? Me? I orright,' said Gurudeva.

There was an awkward pause. Then, as though he should say something more, Gurudeva said: 'Jail ain't bad, you know. It is only the name of jail that is bad.'

'*Shabas, beta*! Bravo, son!' exclaimed Jaimungal. 'I like how you take it.' There was no doubt about it, the old man felt proud and lifted. 'Well, you went to jail, an' you show everybody how you is a man. You din go for t'iefing; you went for fighting. No shame in that, boy.'

'I know,' said Gurudeva.

They passed through the wicket gate, Gurudeva letting the ticket-collector know, in an unnecessarily loud voice, that he didn't have to deliver any ticket. He waved his discharged prisoner's pass.

'Pass on,' said the ticket-collector, a young Negro of about twenty-one. 'Hope this is the last time you passing like that.'

'What you say dey?' asked Gurudeva in sudden umbrage. 'Leh me hear you again.'

'Nothing,' said the ticket-collector. 'I ain' say anything. Go your way.'

'Oh-ho!' said Gurudeva.

They got into a taxi.

'Bap,' said Gurudeva, after he had been settled between Ramnath and the old man – Makhan sat with the driver – 'Bap, I never did know jail was so easy. I was friend of the turnkey. Jus' pickin' dry leaf in the Governor garden. Look at me hand.' He spread out both hands, palms up. 'Sof' an' red like jam!'

'True,' said Jaimungal, who, if he had on glasses, would have seen the fossil remains of some corns.

Makhan said: 'And what about the food, Guru? Is true they does give you beef? You shoun' eat it.' Makhan spat clean out of the taxi.

'Give you beef if you want it,' said Gurudeva. 'It was fowl an' fish an' mutton an' sal'fish for me.'

'Good food,' commented Ramnath. 'I thought they woulda give you beef and po'k!'

'They coun't give me what I didn't want. If you is a Hindu they don't force you to eat beef and po'k. And when you talk 'bout food – well, it is in jail you get food. In the morning a whole big cup full of cocoa or tea or coffee. Depending what you want. And bread and butter. Good butter too. The dam Chineyman kian't tell me 'bout butter now. And the bread they sell in the shop is no good. Too small.'

Ramnath and Makhan chuckled, but the old man dried a tear with a corner of his *koortah*. He wasn't crying, really. He was just glad at Guru's being so brave and uncommon.

'If it wasn't for the family you miss in jail, you won't find jail bad,' Gurudeva said, by way of breaking another awkward silence. 'That is the only thing 'bout jail. You miss you' family like hell.' Then suddenly he asked: 'But what about them boys – I mean Dinnoo and Jairam and Ramlal and the odders. Twice they come to see me. Fust time they make me cry. I suppose they goin' rough on me for that now?'

'Not them,' said Makhan.

Old Jaimungal said: 'All the same, *beta*, I think you better don' have much to do wid them boys now. I woun't like to see you go to jail again.'

Makhan said: 'Bap is right, Guru. Keep away from those boys.'

'Who? Me? I done wid them,' said Guru.

This was not true. He was not done with them, though at the moment he may have meant it. But Gurudeva himself was not certain on his next move. His ideas were as yet more or less nebulous.

The fact is, something had happened to Gurudeva in jail, and that thing had to do with religion. Jail, he had found, was no fun. The very day after his arrival at Carrera, the twenty-acre island settlement, he had found himself pounding coconut husks into fibre. The pestle-like hardwood with which he was working blistered his hands in almost no time. After half an hour he threw away the pounding-stick and blew on his hands as though to cool the burning blisters. A tall, khaki-clad man bent over him, and Gurudeva heard the tall man saying:

'Why you not working?'

Gurudeva looked up and saw it was the warder, leaning on a gun. He thereupon truthfully reminded the officer that he, Gurudeva, was not accustomed to hard work.

The officer equally truthfully informed Gurudeva that there were many on the settlement who at the first were also not accustomed to hard work.

Veiling a bribe, Gurudeva hinted he was not a poor man. The warder replied that jail, like heaven, hell, or the law itself, was no respecter of persons.

'You must work,' he said.

To the warder's great astonishment Gurudeva began to sing.

It was not a loud singing; what he sang was slightly above a crooning. But he sang. He sang the song that he had heard his father sing on waking first thing every morning. In a low voice Gurudeva sang: '*Natha mohi abki bera ubaro*! O Lord, this time save thou me!'

Tall, corrugated Bon-Bon, doing fifteen years for manslaughter, watched Gurudeva open-mouthed. Short, rotund, chubby Ching Fu, doing three months for keeping an opium-smoking den in Charlotte Street, the Chinatown of Port of Spain, exclaimed: 'Wa long, Gulu?' Everybody was aghast.

'What's that you saying?' asked the warder.

Gurudeva said: 'I ain't saying anything; I prayin'. I prayin' for God to help me in me trouble.'

'Oh, all right,' said the warder. 'But don't sing now. You can't sing and work at the same time. Not in jail – you understand?'

And this was how Gurudeva got religion into him. Hitherto he had little, if any, of it. Once in six months or so the old man would offer a puja or worship to Hanuman, the Monkey God. But this was not much. It was not a prayer-service really. It was simply a propitiatory ceremony to win the favour of Hanuman, who is a kind of superman, who could dissipate any evil, conquer any malignant spirit, relieve one of any ugly dreams. All that the old man had to do was to call Pundit Shivlochan, the priest, provide some well-cooked *mohan-bhog* – a sweetmeat of flour, ghee, milk and sugar – and bananas and mangoes or whatever fruit there was in season; fry *soharis* and prepare *tarkaris* of pumpkin and of English potatoes, and offer these to Hanuman at the foot of a fifteen- or twenty-foot tall bamboo staff flying a red flag in honour of the god.

Once a year Jaimungal would sit to a *Satya-Narayan katha*, which was a far bigger puja, to which would be invited all the people in the village; for Satya-Narayan was the God of Truth, the creator and upholder of the universe. And after the *katha* there would be *bhajan* or singing, and a great feasting, in which the Brahmins, members of the priestly caste, would be the first to eat.

And apart from these ceremonies Gurudeva knew little else of religion of any kind, nor did he understand, or care to understand, the significance of these things. In the Canadian Mission school that he had attended there was a period in which the class-teacher took the children in Bible lessons, but Gurudeva had never been keen on that. His father kept warning him that he must never become a Christian. 'If you do, I goin' put you out me house, boy.'

So Gurudeva remained a Hindu, and was proud of his being a Hindu, though he hardly knew what Hinduism meant.

After what the warder said to him, he did not sing while at work, but every morning before the jailer came, he would sing in his cell. He knew no set prayer, but he would sing the devotionals his father sang. He would begin one plaint that had for refrain: '*Tum bin Shri Krishna Deva aur kaun mero*? Apart from Thee, O Krishna, who else is for me?'

And he would reach a stage in the singing when it would be difficult to say whether he was singing or crying. The truth is, he would be doing both. Immediately from the tail-end of one *bhajan* he would go off into another, and from this into yet another, till the jailer would come and say to him, 'Now, you stop being noisy.'

Sometimes, unaccountably enough, in the middle of a *bhajan* a wisp of doubt would rise in him, and this wisp would grow into a dense fog clouding his faith and launching him into confusions of utter doubt. Suppose there was no God? Once or twice he had heard Ching Fu say so. Then, were all his *bhajans* addressed to an airy nothing? He would stop singing and call to Ching Fu in the next cell.

'Ching Fu,' he would call. 'Ei, Ching Fu!'

And when Ching Fu would answer, Gurudeva would ask: 'Tell me, Ching Fu, is true there is no God?'

'Aw!' the Chinese would say. 'Done with that. He awlight.'

But this off-hand cynical reply would not satisfy Gurudeva, and he would turn to Bon-Bon, his cell-mate on the other side.

'Bon-Bon,' he would call; 'you hearin'?' And when Bon-Bon would answer, Gurudeva would say, 'Look, Bon-Bon, Ching Fu playing the fool. You tell me now – you think there is a God?'

'Sure there is a God,' Bon-Bon would say.

'How you know?'

'Well,' Bon-Bon would answer, 'look at me, look at Ching Fu – look at all the people in this jail. If it wasn't for a God we wouldn't be here.'

'I think so too,' Gurudeva would say; and his confidence would be restored for a day or two, and he would go about his task quiet and cheerful, so that he was soon credited by many with a deal of piety. Some of the prisoners even began to call him – albeit facetiously – 'Pundit'. And Gurudeva rather liked being called Pundit, and he strove more and more to make his mien that of a priest, missing to his regret only his dhoti and *koortah* and puggree and caste-marks on forehead and arms and throat – like Pundit Sookhlal, his own father-in-law, or like Pundit Shivlochan, the family priest.

One day, in the middle of his fibre-pounding, Gurudeva let off a painful groan. He dropped the pounding-stick and, bending down, held his belly with both hands. 'Is a pain I get,' he cried. 'Oh, God! Me belly!' This occurred towards the end of his sentence.

A little later he began to throw up; a fever came upon him. That night he rolled and howled a lot in his cell. In the morning the prison doctor ordered him to the Colonial Hospital in Port of Spain: Gurudeva had to be operated upon for appendicitis. After hospital, being too weak for Carrera, he was for the remainder of his sentence kept at the Royal Jail in Port of Spain and was taken to do light labour in Government Gardens, sweeping the paths.

And that was how he had come to have soft hands.

They reached the house, and all the family at home came out in a body to meet Gurudeva at the door. Jhulani, Gurudeva's mother, led the van; behind her were Mira and Dhira. Ratni kept shyly in the rear. Jhulani hung on to Gurudeva's neck and, burying her nose on his chest, began to sob convulsively. He let her for a minute or so, then gently held her off.

'Don' cry, Mai,' he said; 'don' cry. Ain't I orright? Ain't I come back?'

She blew her nose and dabbed her tears. Then Mira, seeing her opportunity, smiled a quiet welcome to Gurudeva, and asked: 'How, Guru?'

'I well, *Bhowji*,' he said. 'I quite orright. But how you, eh?'

There was no answer to this. An answer was not necessary.

Then Dhira, Gurudeva's second sister-in-law, the wife of Makhan, exchanged a smile and a word or two with him; and last of all came Ratni. She gave Gurudeva a brief, shy, affectionate, respectful glance with tearful eyes – as indeed she should – and stooped and touched his toe – as which good Hindu wife would not, in the circumstances?

Gurudeva, looking down on her stooping form, said hastily:

'Is orright, is orright.'

He ought not to have said that – not just that, in that shameful way. He ought to have touched her on the head or the shoulder and given her his benediction. He ought at least to have said 'Live!' in Hindi. The moment and the occasion demanded Hindi. But he was shy, as shy as Ratni herself. He felt acutely embarrassed and awkward and found it difficult to say the right words in the right way and in the right language. One simply did not show one's true feelings to one's wife in the presence of all of one's elder relations.

'Well,' exclaimed Gurudeva, 'at last I home!' He yawned and stretched himself.

9. *Gurudeva Becomes a Vegetarian and Teetotaller*

He left them then, and made for his little room in the gallery back of the house. Ratni had everything spick-and-span. There was a clean, washed sheet of flour-sacks on the charpoy and pillows in new cases of cotton-cloth. The floor and walls were freshly done with a thin wash of greyish earth, and everything in the room seemed to be in the same place, almost as he had last seen them. There, in the corner, at the head of the charpoy, stood his sticks, all in a bunch; and there, hanging from the rusty nail on the wall, was his *gatka* regalia – his satin shorts and shirt – looking a trifle dusty and faded, it was true, but there they were, with the mirrors and bells and all. He did not seem to like the look of them, though; he pressed his under-lip and pulled the things down and kicked them viciously away under the charpoy.

'Who the hell want them things again?' he said.

He gave a short look round, then lay down on the charpoy, not bothering to take off his shoes. He lay flat on his back, hands clasped under his head, eyes staring on the black, sooty galvanized-iron roof. He seemed to be in deep thought, or perhaps he was simply luxuriating in this new freedom. The chatter of the people in the house seemed far away and left him unaffected. They were voices he had longed to hear for twelve months.

It was good to be home again; and, oh, it was sweet to be free. He would be a different Gurudeva now. Yes, no more jail for him. He had enough of it.

Sleep began to steal upon him and he yielded himself to it as the saint gives himself to his God.

A little later Ratni came into the room, and seeing him asleep, she felt a sudden stab of pity for him, and she knelt down and quietly undid the strings and took off his shoes. Then, getting up, she whispered as she might have to a sleeping child she did not want to waken: 'Now sleep.'

It was one in the afternoon and he still slept. Then Ramnath came and looked at him. Gurudeva was sweating and muttering in sleep. He flung out an arm, and waking up suddenly with the jerk, opened his eyes. He looked at Ramnath and said: 'Oh, it is you! T'ank God! I thought it was the warder. I was dreaming. I was still in jail.'

He sat up.

Ramnath said: 'Well, you ain't in jail now. Come eat; food ready. Bap and everybody waitin'.'

Normally the family seldom ate together. Eating together was an exception, not a rule. But today was no ordinary day. The occasion called for an eating-together, as on Christmas Day, or any big feast, such as a *katha* or a wedding. The eating-together did not include the womenfolk, however. Jaimungal himself never allowed this. It was odiously un-Hindu. The women must eat after the men had eaten.

The repast comprised curried chicken, rice, paratha, dahl, and *achar*. Mira attended to the dishing out of the food in the kitchen, Ratni and Dhira saw to the serving, Jhulani stood by and supervised. The menfolk squatted in a line on the floor, a sugar-bag or two folded and put under them. Jaimungal squatted in the middle. On one side of him sat Ramnath and on the other Gurudeva; Makhan sat next to Gurudeva. Before each Dhira placed a brass platter laden with the viands, and next to the brass platter a brass jug full of water.

Jaimungal cast his eyes all sides of him, as though looking for something that he ought to see but didn't. 'Wey the rum?' he asked in an undertone.

'I bringin' it,' said Jhulani, and she went into Jaimungal's room and returned with a quart-bottle and four glasses and set them before the men.

'Now eat and drink,' she said.

The Jaimungal lot never drank openly, for Jaimungal proudly regarded himself a Brahmin, a member of the priestly caste, who should not take intoxicating drinks, nor yet flesh or fish food. Nevertheless, Jaimungal drank, and ate meat, and fish too – quietly and clandestinely – at home. So did the 'boys' whom everybody called 'Maraj', an epithet that only Brahmins could wear, be they priests or be they peasants; be they literate or illiterate.

Jaimungal filled his glass. He looked at Gurudeva and said:

'Today, *beta*, is a great day for we. Once again we be all

together. By the grace of God we be all well. Now, *beta*, leh we eat.'

He sent down his rum, wiped his moustache and broke *roti*. Ramnath and Makhan did likewise, but Gurudeva sat quietly, looking away from his food.

'Eat, Guru,' urged Ramnath.

To everybody's surprise Gurudeva shook his head.

'What you mean?' asked the old man.

Gurudeva smiled amiably. 'I ain't eating, Bap,' he said. 'I ain't eating this kind of food. I done with meat and fish. I done with rum.'

Everybody looked up at Gurudeva in utter mystification. The old man, just about to carry *roti* to mouth, put down his hand. Jhulani exclaimed: 'But . . . but . . . but!'

Makhan said: 'Well, I *never* hear that!'

Ramnath spluttered: 'Well, if you ain't going to eat I ain't going to eat either. Is for you we cook these things, and if you ain't eating, who care to eat?' He turned to the old man and to Makhan and said: 'Bap, don' eat. Makhan, don' eat. Everything turn old mas'.'

Gurudeva, still smiling, shoved away the brass platter, and stood up – 'All – you makin' all this fuss for nothing,' he said. 'Look, Mai,' he added, turning to Jhulani, 'I going tell you the truth – is a pundit I going to be. No mo' meat and drink for me . . . Just bring me some plain *bharth* and dahl . . . And put me food in me own room.'

He walked out.

'Well!' exclaimed the old man.

'I *never* hear that!' put in Makhan.

'Everything turn old mas',' moaned Ramnath.

10. *Gurudeva Girds a Dhoti*

That evening Gurudeva did not have as quiet a time as he would have perhaps preferred. A lot of the villagers came to see him. Most of them came out of sheer curiosity; they wanted to see what changes, if any, jail had wrought in him;

but some came because they felt if they did not, Gurudeva and Gurudeva's household on the whole would bear them ill will.

Jairam was there and Ramlal and Dinnoo – Gurudeva's best friends. Jairam was thirty-five, thin and small, son of Jhagroo the barber. He did not follow his father's calling, however. He said barbering of the old-fashion type did not pay. People wanted you to come to their homes and cut their hair; and, as though this was not enough for the twelve cents they paid you for a haircut, those like Baboo Seemungal, who was India-born, expected you to cut their toe-nails and shave their arm-pits; and those who were still older, and consequently still more old-fashioned than Baboo Seemungal, wanted you to give them a massage – all this on top of the haircut. So he had given up barbering, partly to work in the estate sugar-fields as weeder and cutlasser, and partly to catch crabs in the mangrove. He was married in Hindu fashion, had three small children – a boy and two daughters – and he beat his wife almost every Saturday pay-day.

Ramlal was Raghoo the grass-cutter's son, the best cascadura-catcher in the swamps or in old wells and water-catchments. He was about thirty, with a wife, but without children. He wove his own cascadura net and, if going to fish nearer the sea, paddled his own canoe. As no other fisherman within a radius of a mile owned a canoe, Ramlal was regarded as a well-to-do fellow.

Dinnoo was a bachelor, only twenty-five. He said he did not want a wife. He was the son of Birbal the thatcher, who had no other son and was peeved that Dinnoo had consistently turned down every marriage offer that had come to him within the last decade.

'But why you ain't marriedin', boy Dinnoo?' Gurudeva had asked him more than once. 'Big boy like you should be married. It don't look nice for you to be bachelor. Why you ain't marriedin', eh?'

And Dinnoo would shake his head and say:

'I goin' tell you the truth, Guru. I ain't going lie to you.

Well, is a girl I have . . . Old Jhagroo daughter. Remember? She married and she husband dead. *She* is me girl. Have two child for me a'ready, just at she father. Two son and one daughter. What's the use of marriedin' again, eh?'

And Guru would give a sage-like shaking of his head and say, 'You lucky, boy Dinnoo. You right. You *ain't* married and you have two sons; I married and I ain't have no son.'

So that was that as far as Dinnoo went.

On benches and boxes and chairs sat the visitors in Jaimungal's long, open veranda. Half a dozen or so of the youngsters perched on the veranda rail. Everybody had his eyes on Gurudeva, who sat on a grocery box in the middle of the crowd. Some of them looked at him as upon a wonder; or as though he had gone up to the moon and then dropped to earth without a scratch. Most of them refrained from mentioning jail, knowing they would offend Gurudeva if they did so. But Jairam the barber's son said:

'Well, you lucky for one thing, Guru.'

Guru, looking up, asked: 'And what is that now?'

'I mean to say they ain't give you a bad trim,' said Jairam. 'They ain't give you a jail *coupe*. It is a *la chapelle* I see you have.'

Gurudeva's serenity suddenly collapsed. He glared at Jairam. 'If you don't know what to talk about, why you don' keep you' dam mouth shut?' he snapped.

Jaimungal said: 'Guru don't want to hear that kind of talk any mo', Jairam. You better be careful how you talking. Guru have a different mind now. Fact is, he done give up fish and meat.'

Dinnoo, sitting on the veranda rail, nearly fell over.

Ramlal ejaculated, 'Oh, Lor!' then quickly put two fingers over his lips to signify that he had unwittingly said the wrong thing.

Conversation languished. Nobody knew what to say without giving offence to Gurudeva. It was difficult to keep out reference to jail. One by one, and sometimes in groups, the visitors took their leave. Out on the road they discussed Gurudeva freely and fearlessly. Some said jail had 'cooled'

Gurudeva, some that jail had 'tamed' him, others again that jail had simply turned the fellow into a good man.

'Good man me foot!' said Goonoo, the village lout. 'I t'ink de man jus' playin' de ass. Dat is what he is playin'.'

Old Boodhoo said: 'I think this Goonoo is right for once.' In nearly half a century's residence in the island Boodhoo still spoke nothing but Hindi, and still wore nothing but dhoti and *koortah*, he being India-born. 'I have lived long and seen much,' he said. 'Jail has neither tamed Gurudeva nor cooled him nor made him a good man. At heart he is the same Gurudeva, as militant as ever; but now he will be the crusader, the defender of the *Sanatan Dharma* – the eternal religion. You will see.'

The next morning Gurudeva announced to his father that he was done with trousers. He said he would wear nothing but dhoti. (Except on the occasion of his marriage he had never worn a dhoti; and even on that occasion it was old Jhagroo, the barber, who had girded the drapery round him.)

If this surprised Jaimungal it also pleased him. He had seen which way the wind was blowing. To have a son who was a pundit – a son could bring a father no greater prestige. Still, he asked: 'Why that now, eh?'

'Because trousers is a dirty thing,' answered Gurudeva. 'You kian't make puja in trousers. Week after week you keep in it. Dirty.'

'True,' agreed the old man.

Gurudeva said: 'What I mean, Bap, is that I want you to lend me your dhoti. I ain't got none of me own jus' now. Tomorrow —'

'Is orright, *beta*,' cut in Jaimungal. 'I goin' give you some of mine. I full of them.'

Jaimungal never lacked dhotis, although he seldom wore one. Every religious ceremony he attended – and he was invited to all – he would receive a five-yard-long cotton dhoti, with a florin or a shilling or a sixpence piece tied in it at one corner, as *dakshina*, a Brahminic present, in addition to the cotton cloth. Jhulani would make bedspreads of them, and pillowcases; or *koortahs* for Jaimungal, and underskirts for herself and for Dhira and Mira. But even after all these uses Jaimungal's trunk would still have anything from half a dozen to a dozen dhotis.

The old man went into his room and fetched a new dhoti. 'Heh,' he said, 'jus' put this on.'

Gurudeva took the dhoti and laughed and said: 'But you know, Bap, the dam joke is I don't know how to tie a dhoti. Put this jus' over your pants and leh me see how you do it.'

The old man obliged. In a minute he was girdling the long drapery round him, right over his trousers, saying, with every movement and twist of the cloth, 'You do this, then this, then this . . . It is easy.'

He undid the dhoti and, handing it to Gurudeva once more, urged: 'Heh, you try it now.'

'You mean over me pants.'

'Yes, *beta*.'

So Gurudeva stood there and went through the motions, but when he was finished it turned out a bad job. And Jhulani and Mira and Dhira stood looking on from the doorway, very amused.

'Bad! Bad!' commented the old man. 'Will fall down any time. Try again, *beta*. Don' be shame. Is over your trousers you putting it on. Nothing can happen.'

'No; you do it again, Bap, and leh me see.'

Jaimungal gave another demonstration, and when that was over Gurudeva tried to gird on the dhoti a second time.

'That is better,' commented the old man. 'But tighten the tie round your waist a little mo'. Tighten it, *beta*, or it will drop . . . Ah, it droppin', it droppin' . . . It drop! I tell you so!'

'I ain't care,' said Gurudeva. 'I got me trousers.'

'Try again,' urged Jaimungal.

The third attempt was successful, and Gurudeva took care to tighten the tie round his waist this time; and he and everybody else were satisfied that at last he *could* gird a dhoti.

And with that Gurudeva went right away to bathe,

slinging water over his head and shoulders and legs with a brass jug, out in the yard, dipping the water from a bucket, and murmuring, '*Hari Rama, Hari Rama; Rama, Rama; Hari, Hari*!' – invocations to the Deity, just as he had seen Pundit Shivlochan do a long time ago, when he had spent a night at Jaimungal's.

Of course the old man had to give Gurudeva a second dhoti, and Gurudeva wound that drapery over the wet one, expertly slipping down the drenched dhoti and the trousers under *that* before hitching up the crutch-piece of the dry drapery.

Jaimungal gave him an appraising look, then exclaimed: '*Shabas, beta*! Well done, son!'

11. *Gurudeva Erects a* Kuti

Gurudeva was significantly quiet for a few days. Most of the time he kept in his dhoti and seemed to be pondering some deep question. He would sit under the mango tree back of the house, lean back against the tree, draw his knees up or stretch them in front of him, and keep thinking for hours.

If Ratni and the other members of the household had stood in awe of him when he was a stickman and a bad-John or *badmash*, now they were simply flabbergasted. He refused to eat food prepared in the Jaimungal kitchen. He said he would not have his food contaminated in a kitchen to which dogs and cats and fowls and unbathed and unwashed persons had common access.

Getting hold of some mangrove wood that the old man kept for firewood, and salvaging some discarded grocery boxes and some old and twisted galvanized-iron sheets, he rigged up a shack back of the house, and ordered Ratni to put up a new *chulha* or fireplace in it. Ratni obeyed. He insisted on her taking a bath each day, before preparing his meals, and he saw, too, that she daubed the *chulha* with a wash of cow-dung and earth before she lighted the fire. The first time he came upon a chicken pecking some scattered food grain in the new kitchen, he promptly fetched one of his *gatka* sticks and pelted it at the creature with all his might. The missile missed the chicken by an inch.

Ratni was grinding massala for the currying of *bodee* that she had already cleaned and picked.

'Look,' he said to her in his old, bossy tone, 'you right here with your two eye open, and you allow a chicken to come in this kitchen?'

Ratni stopped the back-and-forth movement of her hands over the massala-stone, and looked at him in a puzzled kind of way and said: 'I din see it. The kitchen ain't have no door. You mus' put a door.'

He ignored her remark and said: 'Now go and *leepey*' – he meant daub – 'the whole *chulha* back again. *Leepey* it, or I won't eat the food you cook on it.' He paused a minute as though not knowing what else to say; then added: 'And look. I just nearly send the daylight out of that dam chicken. Don't leh me see another chicken in here. I want no fowl and nobody in this kitchen. Remember!'

Ratni seemed more puzzled than ever.

He stood back of her, tall, menacing, legs well apart.

She asked: 'What you mean? Nobody to come in the shack? You mean Mai and Baba and Big Sisters and everybody?'

'Yes, that is exactly what I mean,' said Gurudeva. 'Only them who bathe every morning can come in me kitchen. And them who don't eat meat and fish. Like me.'

'But I kian't stop them,' Ratni argued. 'I will be shame to stop them. Them is not fowl and dog. You better stop them you'self.'

He scowled and pulled his under-lip; then left her.

Most of that day he remained in deep cogitation, leaving everybody to wonder whether he was ill. Jaimungal was visited by an awful suspicion.

'I wonder,' he said. He was speaking to Jhulani, who sat on the doorstep mending a *cocoye* broom.

'Wonder what?'

'I wonder if Guru right in he head. Whole day he remaining quiet; whole day he thinking and mumbling to heself; he putting on dhoti – and he ain't want to see a chicken in he kitchen. I hear him jus' now. I hear him playin' hell with Ratni. I don't know what to say.'

Jhulani said: 'Don't talk like that. You should be glad you have a son like Guru. Is a pundit he goin' to be. He kian't have chicken in he kitchen. Don' worry, man; he orright.'

Jhulani was right. Gurudeva's cogitations bore fruit. Within a week of his home-coming he put up a *kuti*. That was where, he explained, he would perform his puja – his worship.

He erected the *kuti* in his father's ample yard, facing the road. Jairam, Ramlal and Dinnoo, his best friends, helped him to put it up. It was a grass-thatched hut some twelve feet square, half-walled on all sides, except for a doorway. The floor, like the walls, was of earth.

In the middle of the *kuti* Gurudeva raised an earthen altar, one foot high, three feet long, and two feet wide. Then with Jairam and Ramlal and Dinnoo he went to the bamboo patch from which he had obtained his bamboo for his stick-receptacle in the days when he was eager to be an able stickman and a don't-care-a-damn bad-John. There they cut some long, ripe bamboos and toted them half a mile to the *kuti*. They cut the bamboo into various lengths and made a continuous line of bench against the short walls inside the *kuti*.

'This is the *baithaka*,' Gurudeva told his father when he came to inspect the *kuti*. 'When I doing me puja or singing me *bhajan*, people could sit down and watch and listen.'

'*Shabas, beta!*' said Jaimungal, and patted Gurudeva on the back.

When all was finished he made Ratni daub the walls, in and out, with the earth-and-cowdung wash; also the floor and the altar, which later Gurudeva called the *singhasan*, which was another name for an altar or throne. He knew cow's dung, when fresh, was sacred; dry, it was only good for fuel. He couldn't say why it was sacred; it had always seemed most unaccountable and peculiar to him; but he had not paused to reason. He had seen it used in every important religious ceremony, and that was authority enough for him. And he knew that, more than being sacred, cow's dung mixed with earth prevented cracks in earthen walls and floors.

He draped the *singhasan* with red cotton, and placed upon it a brass image of God Krishna, and another of Krishna's other half, Radha, borrowing these from Pundit Sookhlal. At the foot of the *singhasan* he placed a short slab of stone that he had picked up in the river, and on the flat stone a four-inch stick of sandalwood. His delight would have been complete had he had a tiny bell and a white conch-shell; for the whole idea of the *kuti* he had had from Pundit Sookhlal, only he was determined to make his *kuti* even more impressive. The tiny bell and the conch, and pictures of the four-armed Vishnu and of Shiva the destroyer and of Hanuman the Monkey God, and maybe a print or two of Goddess Kali – he would obtain from Kalinath, the dealer in Indian goods, the first time he went to Port of Spain.

He stood back and surveyed the *singhasan* and clapped his hands. The *kuti* looked neat and pretty and he was very pleased.

'But I will make it prettier yet,' he said to Jairam, who, with Ramlal and Dinnoo, was taking it easy on the bamboo bench. 'You will see.'

Then he called Ratni, and when she came he told her to bring him some slabs of Oxford blue, which she used for her washing. He mixed the blue in some coconut oil in a calabash, stirring the mixture with his long finger.

Jairam, assailed by curiosity, asked: 'What you goin' do with that, Guru?'

'You will see,' Gurudeva said mysteriously.

He stood up, calabash in hand, and went up to the *singhasan* and dropped on his knees, ready to write on the

wall, above the *singhasan*. Then he hesitated, laughed and
said:

'Joke is, I don't know how to write *Ram-nam* in Hindi. Is
Ram-nam I was going to write. I want to write *Ram-nam* right
round the walls. Well, I think I will call Bap.'

Jaimungal himself could hardly cope with the simplest
book or booklet in Hindi. When a boy he had gone through
the first primer and had tackled the second about half-way.
Then he had given up. He said that his head was 'too hard'
and that he preferred to earn his livelihood with a cutlass and
a hoe in cane- or rice-field, if it came to that, rather than to
have to read and write Hindi. He said what was in his karma
was bound to come his way, anyway. He was cheeky; and
when the teacher, Ramdhan by name, tweaked his ear one
evening in the course of a reading lesson, Jaimungal spun
upon his bottom and thus most disrespectfully turned his
back to the teacher.

'I ain't readin',' he said. 'I ain't *want* to learn to read.'

'Give the boy another tweak in the ear,' Jaimungal's
father had said to Ramdhan; but that man had simply shaken
his head to say no, he couldn't do it – not if the boy was
really angered against him.

That night a scorpion stung Ramdhan, and he said he was
sure that what had happened was a punishment from on high
for his tweaking the ear of a Brahmin boy. In the morning
Ramdhan took hold of his own right ear between thumb and
forefinger and gave it a sharp twist. 'I vow,' he told himself,
'to have nothing to say to that boy, he a Brahmin, and I a
chamar.' A *chamar*, a sweeper and worker in leather.

Nevertheless, ultimately Jaimungal acquired a reputation
as a reader and writer of Hindi. And, in fact, he did read. He
read the *Hanuman Ashtak,* a eulogy on the Monkey God,
printed in large, bold letters in a five-inch by three-inch
twelve-page booklet. He read this whenever he was visited by
ugly dreams, or whenever he had a difficult problem to solve,
or a stubborn enemy or a stubborn spirit to overcome. In his
more religious mood he would stumble and stammer over a

page or two of the *Ramayana*, or bravely tackle the *Prem Sagar* or the *Arjuna Gita*. All the simplest of simple books in Hindi. Other than these he read nothing. It was beyond him to read anything else. And if he read badly, he wrote worse. Though visually he knew all the letters in the Hindi alphabet, when it came to writing them their individual shapes and twists eluded him. He mistook a *pa* for a *pha*, a *bha* for a *jha*, a *ya* for a *tha*. They were so nearly alike. But this puzzlement the old man would hardly admit even to himself, leave alone his admitting it to others. Surely, if one could read and speak a language one could just as well write in it.

'Bap!' called Gurudeva.

The old man did not hear. He was cleaning a clump of sugar-cane back of the house, and the rustle of the crisp, dry trash drowned Gurudeva's voice.

He called again, louder this time. The old fellow came, puffing and sweating.

Gurudeva said: 'Look, Bap, the *kuti* finish. Only some pictures I want on the walls. And a *sanch*' – a conch-shell – 'and a *ghanti*.' A tiny bell.

The old man put his palms together and bowed to the images of Krishna and Radha on the altar.

'Look, Bap,' added Gurudeva, 'is *Ram-nam* I want you to mark on the walls . . .'

'Yes, *beta*.'

It took Jaimungal the better part of half a day to finish inscribing *Ram-nam* in some six places, and when he was finished only he or a very good reader could decipher what he had inscribed.

Gurudeva contented himself by making an outline drawing of the Monkey God: Hanuman flying across ocean, bearing aloft on one mighty hand a whole peak of the Himalaya.

'Good, *beta*,' exclaimed Jaimungal. 'That is a good Hanuman.'

'Yes, Bap,' said Gurudeva.

12. *Gurudeva Becomes a Pundit*

'Say, *ka* – say, *ka-kabirkane-kah.*'

Pundit Shivlochan deliberately opened his mouth high and wide to utter the last syllable. He was teaching Gurudeva to read Hindi and he wanted him to understand that *kah* had the long sound.

They were in the *kuti*. It was dusk and the little earthen lamp on the *singhasan* had already been lit; and Gurudeva was being taken in his reading lesson in the light of an un-shaded oil-lamp. The pundit sat on a charpoy, his feet on the earthen floor, his elbows on his knees, his chin on his hands. He was looking down on the booklet that lay open before Gurudeva, who sat cross-legged, like a true *chela* or disciple, at the teacher's feet. He was in dhoti but nothing else. It was the beginning of the second week since he had embarked on his learning to read and write Hindi. Instead of his going to Pundit Shivlochan's he had induced the pundit to come to him.

The pundit was a tall, thin, mild-looking person of about sixty or sixty-five. He had small rheumy eyes below a bush of grey eyebrows. His moustache was all grey too; and he had a hawk's nose, pitted with what might have been small-pox some time in his early life.

'Say, *ka-kabirkane-kah.*'

Gurudeva tried to say the words but the sounds he uttered amounted to something totally different to the sounds uttered by Pundit Shivlochan.

The pundit frowned.

'Open your mouth like this,' he said, giving Gurudeva a demonstration. 'Say, *ka-kabirkane-kah.*'

Gurudeva tried again but nearly bit his tongue.

The pundit turned the Hindi primer face down. He, rather than Gurudeva, seemed discouraged. Gurudeva was not proving as apt a pupil as he would have wished. True, Gurudeva had arranged to pay him fifty dollars at the end of the course, which, it was stipulated, would last about three months; but it seemed to him now that at the rate at which Gurudeva was progressing he would have to be teaching him a whole year to earn that fifty dollars, if he would earn it even then.

Pundit Shivlochan lived in Penal, some thirty miles away from Gurudeva's village. He was beginning to regret that Gurudeva had somehow succeeded in making him leave home. Now he shook a lank forefinger and said to the pupil:

'Unless you do better I do not think I, or anybody else, can do much for you. I am not a rich man; far from it. I cannot prolong my stay here indefinitely. I have my wife and four children to see about. Lakhna is wayward, and Chandariah is too big a girl to be left only to the care and protection of her mother. Raise the wick of that lamp.'

He took up the primer once more and placed it back on the floor, face up.

'Now try again,' he said. 'I will make it simpler for you. Look at me: keep your mouth nearly shut to say *ka*; open it wide to say *kah*.'

'*Achcha, Nana.* Yes, grandfather,' said Gurudeva. '*Ka-kah.*'

'Now you have it,' commented Pundit Shivlochan. 'Now go on to *kih-kee, kuh-koo, kay-kai, ko-kow, kang-kanh.*'

Gurudeva managed it.

Pundit Shivlochan slapped his thigh with one hand and tugged his moustache with the other.

'Now that is fine,' he said. 'Now you will learn fast enough.'

It surprised a lot of people that in just two months Gurudeva was reading all the books that Jaimungal kept on his little shelf. One month more and he was reciting the *Ramayana* itself; and not only the *Ramayana*, but the *Bhagavad-Gita* too – in Sanskrit.

You might say he made the villagers bawl.

Further into the subtleties of Hinduism he did not penetrate. He dared not. He was keen – and oh, how keen! – only on his being acknowledged a pundit, not necessarily a priest, though every Hindu priest in Trinidad is also called Pundit. He had neither the patience nor the inclination to learn by rote all the multifarious details that centred on even a simple puja, leave alone the details of rituals on, say, a marriage ceremony.

After all, a priest was only a kind of tradesman, so to speak. He did a job and was paid for it, in cash or in kind, or in both. So reasoned Gurudeva, for so he had heard his own father say. His father had said, moreover, that in some parts of India itself priests were looked down on as mere ritualists – a low class of Brahmins . . .

Now Gurudeva would do a puja every morning, and then sit or recline or sleep on his charpoy in the *kuti* till noon. (Pundit Shivlochan had packed and gone.) Then he would wake up and go and eat alone in his kitchen priest-fashion, that is to say, he would eat squatting on the mud floor, clad only in his dhoti, naked from the waist up. Then he would come out once more to the *kuti* and take to his charpoy and talk or argue about the *Sanatan Dharma* – the orthodox religion. Mostly it would be Dinnoo or Ramlal or Jairam that he would talk or argue with when they were freed from their work in sugar- or paddy-field. He said a lot of things were going wrong with the *Sanatan Dharma*. And if anyone said or did a thing against the *Sanatan Dharma*, Gurudeva felt he was the man to bring the offender to book. He seemed to be ever on the look-out for such offenders.

Just now he had his eye on Ramdas. The week before Gurudeva had put up a *jhandi* – a flag – to the Monkey God. He had invited almost the whole village to the ceremony, but, it being paddy-reaping time and a sun-blazing day after days of intermittent rain, only about a dozen people had turned up. The puja was therefore not as much a success as he had hoped it would be, and this had embittered him against many.

Ramdas was one of those who had not come to the puja. Gurudeva was sure the fellow entertained anti-Sanatanist sympathies. So he had his eye on Ramdas, who lived within sight and hailing distance of the *kuti*. He knew Ramdas had a cow. He knew —

13. *Gurudeva, Ramdas, and the Cow*

Ramdas was a short, thin person of about forty-five, with a prominent Adam's apple and a sharp, pointed nose. Mostly you saw him in trousers and shirt, with the shirt tail almost always out. Everybody called him 'Maraj', and in a quiet, confident sort of way he was rather proud of this. He knew it was not so much a name as an honorific epithet. He knew he was called Maraj because he was a Brahmin, a member of the priestly caste, the highest place in the Hindu social set-up.

He could neither read nor write, though he sometimes recalled, with some show of pride, that at one time he used to know all the letters in the English alphabet – all.

Knowing he was a Brahmin, he avoided as best he could doing those things that Brahmins should not do. He did not eat beef, did not even touch it; he observed the same taboo on pork or on any other product of the pig. He was careful not to touch the wives of his younger brothers, nor yet to joke with them. This, he knew, was also most improper.

And he carried out those duties that Brahmins *should* carry out. He looked upon cows as *gow-matas* – as mother-cows; and at times, in his most Brahminic moments, quite meant it. On *Divali* night – the festival of lights – he lit, like any good Hindu, at least a dozen little earthen lamps to Lakshmi, the goddess of luck and prosperity; and on the approach of the holy festival of *Shiva-Ratri* he walked barefooted, brass jug in hand, to the nearest temple and there performed an ablution on the idol of Shiva. If he could spare himself from cane- or paddy-field, he went to *Rama-Leela*, the annual pageant of Rama, on the last day of the ten-day festival, and offered a pound or so of *meethai*, sweets, to God Rama or to the boy who performed as God Rama. And once every six months or so he put up a red flag to Hanuman, the Monkey God, and sometimes a white flag, too, to Suraj-Narayan, the Sun God.

On these occasions Ramdas lived completely as a high-caste Hindu: no rum, no fish or flesh food of any kind, no cuss-word. For the duration of the puja he would perforce gird a dhoti round him and allow the priest to smear his forehead with a pinch of sacred ash. He would feel more holy then than comfortable, and as soon as the puja was over, or the priest gone, he would get back into his trousers (though not necessarily into his shirt) and return to his normal life. It would be up to him then to drink his rum – after wiping off the sacred ash – or administer a clout or two to one or more of his smaller children for their not behaving well enough during the puja, or give Mrs Ramdas a short but emphatic bawling down for her not having some of the puja things ready at hand.

All in all, he was not a bad man. He worked hard in cane or paddy-land, reared his family – a wife and ten sons – looked after his donkey and his cow, and on the whole minded his own business.

But of late he was not a happy man. It was the cow that made him unhappy. He was more than unhappy. He felt bitter, cut-up and frustrated. Today he was in one of his sour moods. At the moment he was sitting on a short log on which he had just finished chopping chop-chop, or cane-tops, for the donkey. He sat on the log, his cutlass at his side, and looked at the cow with extreme distaste. The cow was tethered to a stump in his backyard, about ten feet away from the donkey.

It was a pretty red-and-white cow. Two years ago Ramdas had bought it from Agnoo, who lived three miles away in Bejucal. Because the cow was red-and-white he called it Chitkabari. Everybody called it Chitkabari. It was sleek and big all over, and Agnoo said it was like that because it wanted just three months to deliver calf.

A tear trickled down Agnoo's cheek. He was a short man with a bony squareness of shoulders, an amiable fellow of about sixty in a scanty dhoti and merino, his head almost bare of hair.

'I tell you, O Ramdas,' he said, 'I would never part with this cow but that I stand in urgent need of money for a pressing cause. Thou art lucky!'

'Art thou sure about this, O Agnoo? That this cow will put down in just about three months?' asked Ramdas, for he was a careful man.

'God knows,' said Agnoo, truthfully. 'Take it home and thou wilt see.'

'Orright,' said Ramdas, in English this time. 'I will buy she.'

He did. He paid sixty dollars for the cow and regarded the deal a bargain. He and his eldest son, Dipraj, led the cow home. Ramdas drove a stout stump of hardwood back of his house, and tethered the cow thereto. He fed it well. He fed it on chop-chop, he fed it on para-grass, on giant grass, on guinea-grass, corn-grass – and on quite a variety of other grasses, besides.

The cow, already fat, grew fatter. It shone. Ramdas, for some reason known only to himself, kept the animal tethered to the same stump, on the same spot, month after month, only throwing it fresh beddings of dried grass every evening. In a month the bedding heap rose high and with it the cow. Two months went by, three, four, five . . . six . . .

'Eh, eh!' exclaimed Ramdas. 'Wha' wrong wid this cow? Man say she will put down in t'ree months. Cow here six months now – and no calf. Eh, eh!'

He would look at the cow often, watching to see whether its belly was growing, or had grown, bigger. He would stoop and look at its udder, knowing that a cow developed that organ near calving time. He saw no change. He could hardly believe his eye. The cow remained as sleek and round and sweet as ever. He began to suspect that Agnoo had fooled him; and as many people as would come to his house he would ask to look at the cow.

'Look at this cow,' he would say in an off-hand sort of way. 'T"ink she full?'

Some said yes, some said no, some said they just couldn't say. Ramdas would look at the cow open-mouthed and pass one finger over his lower lip in a thoughtful, sawing fashion. Then he would curse Agnoo, and when he was done with Agnoo, would tremble to curse the cow itself; but would desist. *Gow-mata*. And perhaps the cow *was* in calf. He didn't know.

'Is a hell of a thing,' Ramdas would say, instead.

Then he called Jagoo. Jagoo being an *ahir* – an India-born cowherd – was supposed to know everything that one could possibly know about cows. He was a kind of local vet for cattle.

This Jagoo gave the cow a thorough look-over, felt it all over too. Then he looked at Ramdas and shook his head dolefully and said: 'Well, Maharaj, I do not want to hurt your feelings, but the truth is the truth. This cow is no more in calf than my own bull in its pen.'

'No?'

'No.'

'But Agnoo who sold it to me, Agnoo said she would put down in three months.'

'Agnoo is a liar,' said Jagoo. 'I know the man. What you have to do now, Maharaj, is to take the cow to a bull-pasture; and when you have brought it back – say after a month – do *not* feed it high. High feeding will make her lose calf – will make her fat.'

Ramdas obeyed. He took the cow to the leanest pastures he knew in his area; and when he brought the cow back home he was pleased to see that the animal, like the pasture it had come from, looked a good deal lean. He tethered it to the same old stump and took good care that the cow had as little to chew as possible. He warned his wife and the first three of his ten boy-children that they 'must not ever forget and feed it high'.

'Jus' give she a cane-top or two – and some plain water,' he said. 'That is all.'

The grace of the Almighty was upon that cow. For three months the sun blazed upon it; then the rains descended, and the wind blew; mosquitoes kept up their infernal chant upon her; flies lived, buzzed, and had their fill of her. But that cow, tethered to its stump, stood its ground. It neither mooed nor collapsed. But it had shrunk. Its ribs stood out in bands. Its red-and-white hair no longer shone, but stood in scrubby, lustreless patches on its tawny hide.

'Bhagavan be praised!' said Ramdas in Hindi; 'now this cow cannot but be in calf. I took good care to see that it was not overfed. Yes, this time she *is* in calf.'

But the cow was not in calf. It took Ramdas another nine months to be convinced of this; and when he was, he (not the cow) nearly collapsed. He called in Jagoo again, and Jagoo obliged; but, as before, shook his head to say that the cow was not *garbhin* – was not in calf, never was and never would be.

'It is a barren cow that you have got here now, O Ramdas,' said Jagoo.

'You bitch! You good-for-nothing!' spluttered Ramdas from the chop-chop log. 'Now what the hell I going do with you?'

The expletives were directed to the cow, of course (which stood looking at Ramdas with great streaks of *yampi* running down its eyes). He had stopped calling it Chitkabari; it was too much of a pet name, and he could no longer find it easy to pet that cow. He referred to it by all sorts of crazy names and cuss-words, the most common of which was 'bitch'. He knew bitch was a bad word for a cow, and that calling a cow a bitch was as sinful and shameful as calling one's own mother a bitch: a cow was *gow-mata*. Still, he could not help it. His chagrin got the better of him.

'Now,' he vituperated again, 'what the devil I going do

wid she? Can't keep feeding she all the time for nothing. Can't sell she; nobody would want a cow that don't give young.'

Mrs Ramdas came and grudgingly threw the cow a couple of cane-tops. She turned to Ramdas. She had heard what he had said.

'Some people would sell she to a butcher and be done wid she,' she said.

Ramdas gave her a quick glance. The thought had crossed his mind too, but he had not dared express it.

'Careful!' he said. 'Don' use them words. Is a sin. *Gowhatia*. Cow-murder. Thousand and thousand of years in hell for that. Careful!'

Mrs Ramdas, a biggish, brownish woman of about forty, with long, oily black hair and a gold ring on the left side of her nose, exclaimed, 'Chut!'

She looked at the cow again – this time with a pitiful eye. 'Look to me that starving she like that is worse than *hatia*,' she said. 'Sell she and be done, is what I say. Just common sense, man.'

He said: 'Trouble in that. People will know. If nobody know, Gurudeva *bound* to know. And when *he* know, everybody know.' He looked toward Gurudeva's *kuti*, and added: 'He have a spite for me, too; think I ain' go to he *jhandi* for sake of malice.'

Mrs Ramdas cut in with: 'Orright, suppose he know – what then?'

'Well, it will be panchayat 'gainst we,' Ramdas said. 'Put we *ku-jat* – make everybody outcaste; 'cept we feed him and all the other Brahmins and priests. Shame in that.'

Ramdas knew what he was talking about. He knew he ought not to sell a cow to a butcher. He was a Brahmin; in virtue of which fact he was made to sit at every feast and ceremony exclusively with Brahmins; and after feasting, received his Brahminic presents of silver and cotton cloth. People respected him; and this respect that he enjoyed flowed mainly from the fact of his being a Brahmin. As such it was his duty to protect cows. To sell a cow to a butcher, even unknowingly, was a monstrous sin – as monstrous a sin as Brahmin-murder itself, than which no other murder was more hell-begetting.

He shuddered.

He knew, of course, that most Hindus in Trinidad no longer paid much heed to this aspect of the matter. Times had changed. If you lived in St James or San Fernando or Arima, or in any of the other hotchpotch and polyglot towns of the island, you could be a Hindu and yet sell your cow to a butcher without anybody asking you a word about it. Or if, by chance, a meddlesome Hindu did question you, you could frankly tell the man to go to hell. After that the only action he could take against you would be, perhaps, to bring you up before a magistrate on a charge of your using insulting language to him. Even so, the magistrate, hearing the circumstances of the case, would most probably dismiss the charge. He might even advise the plaintiff to mind his own business in the future; and tell him, moreover, that he – the magistrate – might have himself used the same three words to one who could be so beside himself as to question him why he had sold his own cow – supposing he had one.

But Cacande was not like St James or Arima or San Fernando. Cacande was not polyglot. Cacande was a little India, almost wholly Hindu-populated, and cows there are as sacred today as they are in India itself. In Cacande, as in Debe and Penal, in matters such as *gow-hatia*, if you offended one you offended all. Of course you were made to feast a company of Brahmins and priests, but that didn't put matters entirely right for you. The *panch* or community never forgot you as one who sold cows to butchers. Everybody laughed and talked with you as before, but behind people's amiability lurked a grudge and distrust. Ramdas knew well enough that in his own case – supposing he was caught – many would grudge him his epithet of Maraj – feast or no feast. And it was by no means easy to dispose of a cow such as his without somebody in the village getting wind of the transaction.

Ramdas shook his head.

'In this place,' he told Mrs Ramdas, 'you could only sell your cow to a butcher and still be friendly wid everybody, if you you'self is *not* a Hindu. Which can't be. Not in Cacande. Or you mus' be friendly wid the butcher, very friendly – and yet not so friendly that everybody should know. That would spoil everything.'

The butcher's motor-lorry passed and re-passed Ramdas's house once or twice every week. Ramdas knew the lorry well enough. It was a green-painted thing, with tall, stout pickets on all sides. The lorry would go empty towards Brasso Caparo; it would return, late in the afternoon, with one or two bulls tied closely to one or two of the pickets. He knew the bulls were intended for slaughter. Once or twice he had seen cows in the lorry. That sight had made him wince.

Yet, of late, Ramdas would find himself deliberately looking at the lorry as it passed. Then he would turn away. 'No,' he would tell himself. 'No; it will be a sin. *Gow-hatia*.'

The bearded Indian driving the lorry would look at Ramdas, then he would look at Ramdas's cow. He had, in fact, eyed that cow often, ever since the days it had been well-fed and sleek; but he knew Ramdas was a Maraj and would never sell *him* the cow – the more so if the cow was in calf. But in nearly two years he had seen no calf, and the cow had dwindled from day to day. Clearly, something had gone awry with that cow. Perhaps . . .

One day the lorry stopped before Ramdas's house. It was on the return trip from Brasso Caparo and it was empty. Ramdas was chopping firewood in the yard, in front the house. The bearded man leaned out of the cab and looked at Ramdas. Ramdas gave him one glance and went on chopping his wood.

'Say, Maraj,' called the butcher, in a low voice, 'you sellin' that cow?'

Ramdas looked up, wiped some sweat off his forehead, and said:

'Sellin' it, yes; but not to a butcher. I can't sell to a butcher. Me is a Maraj.'

The butcher grimaced in a friendly way. 'Who else you think will buy a barren cow?'

'Go, go your way,' said Ramdas, frightened. 'Don' let people see you talking to me. Is trouble you going put me in.'

The butcher said: 'I will give you a good price ... I will give you – well, say fifty dollars.'

'No, no; I not sellin',' said Ramdas, sweating hard. 'Go, go your way. I don't want anybody to make me *ku-jat*.'

'You can trust me. I won't talk,' insisted the butcher ... 'All right ... Sixty dollars. Now, that's a good figure. The cow ain't got much on it.'

Mrs Ramdas came out quickly and whispered to Ramdas: 'It is a good price. It is the same price you buy the cow for. Don' be foolish. Tell the man orright.'

Fresh sweat broke on Ramdas's face. He looked up and down the road. Nobody was in sight, but there was Gurudeva's *kuti*.

'Orright,' he said, 'but go now. See me another time. Go, go now.'

The butcher-man smiled and drove off.

Ramdas sat down on the pile of wood and gave himself to a host of extremely disturbing misgivings. He looked accusingly at his wife, who was now steadily chipping pumpkin in a calabash, and said:

'Is you ... is you make me do it.' He wrung his hands. 'Now, what we going do?' he asked. 'I sure the butcher-man will come back. I hope he will have sense enough to come by the back street. I hope he will have sense enough not to come in daylight ... Is you ... is you ...'

Mrs Ramdas stopped chipping the pumpkin and dropped the knife in the calabash. She looked at her husband with a hurt look in her eyes and said: 'Don' talk like that, man. Just take the fork and dig a big hole in the yard. Make the place look like a cow bury there. If anybody ask – the cow dead, that's all.'

The eldest son said: 'Yes, Bap, leh we do it.'

Father and son worked late with fork and shovel that night. They dug the ground as though they really had to bury a dead cow in it. They threw up a lot of earth. Then they began refilling the hole, and after that to shape up the mound. Suddenly back of them something crashed to earth with a tremendous thud.

The boy cried out: 'Oh God, Bap! The cow fall down!'

Indeed, it was Chitkabari.

They both ran to it. The creature was stretched out on its side. Its legs twitched once, it frothed at the mouth, emitted a faint moo. Then it died.

'It dead,' said Ramdas.

'It dead,' said the boy, with a sob.

Then they set to digging the hole all over again.

In the morning Gurudeva looked out of his *kuti* and his belly gave a jump: Chitkabari was not in its accustomed place; at any rate he did not see the cow. Having had the full history of the animal from Dinnoo and Ramlal, he had been on the look-out to see that cow go. He knew if it went at all it would go only to a butcher. And he knew if that happened Ramdas would be at fault.

'Ah-hah!' he exclaimed. 'I catch 'im today!'

He called for Dookhwa, the general factotum in the Jai-mungal household – a young, ill-clad fellow of about seven-teen, with matted hair begging for a cut, and a grimy face begging for a wash.

'Go and tell Ramdas that I call him right away,' Gurudeva told Dookhwa. 'Tell him that if he don't come right away, is trouble for him – is water more than flour for him.'

Dookhwa found Ramdas sitting on a bench, looking sad, vexed and tired.

'Pundit call you,' said Dookhwa.

'What the hell he want?' asked Ramdas. 'I ain't do him nothing.'

But he went.

Gurudeva had just finished his puja and sat on his charpoy exuding a mixed odour of incense, sandalwood paste and marigold.

Without any preamble he said to Ramdas:

'I suppose you know why I call you, eh?'

'I don't know why. I ain't do no wrong.'

'You is a Brahmin, ain't so?'

'That is so. I is a Brahmin, me poopa was a Brahmin, me gran'poopa was a Brahmin. What wrong with that?'

'You will know just now,' said Gurudeva. 'I will make water more than flour for you. You know a Brahmin must look on a cow like he looking on he own mooma?'

'I know that.'

'You had a red-and-white cow?'

'I *had* a red-and-white cow. Chitkabari.'

'It was a *bahila* – a cow that *don't* put down?'

'If you say a cow is like your own mooma, you shou'n't call it *bahila*. Is not a good word. It don't sound nice,' Ramdas said.

'Shut your mouth and answer me question.'

'I kian't shut me mouth and answer question. Nobody can do that.'

'I going fix you up,' said Gurudeva, in parenthesis. 'You playing smart. Up to yesterday I see that cow from me *kuti* here. This morning it ain't there. What you do with the cow?'

'I ain't do nothing with the cow.'

'You lie. Yesterday I see you talking with the butcher-man. I see you from me *kuti* with me own eye. Where the cow?'

'It dead,' said Ramdas.

'You lie.'

'Come and see, then,' Ramdas said.

Gurudeva jumped out of the charpoy.

'Orright,' he said, 'leh we go.'

At Ramdas's he saw, to his great disappointment, that after all Ramdas hadn't sold the cow to a butcher; he hadn't sold the cow to anybody. The cow *was* dead. It sprawled on its bedding-heap.

'But it is true!' he said, very surprised.

'She dead last night,' said Ramdas. 'The hole dig a'ready. Come now, Pundit, and give a hand to help bury she.'

'Who? Me? Not me!' said Gurudeva. 'I just make puja. Kian't touch dead cow.'

14 *Gurudeva Issues a Challenge*

It was a Sunday, and Dinnoo and Ramlal and Jairam were at the *kuti* since puja-time. Jairam gathered some flowers for Gurudeva off the hibiscus hedge, for he knew that gathering flowers for Gurudeva was a meritorious act: Gurudeva would offer the flowers to the gods; part of the blessings of Krishna and Radha would come his way, not to speak of the benign protection of the Monkey God and of the other deities.

Ramlal split some firewood for Ratni; for Gurudeva, though insisting on his food being prepared in his own special kitchen, would nevertheless touch nothing like an axe. Any very laborious work was not for him, he said. Ramnath and Makhan had begun to grumble at this sort of thing, but old Jaimungal did his best to prevent a row.

'All-you is not like he, *beta*,' he would say cajolingly to his younger sons. 'All-you make for work in field, but Guru is different. Is brain he got and good sense.'

Makhan would ask: 'So who going work for he and he wife? Me?' And before the old man would answer that, Ramnath would add: 'It is good time to finish plant the paddy. The water in the rice-field is fine and nice. Now is the time to do the planting. We want help, Bap. I don't see why Guru shou'n't give we a hand for a day or two.'

But the old man, afraid of his offending Gurudeva, would

not ask him to help Makhan and Ramnath in the rice-field, but would go himself and help plant the seedlings.

Now Ramlal, Jairam and Dinnoo sat on the bamboo bench to watch Gurudeva do his puja. He performed an ablution on the images of Krishna and Radha, apparelled them with fresh garments – a six-inch strip of dhoti round Krishna, a doll's sari round Radha. He offered flowers to the deities and put the ceremonial marks of sandal-paste on the foreheads of the images; then he swung incense over them in an earthen incense-burner that he had bought on market-day from the Indian potter on the roadside. He rang his little bell and blew his conch-shell, and everybody stood up and clasped his palms and bowed his head to the deities. Then Gurudeva performed *arti* – moving a lighted camphor on a brass platter circularly round the images; first round Krishna and Radha, then over the pictures of Vishnu and Shiva, and last of all over his own drawing of the Monkey God. This done, he brought the *arti* to his father, who very reverently put his palms over the burning camphor for a moment, then carried them to his forehead; Jairam and Ramlal and Dinnoo did likewise. Then Gurudeva handed the *arti* to Dinnoo, and said:

'Carry it now, Dinnoo, to the others in the house.'

And when all this was over, they sat and talked – talking mostly of the *Sanatan Dharma* – the ancient religion – and of the people in the village who, they said, were going disgracefully to the gutter, outside the pale of the *Sanatan Dharma*.

Gurudeva sat on his charpoy, naked-back, the caste-mark still damp on his forehead, throat, arms and chest; looking every inch a holy man and a pundit, and such, indeed, he was already acknowledged to be.

Jairam said: 'That Kalpoo daughter, Ramdayah, she going to school with she hair cut. Just like a boy. She wearing low-neck dress that making most of she breasts show up. Morning and evening she walking to school with a boy on she side.'

Grim displeasure spread on Gurudeva's face. 'Kalpoo want he backside cut,' he said. 'Shou'n't allow he daughter to walk about with she breasts showing and she hair cut. *That* is not the *Sanatan Dharma*.'

'She ain't have no right to walk with a man she ain't married to,' put in Jaimungal. 'She father ain't have no right to let she choose she own man. I tellin' you, Guru, Kalpoo really want he tail cut.'

'We going fix him up,' said Dinnoo.

Gurudeva pondered. His eyebrows arched and his forehead creased. The *chandan* or caste-mark, having dried, broke into microscopic flakes on his forehead. He said:

'A lot of things going wrong with we religion in this village. People doing just as they want. Something must be done about it ... A *Bhagawat* now ... for seven days, and lecture at the end of the *Bhagawat* every night ... We could teach the people, tell them right from wrong.'

'Now you talking, *beta*!' said Jaimungal, ecstatically.

Dinnoo scratched a naked toe. 'A lot of things going wrong for truth, Guru,' he said. 'Pundit Biswas, the man that come from India –'

'Yes, what about him?' It was Gurudeva, alert, eager, bending forward. 'I hear 'bout him a lil bit. What more, eh?'

'He lecturin',' replied Dinnoo. 'I hear him last night. He condemning what he call idol worship. He saying Rama was *rishi* or prophet, not God; he saying a woman who married a'ready could be married again. And he sayin' there is nobody like Brahma and Vishnu and Shiva. He saying a lot of things. He saying anybody who is educated is a Brahmin and anybody who is *not* educated is *not* a Brahmin.'

'He saying all that?' asked Gurudeva, hotly.

'He saying all that,' said Dinnoo. 'I ain't lying.'

'Well, he want he backside cut too,' said Gurudeva. 'All these things he condemning is *Sanatan Dharma* – come from the beginning – is all in black and white. Me *Gita* say ... Orright –'

He broke off and called on Ratni to bring him pen, ink

and paper. Promptly Ratni brought him the things. He put
the paper on one dhoti-clad thigh and began to write.

Jaimungal watched him a minute in wonder and admiration, then asked: 'What you writing, *beta*?'

Meditatively biting the end of his pen-holder, Gurudeva
looked at the old man. 'Is a challenge I writing, Bap,' he
said. 'I calling a meeting and I giving a lecture. I challenging
Biswas. Beating him wid his own whip. He got to prove what
he saying. He got to prove how Rama is not God. He got to
prove how married woman can be married again. He got to
prove how a man born a Brahmin kian't be a Brahmin just
because he kian't read and write. He got to prove all this . . .
Don' trouble me, Bap; is think I thinking.'

He lowered his head and went on writing; then he stopped
and looked at Jairam and asked:

'How to spell "challenge", eh? I just forget it. Spell
"challenge" for me.'

'C-h-a-l-i-n-j. Challenge. That is how to spell the word,'
said Jairam.

'Sure?' asked Gurudeva.

'Sure,' replied Jairam. 'I know how I spelling. I ain't read
t'ird standard just for so. I know.'

'Orright,' said Gurudeva, and went on writing, every now
and then stopping to bite the end of his pen-stick.

He laboured for about fifteen minutes; then took a long
breath and put away the pen.

'I done,' he said, with triumph.

'Read it, *beta*,' said Jaimungal. 'Read it and leh we hear.'

'Orright,' said Gurudeva. 'Listen. "A challenge. Look out
for preachers in sheep clothing. What is the *Sanatan Dharma*?
Come and hear the truth revealed by Pundit Gurudeva
Sharma. At the *kuti*, Cacande Village. On Thursday 13th
instant at two-thirty p.m. A challenge to Pundit Biswas. If he
know his religion let him prove to Pundit Gurudeva Sharma
the wrong of idol worship. What is caste? What is everything? Come one, come all."'

'A strong challenge,' commented Jaimungal. 'I ain't send

you to school for nothing, boy ... This will teach Biswas
sense. He will know who he playing with. Now what you
goin' do with it, *beta*?'

'Print handbills,' said Gurudeva. 'A t'ousand handbills.
Stick them up all about. Dinnoo here can stick them up ...
'pon walls and shops and things. Ramlal can help. One of
them I postin' straight to Pundit Biswas. Bet he ain't come.'

'These people, *beta*,' said Jaimungal, 'they don't know
their head from their toe. Anyway, what you do there is the
right thing.

'*Shabas, beta*!'

15. *Gurudeva as a Lecturer*

They made painstaking preparations for the lecture. Gurudeva and his friends brought in two cart-loads of bamboo
from the bamboo patch and as many loads of coconut-palm
leaves. On three sides of the *kuti* they put up a huge tent,
using the bamboo as poles and the long, green palm leaves as
the covering. A whole day they sweated to finish the tent;
then Gurudeva looked around him and said:

'But on what will the people sit down?'

Jaimungal said: 'It is a lecture you giving, *beta*. It is not
a wedding. The men and them can stand up and listen; the
women and them can sit down on the ground. 'Cept for a
bench or two for those who will be in the *kuti* with you, don'
worry you' head 'bout benches and chairs. This is not a
Crishtan meeting. This is a lecture on the *Sanatan Dharma* ...
Yes, only a few benches you want, and I sure Schoolmaster
will lend you them. School is in holiday. He is you' own
schoolmaster, and I sure he will be proud is a lecture you
giving! You just go and ask him to lend you some bench.
Go, *beta*.'

Mr Sohun lived in a cottage half a mile away from the
Jaimungals'. The house was fronted by a strip of flower garden, with roses and pinks and zinnias. Over the wicket gate
rose an arch of flaming bougainvilia. Mr Sohun, in old

khaki shorts and shirt, was mooching around this garden when Gurudeva came.

'Good evenin', Schoolmaster,' he said.

Mr Sohun jumped.

He had neither heard nor seen Gurudeva coming, and it was the first time he was seeing him in dhoti. The fact that Gurudeva was in dhoti was surprising enough to Mr Sohun, but the fact that he was naked from the waist up, the fact that he had on broad patches of caste-marks on forehead, temples, throat, chest and arms; the fact that he was bare-footed – these things alarmed Mr Sohun. He looked at the visitor from head to foot, then from foot to head. Mr Sohun gasped.

'I say good evenin', Schoolmaster,' Gurudeva said again.

'Good evenin',' answered Mr Sohun at last. 'You gave me such a fright. I had to make sure it was you. Where are your trousers?'

To many of the young villagers Mr Sohun habitually retained the classroom attitude and he spoke to Gurudeva as though he were still a boy in his school. He had crossed his fifty-year span and could be disconcertingly outspoken.

'Trousers, Schoolmaster?' said Gurudeva. 'I done with trousers. Is dhoti I putting on these days.'

Mr Sohun put away the garden fork and leisurely wiped his face and neck with a broad kerchief.

'But why?'

'Well, Schoolmaster, I – I is a pundit now.'

'I see,' said Mr Sohun, and repeated more slowly and thoughtfully, 'I see! Wonders will never cease. I didn't know – I meant to say, you are certainly not slow. You *are* going the pace. Let me see ... Married at fourteen – at *fourteen*, if you please – to jail at twenty – and now, at twenty-two or twenty-three, a pundit! You amaze me. Besides, I didn't know you could read Hindi.'

'But now I can read Hindi, Schoolmaster,' Gurudeva said. 'I learn it a'ready.'

'Quick work,' said Mr Sohun. 'In school you never were

keen on Hindi. Your father felt that teaching you Hindi was only a ruse on my part to teach you the Bible. He preferred his sons to grow up as ignorant Hindus rather than as intelligent Christians. A strange process of reasoning. But there you are! . . . Anyway, come, come into the house. Don't let me keep you sweating in the sun.'

Mr Sohun led Gurudeva into his short veranda and pointed him to a chair. He himself reclined back on a rocker.

'Dhoti is all right,' said Mr Sohun, 'but I dare say trousers are better.'

Gurudeva, a trifle piqued, said: 'But I is a pundit now, Schoolmaster. I tell you so a'ready.'

'What of it?' asked Mr Sohun. 'I will not do your God the injustice of thinking that He will not recognize you in any other clothes but dhoti. What I say is, when in Rome do like the Romans.'

'What you mean, Schoolmaster? Rome and Romans?'

'It means that in a country such as the West Indies, Western culture and habits are the passport to progress. You people want to build a little India of your own in Trinidad. You are trying to dance top in mud. It cannot be done. The difficulty lies in the fact that you are too much of a majority to assimilate, too much of a minority to dominate. On every hand you are pressed by Western influences. You cannot be entirely Oriental, nor entirely Occidental; you can no more be entirely Western than you can be entirely Eastern; neither a hundred per cent European nor a hundred per cent Indian. You will be distinctly West Indian . . . Anyway, what can I do for you?'

Gurudeva was relieved.

He said: 'Schoolmaster, it is a favour I come to ask you.'

'Anything in reason,' said Mr Sohun. 'Glad to oblige.'

He called for a drink of water and when Mrs Sohun brought it, he drank it and dried his mouth. A black-and-white mongrel sat on its haunches at the end of the veranda, briskly scratching its ear. Back of the house Mr Sohun's sixteen-year-old-son, Ellway, was noisily tacking up a fowl-run. Mr Sohun called to him to cease his hammering a while. 'It's an old pupil I have here, boy,' he said.

'Is some benches I want you to lend me, Schoolmaster,' Gurudeva said.

'Benches? What for?'

'Is a lecture I giving. Tomorrow night, Schoolmaster.'

Again Mr Sohun was alarmed. '*You*? Giving a lecture?'

'*Me* giving it, Schoolmaster,' answered Gurudeva, with emphasis.

'What on?'

'Me religion. On the *Sanatan Dharma*,' Gurudeva said. 'I challenging Pundit Biswas. He condemning we religion, Schoolmaster.'

'Well,' said Mr Sohun, 'I don't know whether I can lend you the school benches. I would have to get permission of the manager . . . But benches apart . . . Look here, why not let this man Biswas go ahead with his preaching? He can't possibly do more harm than you and others are already doing.'

'But he condemning idol worship,' Gurudeva said. 'He saying Rama is not God. He –'

'Well, he is not altogether wrong. It depends on one's point of view – on one's temperament. In Hinduism idols are permissible, but not indispensable. They are a concession –'

'You puzzling me, Schoolmaster. That is a big word. Con – concession. What is concession? What you mean, Schoolmaster?'

'Well, I mean you are just allowed to use idols or images if you can't do better. It is a low – a gross – form of worship. You are expected to grow out of it. The trouble with you is that because you began with idols, on the principle of bottles for babes, you want to remain with them throughout life. They become a vice rather than a virtue. Enlightened Hindus do not necessarily use idols, nor do they worship many gods. But all Hindus, however numerous the gods they worship, whatever the forms through which they choose to do so, nevertheless believe in *Para-Brahm*, the formless Absolute, the One without a second. The gods are simply regarded as so many self-statements of the one Supreme. What is at once the glory and tragedy of Hinduism is that you are no more bound to worship through images than you are bound to worship through many gods.'

Gurudeva was visibly perplexed.

Much of what Mr Sohun was saying went clean over his head. It was like throwing water on a duck's back. But Mr Sohun was talking more to himself than to Gurudeva. He had read widely on Indian philosophy and religion and must needs talk it out. His bookshelves carried bound volumes of Gandhi's *Young India* articles; books by Radhakrishnan, Babu Bhagwandas, and Tagore; English translations of the *Ramayana*, the *Mahabharat*, the *Bhagavad Gita*, and some of the *Upanishads*.

Gurudeva shifted uneasily in his chair. 'Not bound to worship idols, Schoolmaster?' he asked. 'Not bound to worship gods? Well, I *never* hear that!'

'I believe you,' said Mr Sohun dryly. 'It just shows ... If you knew, there wouldn't be all this quarrelling among you. You would worship Rama and Krishna, or Shiva, or *Para-Brahm*, and nobody would say a word.'

Gurudeva said: 'But Pundit Biswas condemning Rama too; and Krishna and Jesus and everybody. He saying them was *rishis* or prophets, not God. He saying God ain't have no hand and foot. He saying God is like nothing. Ain't he talking like a fool, Schoolmaster? Say the truth.'

Mr Sohun pondered.

'He isn't talking like a fool,' he said. 'He is talking like a sectarian. Some people would claim to know God as He is. Others, like myself, would prefer to meet him face to face in a Jesus; you, no doubt, would prefer to meet Him in a Rama or a Krishna. The one God appears to different minds in different ways. Radhakrishnan quotes an ancient text as saying that forms are given to the formless Absolute for the benefit of the aspirant. Another text says that some men find their gods in waters, others in the heavens, others in the objects of the world, but the wise find the true God, whose glory is manifest everywhere, in the *Atman* – Brahma, Vishnu and Shiva; God the Father, God the Son and God the Holy Ghost – the one concept means much the same to me as the other.'

'I going try to remember what you say, Schoolmaster,' Gurudeva said. 'But one thing more. You think woman who married a'ready should be married again? Me *Gita* say –'

'I know what your *Gita* says, but in Trinidad every Hindu woman whose husband is dead, or whose husband has deserted her, or she deserted him – quite common features of the family structure – takes a second, if not a third or a fourth husband. Only there is no second marriage ceremony. You keep the letter, but quite ignore the spirit of the law. It's just a farce.'

'What is a farce?' asked Gurudeva.

'Tomfoolery,' answered Mr Sohun.

'Oh,' said Gurudeva.

'And all this quarrel and debate about the goodness or wickedness of caste is another farce. Nobody ever observes caste-rules in the West Indies.'

'Pundit Biswas condemning caste too,' Gurudeva said. 'Man saying anybody who can read and write can be a Brahmin. He saying he can be a Brahmin even if he father is a *chamar*.' A low-caste sweeper or worker in leather. 'What you think of that?'

Mr Sohun chuckled.

'I suppose that must be rather hard on you,' he said. 'But a Brahmin should be a man of knowledge and piety; yet ninety-nine in every hundred of you who pride yourselves on your being called Pundit and Maharaj are, in fact, neither the one nor the other. Caste, thank goodness, is non-existent in the West Indies. Nobody really keeps caste-rules, yet, ridiculously enough, most of you keep quarrelling over caste – as though you were still in some very remote village in India. Those of you who call yourselves Brahmins are not always priests, and seldom, if at all, pundits. The average pundit in the West Indies looks a pundit without being one.

In most cases the epithet is a misnomer. It has come to mean anyone who goes about in dhoti and turban and caste-marks of sandal-paste. Not ten in the whole mass, numbering hundreds, could pass an examination in Hindi that equals the test of a second-standard boy in my school. Again, thousands, claiming to be Kshatriyas – the military caste – call themselves *Singhs*, yet I know not one who follows the calling of a soldier. They are not even policemen. In the same way *chamars* are not sweepers – they are often school teachers, and so can be said to have changed place with Brahmins; *ahirs* do not necessarily rear cattle; *barahis* are seldom, if at all, workers in wood. Not caste, but the shadow of caste remains in the West Indies. Its only use here is to inflate some people's ego.'

Mr Sohun stopped talking and called for another drink of water. 'You may have the benches,' he said, 'though I should have first obtained the manager's permission.'

Gurudeva stood up.

'Thank you, Schoolmaster,' he said; 'and I hope you coming to the lecture. Dinnoo and Ramlal will be coming for the benches.'

Mr Sohun said: 'Don't know about coming to your lecture. However, I wish you luck. I'm sure it will be very amusing.'

'Yes, Schoolmaster,' said Gurudeva, thinking he was paid a compliment.

Gurudeva was giving his first lecture; his first, because of course he was to give many more. Ramlal and Dinnoo had done a thorough job distributing the handbills. So everybody knew of the lecture, and the whole village, it seemed, turned out, and scores came from beyond Cacande too, so that the long tent was crowded.

Gurudeva was specially garbed for the occasion: long white dhoti, pink *koortah*, caste-marks on forehead, topped with a yellow puggree. He looked a pundit and a Prince Charming in one, and he knew it. Six or seven pundits, more or less similarly garbed, but aged and decrepit compared to

Gurudeva, occupied the *kuti*, from which stemmed forward the huge tent. Pundit Shivlochan was there and Pundit Ramdut had come from Debe, and Mahant Gangaram from the adjoining village of Bejucal.

For these to sit on, Gurudeva spread sugar-bags on the earthen floor of the *kuti*, and on top of the sugar-bags washed sheets of flour-sacks, for they would not sit on a bench; they said that their doing so would be to put themselves higher than the gods on the *singhasan*.

A dozen flambeaux sticking out of a dozen bamboo poles lit the scene. From the green thatch hung festoons of bougainvilia, and between these floral decorations hung mangoes and green coconuts and bananas and oranges. It was Gurudeva's idea of a grand decoration. He warned everybody, though, that anyone snatching a fruit or a flower before the end of the lecture would be put out of the tent forthwith.

'If you don't believe me, just try it,' he said. 'So don't say I din warn you. Just keep quiet and listen, and after me lecture is over you can take what you want.'

There was a murmur of approval.

Gurudeva decided to give his lecture in Hindi. During the last week or so he had made it known that he was done with English. Without saying it in so many words he had made it known that English was beneath his consideration. Since recently he had been speaking only in Hindi – even with Jaimungal, with whom he had habitually spoken in English – and, still more strange, with Ratni. And he spoke not the mongrel, patois Hindi. No; he spoke, or tried to speak, the Hindi of the vernacular weekly paper that he had recently begun receiving in batches from Pundit Shivlochan, who got these every three months or so from India. It was a clever decision. He knew well enough that his Hindi, in spite of the *Ventekshwar Samachar*, the Indian weekly newspaper, was more or less on a par with his English; but whereas his bad English would be glaringly patent to many, his bad Hindi, particularly if he applied the *Samachar's* pronunciation and intonation, would be patent to none. Those who

knew Hindi knew little of it to be able to correct him; those
who didn't know – well, they didn't know.

Gurudeva coughed. He coughed twice. Then he began.

'Reverend pundits, brothers and sisters, this is a memo-
rable day in Cacande. Cacande is blessed; for in Cacande are
gathered this evening the cream of the Hindu community.
I thank them for their presence.'

He coughed once more, looked round him, then took a sip
of water from a brass jug.

'This meeting is called so I could tell you of our *Sanatan
Dharma*; so we could protect our *Sanatan Dharma*. Protect
it from whom? I say protect it from the mischievous propa-
ganda of Pundit Biswas. I think you have all heard of Pundit
Biswas –'

Dinnoo from the rear of the audience shouted: 'We know
'im. He is the enemy of the *Sanatan Dharma*.'

Gurudeva raised his hands for quiet.

'That's right,' he said. 'That is the truth. But I forget. Is
Hindi I speaking tonight; no English at all. I don't know
English.' He went on in Hindi:

'This man, this Pundit Biswas – he is a bad man. He is an
enemy of the *Sanatan Dharma*. And all who belong to his
clique are the enemies of the *Sanatan Dharma*.'

Prolonged applause.

'I repeat: this man is an enemy of the *Sanatan Dharma*.
He is telling the people that Rama is not God. He is telling
the people that there is no one like Brahma and Vishnu and
Shiva. He is saying that a woman can marry more than once.
He is saying that idol worship is sin . . . All these things that
Pundit Biswas is condemning comprise the sum and substance
of the *Sanatan Dharma*. And the *Sanatan Dharma* is from
the beginning. It is the oldest religion. It is eternal . . .

'Pundit Biswas is a fool. I challenged him to come to this
meeting to prove that what he is saying is right. He has not
come. I knew he would not come. And why? Because he
cannot prove what he is saying . . . Dinnoo, bring me
another *lotah*-ful of water.'

He drank his water, wiped his mouth with the sleeve of his *koortah*, and resumed:

'Yesterday I was talking to Schoolmaster Mr Sohun. You all know Schoolmaster Mr Sohun. Most of you at one time or another have been his pupils. I have been his pupil too; otherwise I would not have been here lecturing this evening. In only one thing I disagree with Schoolmaster. Schoolmaster says we must all become Romans. I say we should not become Romans. All the same I am proud of having been his pupil. He taught me *Angrezi*, though I no longer care to speak or write in that language. He taught me geography, he taught me grammar, he taught me hygiene and arithmetic. Dinnoo and Jairam and Ramlal were going to the same school – to Schoolmaster's school. They can prove what I am saying. Schoolmaster is a Christian but he knows plenty more about the *Sanatan Dharma* than do most of you. He certainly knows more about the *Sanatan Dharma* than does Pundit Biswas. Pundit Biswas does not know anything. You could take that from me. I am not fooling you. The man who is fooling you is Pundit Biswas. But why did he turn Christian – I mean Schoolmaster Sohun? I will tell you: Schoolmaster turned Christian for his *roti* . . . And, as I was saying, Schoolmaster knows about the *Sanatan Dharma*. He is a schoolmaster. He is bound to know . . .

'And what does Schoolmaster say about idol worship? He says it is a concession. That means it is proper for the worship of poor people who cannot read and write. And what does he say about Brahma, Vishnu and Shiva? He says they are the same as the Holy Ghost. And what does he say about the *devatas*, the gods? He says they are all God, but just different spectacles.

'Pundit Biswas is saying that a woman who is married can be married again. Schoolmaster told me this is only the letter of the spirit, not the spirit of the letter. He says Pundit Biswas is trying to dance top in mud . . .

'Now I ask you people – my brothers and sisters – to stick to the *Sanatan Dharma*, and not be influenced by Pundit

Biswas. I beg my brothers and sisters not to send their daughters to school with their hair cut; not let them choose their own husbands; not let them put red paint on their lips. All these things are against the *Sanatan Dharma*. If a girl must look pretty, she must make herself pretty only for her husband, not for anybody else; but if a girl is not married she should not cut her hair and paint her lips.

'Another thing. Lots of Hindu boys are going to school these days. Nothing wrong in that. They are all going to Schoolmaster's school; but what I am against is that none of them is keeping the *churki* – the long tuft of hair back of the skull. I have something more to say about girls. Lots of them are getting married. Nothing wrong in that; but they do not wear *orhanis*. They go about bareheaded. Some of them are even putting on hats. Hats! Well, all these things are against the *Sanatan Dharma* . . .'

He went on speaking for about half an hour, mostly repeating himself; then he said:

'Now I am going to ask Pundit Shivlochan to say a few words.'

Pundit Shivlochan stood up.

He faced the audience bravely enough, but said he did not know what to say. He confessed that if he told them he knew what he had to say he would be telling them a lie. But he was not a liar. The fact was, everything that he could have said Pundit Gurudeva had already said it. The night was getting on and most of them were, no doubt, sleepy. He himself was feeling sleepy. To tell the truth, he had been asleep during a part of Pundit Gurudeva's very inspiring lecture. He could only say – and, indeed, he was anxious to say it – that he was proud of his being Pundit Gurudeva's *nana*, and still more proud of his being Pundit Gurudeva's teacher. He hoped Pundit Gurudeva would continue to give such lectures as he had given them that night. A lot of Indians in Trinidad wanted waking up. He was sure Pundit Gurudeva was the man to do that. He —

A shower of stones came pattering down on the tent.

Pundit Shivlochan ducked. Gurudeva looked up and then looked all round. The people stampeded. Somebody cried: 'They peltin' stone!' And before the crier could run out another shower of the missiles fell about with heavy, staccato thuds. One stone, big as a mango, fell on Dinnoo's shoulder.

Dinnoo shouted: 'All you sons of bitches! All-you peltin' stone? Leh me catch one of you –' And he made a dash outside the tent.

Pundit Shivlochan, crying out, '*Ari, Mai*! O my mother!' suddenly hunched down on his bag-spread. The other pundits tittupped.

Gurudeva, forgetting his vow against the English language, exclaimed: 'It is the doing of Pundit Biswas. Wait leh me catch him! Ramlal! Jairam! Dinnoo! See who peltin' them stones.'

He ran out to look for himself . . .

Something moved on the thatch of the *kuti*, just over the *singhasan*. The pundits looked up.

The 'something' was making a sink in the thatch. Ah, now it could be seen. Something black and macabre, dripping blood, punching earthward through the thatch. Gurudeva fetched a bamboo rod and poked the thing with it. The turf parted, the black object fell on to the *singhasan*, spattering blood. It was the head of a hog!

The pundits scampered, fearful of defilement. The meeting broke up in disorder.

'All this,' repeated Gurudeva, 'is the work of Pundit Biswas. I know. But I will show him. I going put the whole thing in the papers.'

The next day the *Trinidad Guardian* reported:

Amazing scenes were witnessed at a meeting of Hindus at the kuti *of Pundit Gurudeva Sharma at Cacande last night, when fist-size stones came flying through space and fell on to a tent packed with people listening to a lecture on the Sanatan*

*Dharma (orthodox Hinduism). The incident occurred near the
end of the lecture, which was being delivered by Pundit Gurudeva
Sharma.*

*The meeting broke up in pandemonium when a freshly severed
hog's head, still dripping blood, mysteriously fell through the
thatch of the* kuti, *defiling a sacred altar.*

*Pundit Sharma attributed the mischief to unidentified enemies
of the Sanatan Dharma.*

The incident, far from hampering Gurudeva or his course,
endeared him to the followers of the *Sanatan Dharma*. Over-
night he became a celebrity. The whole community sympa-
thized with him. They flocked round his banner. He gave
more lectures. Within a month some of those who had attended his first lecture became his *chelas* or disciples. They included Jairam, Dinnoo, and Ramlal.

16. *Gurudeva Falls in Love*

Gurudeva looked at the alarm clock at the foot of the *singhasan* and frowned. It wanted ten minutes to seven in the
evening and Daisy Seetoolal had not yet arrived. She ought
to have been at the *kuti* since half-past six. So Gurudeva
frowned. He was teaching Hindi to Daisy Seetoolal; also to
a group of boys and girls. But for Daisy he had arranged a
separate hour. He did not charge for tuition. He said he
would not demean himself to that extent.

By now few of the villagers doubted that Gurudeva was
uncommonly learned in Hindi. None of them could say just
why he thought so. One just felt it in one's bone. For one
thing, nobody else could talk on high religious themes as
bravely and as well – and one might say, as militantly – as
could Gurudeva. He had delivered some half a dozen lectures
within the last month or so and not once had anyone ques-
tioned even a single point in his perorations. There was certainly no greater champion of the *Sanatan Dharma*. Small

wonder everybody called him Pundit now, or Pundit Gurudeva, or Pundit Gurudeva Sharma; and some even addressed
him as Pundit Gurudeva Shastri. *Shastri* was a title for one
who was versed in the Shastras, the Hindu institutes of religion; and Gurudeva held that the books and booklets he
had read all formed part of the Shastras, and therefore he
could legitimately take the title of *Shastri*.

'You right, *beta*,' said old Jaimungal. 'Them is all Shastras.'

'Yes, Bap,' said Gurudeva.

Ratni was not pleased at his setting apart a separate time
for Daisy Seetoolal. She had her suspicions, but Gurudeva
insisted that when he was teaching Daisy he wanted nobody
else in the *kuti*. He said that the presence of others dis-
tracted him and she whom he taught.

'It is not fair to the girl,' he said.

Ratni shrugged her shoulders and pressed her under-lip
but dared not make a verbal protest.

Consider Daisy. She was not at all like Ratni. Daisy was
about twenty-three or twenty-five, tall and slim, the colour
of ripe corn. She had large dark eyes, and she plucked her
brows and painted her lips and rouged her cheeks – things
that Ratni had not even dreamed of doing; things, in fact,
that she would never have been allowed to do, supposing she
had thought of doing them at all.

As though all this wasn't enough to make her uproariously
different from the other girls in the village, Daisy wore short,
tight frocks that clean showed up the shape and contours of
her body; and she used brassieres that jutted out her breasts
in an aggressive, forward thrust that made Gurudeva take
notice of them under Daisy's thin, often diaphanous, bodice.
She bobbed her hair, too, and periodically went to Port of
Spain for a hair-do, so that far from covering her head with
an *orhani*, as well-brought-up Hindu girls do, she went about
bareheaded, proud to show off the waves and curls that her
hair had taken on.

And the villagers wondered how it could be that a big,
pretty girl like her wasn't married. But the next moment they

would cease wondering, for they remembered she was a Christian, a member of the Presbyterian church two miles away in Chaguanas. On Sundays she went to church; then was the time she wore a hat, or what passed for a hat – a patch of lace-like cloth that in truth was neither hat nor *orhani*.

Daisy spoke and read English, for she had attended Mr Sohun's school with Gurudeva; and there was a swoosh about her that Ratni, and in fact all the other girls in the village, entirely lacked. What amazed the villagers, the more so the youngsters, was the way she walked. Daisy walked as though she trod on springs. She swayed at the middle, as a coconut tree sways in a not-too-heavy wind. Her shoes had such high heels that Gurudeva had often wondered how she walked in them at all. The fact that she not only walked in them, but walked rather prettily, was a thing that quite fascinated him.

The villagers didn't like Daisy. They all admitted that she was pretty, but by the same token they all said she was bad. 'Good looks and dotty tricks' was how some of them put it.

What made Daisy bad, they said, was the fact that she had gone to work with the Americans (when, after Pearl Harbor, the U.S.A. was putting up a defence base at Edinburgh, some four miles from Cacande). She was the youngest of three daughters of Mr James Seetoolal, retired catechist of the Presbyterian Mission. Mrs Seetoolal had died some two years before World War Second and Mr Seetoolal was disabled from paralysis for years. His two older daughters had married and settled on their own, away from Cacande, so that Daisy alone remained with him. For a year or two she had taught school; then, tiring of school-teaching, she had worked as a sales-girl in Mr Boodlal's dry-goods store at Chaguanas.

Then, with the coming of the Americans, she got some kind of job at Carlsen Field at Edinburgh; and soon enough Daisy had become shockingly modern. For the first week or so she cycled to and from work like a good girl; then almost every afternoon got an American 'boy friend' to bring her home in a jeep. Then Daisy would not come home for days on end, but would get into slacks and get in a jeep and go away to Port of Spain with the Americans. When she returned old Seetoolal would let her know he did not approve of that sort of thing. Decent girls, he would say, came home immediately after work; only bad girls went away to spend nights in town. What would people say of her goings-on with the Yankees?

'But is war, Pa!' Daisy would say. 'I have to work overtime. Everybody has to; can't say no; it's war. And, besides, they pay well. Why, I often make more from overtime than from my regular job . . . Look –' And Daisy would promptly unclasp her large shining purse and bring out banknotes from it. Mr Seetoolal would shake his head half disapprovingly and mumble he still didn't like the look of things. But Daisy, humming 'Rum and Coca-Cola', would make for the small wooden enclosure in the backyard which was the bathroom, and after her ablution – from water in a bucket – she would eat and go to sleep, and after sleep would begin to get ready to get to the base once more.

'Coming home this evening, Daisy?' Mr Seetoolal would ask; and invariably Daisy would answer, 'Well, I don' know, Pa. Depending on whether there will be overtime.' And once more Mr Seetoolal would shake his head hopelessly on his pillow as much as to say he really didn't know what to make of her behaviour.

But after the war was over and the Americans had gone back home and the bases disposed of as so much scrap, Daisy had found herself at a loose end. She had indeed fallen on hard times. During the war she had contemptuously shunned and snubbed the local boys. She regarded them as cheap, oily-looking fellows. Now she was on the rebound from one village swain to the other, but still looking very much a 'hot girl'. She was a thorough mixer, and for this as much as for other reasons was looked at askance by her own Christian community – that numbered some ten or twelve households in the village – as well as by the non-Christian Indian community.

But Daisy didn't care.

In the course of one of his lectures Gurudeva had made it known that the boys and girls of Cacande must regard it their duty to learn Hindi. He said he had discovered to his shame that not two in a hundred knew their mother tongue. He said hitherto they might have had excuses in the fact that they had no one to teach them; but now they had no such excuse. He was at the service of every boy or girl – if he or she would come to his *kuti*.

A voice near to Gurudeva asked in an aside:

'True? You will teach me?'

It was Daisy Seetoolal. Soon enough Gurudeva had found himself stammering, 'Lecture is over for this evening. I shall lecture again tomorrow.'

Then he had turned to Daisy. 'Is true, nuh? You really want to learn Hindi? I kian't believe it.'

'It is true, though,' said Daisy. 'I mean it.'

Gurudeva took a walk with her – to her home – and found himself saying again and again, 'Come tomorrow, Daisy; come tomorrow.'

And she came.

From the outset he found her a prodigy at Hindi. He had to show her a thing but once and she never forgot it. Jaimungal had been watching them, and at the end of a week Gurudeva had found himself saying to the old man, 'Bap, well, I never see a girl like that. She have a good head. In t'ree weeks I going to make she as able as meself, for I have only to teach she once and she up and know it as good as me, sometimes even better.'

Jaimungal said: 'Careful, *beta*. Look to me like she know to read a'ready. Look to me she only pretending she ain't know. Look to me it is a man she want. Careful, *beta*; you have a wife.'

Gurudeva laughed. 'You making joke, Bap,' he said. 'You think is that I thinking? I ain't thinking that yet.'

The old man scratched his chin, and Ratni, passing by, stopped for just a second.

'Fact is,' Jaimungal said. 'She is a Chrishtan. I wonder, *beta* . . .'

'You mean 'bout she turning a Hindu?' asked Gurudeva. 'You leave that to me, Bap.'

The old man walked away with a troubled look in his eyes.

The hands of the clock now pointed to eight o'clock . . . There was the sound of approaching footsteps. Gurudeva sighed with relief: it was Daisy. She knew by now that she had to slip her shoes off before entering the *kuti*. This she did. She knew, too, that she must sit flat on the ground on the bag-spread, her legs drawn in under her skirts, facing Gurudeva. With consummate care she managed this too. She smiled, quietly, shyly, meaningfully. The smile said: 'Well, I *have* managed it, and you haven't seen a thing!'

'Where you been?' asked Gurudeva. 'God, I thought you wasn't coming. I thought –'

'It was Pa,' said Daisy. 'He kept me back.'

'He – he ain't stopping you, Daisy?' asked Gurudeva, with great concern. 'Tell me, because if it is that, I is just the man to go to him. I is just the man to tell him to he face what I feel about you. What you saying, Dais?'

'Careful,' said Daisy. 'You' wife watching.'

Ratni stood before the kitchen and gave Daisy an accusing look. In the dull light cast on her by the oil-lamp, Ratni's figure was a silhouette.

Gurudeva looked at her and scowled.

'What you doing there?' he asked. 'Go inside. Go away!'

'I watchin' all-you,' said Ratni. 'I seein' what all-you doin'. I ain't blind.'

Gurudeva made to get up, but before he could do so Ratni stamped her foot and jerked her chin towards them and disappeared into the kitchen.

'Hell wid she!' said Gurudeva. Then on Daisy's slate he wrote in Hindi: 'I love you. Do you love me?' He handed her the slate, saying, 'Now, try and read that and write down the answer – the true answer.'

Daisy read the sentence, broke into a giggle, covered her face with both hands as though shamed to suffocation.

'You, eh!' she said. 'You too bad.'

'That is not the answer,' said Gurudeva. 'I waiting for the answer – the true answer.'

'You can't have two wives in this country,' Daisy said. 'Jail for that.' She laughed out again.

He asked: 'You mean Ratni?'

She said: 'And who else?'

'Chut!' said Gurudeva. 'You shouldn't mind she. She is not me legal wife. Bamboo wedding.'

Once more she broke into a giggle, once more she covered her face with both hands, once more she exclaimed, 'You too bad!'

Gurudeva blew out the lamp.

A little later Jaimungal came out and stood on the step of the big house and, looking towards the *kuti*, called: 'But, eh-eh, *beta*! All-you in the dark. How all-you can read in the dark, eh?'

He came to the *kuti* and handed Gurudeva a box of matches. 'Light that lamp, *beta*,' he said.

'Yes, Bap,' said Gurudeva; 'it was the wind.'

'I know,' said Jaimungal, turning to regain the house.

They started the lesson afresh; then Gurudeva decided to reach Daisy home.

Daisy opened wide her eyes and said: 'But what will the people say? You walking with me – in dhoti, too, and at night time.'

He said: 'Leh them say anything. I don't care.'

It may not have been Gurudeva's deliberate intention to make a row with Ratni, not that same evening at any rate; but a row with her he did make, and it came about in a peculiarly spontaneous way.

He had returned after seeing Daisy home, and was sitting

before his little table in his room; and, perhaps he had nothing to do just then, his mind somehow ran on to his father-in-law, Pundit Sookhlal; and as he thought of Pundit Sookhlal his eyebrows knitted and he heard himself saying, 'The donkey!' He spat out the expletive as he might have spat out two hot, putrid bits of potato. There was a sheet of paper on the table, and a stub of pencil, and in a rather doodling way he found himself writing –

The Donkey.

He thought over this and found, to his great satisfaction, that Pundit Sookhlal was indeed much like a donkey. Pundit Sookhlal, he found, was stupid like a donkey, grey as a donkey, pot-bellied as a donkey. Then, without knowing it perhaps, he began thinking of the other members of Ratni's family, in sequence, and the next thing he wrote down on the paper before him was –

The Old She-Fox.

'Ha!' he exclaimed. 'She is a fox!'

It is true he had never seen a real fox, but he had seen a picture of that animal in his *McDougall's First Reader* and he knew from the story in the book that foxes were notoriously cunning creatures, and nothing could beat him off the conviction that Phulmati was cunning and mean.

A moment ago he was hating every member of his wife's family with a burning hatred; now he wanted to be fair. He was careful not to let his prejudices interfere with his fitting the right animal to the right person. He went to work with the detachment of a scientist spotting his microbes without getting himself into a jitter. He was getting a great deal of fun out of the exercise. He went on writing and soon enough had produced the following list:

> *The Old She-Fox*
> *The Old Donkey*
> *The Scorpion*

The Thug
The Human
The Hippo
The Donkey
The Donkey
The Donkey

He put down the pencil and sighed his satisfaction. He knew that in two cases he could find no animal or non-human counterparts. A thug was not an animal, but he could think of nothing apter when it came to the husband of Ratni's eldest sister; and when he came to think of this woman herself – well, he simply had to let her pass as human: he could find no fault in her.

Ratni came in.

It was never her way to want to know what he was doing. There ever had been something forbidding in Gurudeva's attitude that rendered such curiosity superfluous and offensive, a sign of bad manners. So, without a word she began to slip off her outer garment preparatory to her going to sleep.

He said, without looking at her: 'Don' sleep yet. Is something I write here. Listen to it. I get a lot of fun writing it.'

She hung her skirt and bodice on a nail on the wall and sat down on the charpoy.

'What is it? I listening,' she said.

He read out the list, and she asked: 'But what is all that? Fox and donkey and scorpion? I kian't make out a thing.'

He said: 'Well, I going tell you. Listen. The old donkey. That is your father. He just like a donkey, ain't so? I ain't making no joke. I try to fit him exactly where he belong, and I find your father is exactly a donkey.'

She made no answer. She knew it would be looking for trouble if she contradicted him; but she took courage and said in a mild abandon, 'Orright, me father is a donkey; but don't tell me; tell him.'

He said: 'But listen to the rest. I telling you is a pleasure I get writing them.'

She said, lying down, 'I ain't want to hear no more. I hear enough a'ready. Let me sleep. Is tired I tired.'

He was adamant. 'No; listen to what I saying. Listen or I going do for you right now.'

She sat up.

'"The old she-fox",' he read aloud. 'That is your mother. Ain't she just like a old she-fox? I ain't 'zaggerating. Promise me land, promise me house, promise me shop: promise me this and promise me that. Never give a thing. She think she smart; but she is just a dam old fox – stingy like hell.'

Ratni said not a word; just propped her chin on her hand, looking down at her feet, brows down.

'Then your brother,' said Gurudeva. 'I put him down as a scorpion. He *is* a scorpion. Don't talk much, but you never know when he going up and sting you. Want everything for heself; don't care a fart 'bout anybody else.

'Well, I sorry I kian't place your smaller brother, so I just put him down as a thug. Kian't think of any animal that is exactly like him. He is *just* a thug. Want to fool everybody and take everything for heself. Full of sweet-mouth. Want to be boss. Boss me eye!'

He blew his nose and added: 'Then he wife. Fact is, I kian't find nothing against she. She is a good woman. Well, I let she pass as a human. But your third brother . . . Mohana . . . I put him down as a hippo. Hippo is a animal. Well, he big like a hippo, stupid like a hippo, tough like a hippo. He is a hippo, he wife is a donkey . . . Then them two sisters of yours – Durgi and Rajiah – them is donkeys, too. Your family full of donkeys . . . Let me see . . . one donkey, two donkey, three donkey, four donkey. Altogether four donkeys; then one fox, one scorpion, one thug, one human, one hippo . . .'

Ratni began to cry.

'You forget me,' she said. 'You shou'n't forget me.'

And suddenly Gurudeva found it difficult to say what he had to say – which was to tell her to go away – to tell her that he no longer wanted. her. When he came to think of it, *he* found no fault in her – except for the one fault – the fault from which other faults flowed: she did not bear him a son; she did not bear him even a daughter; she seemed incapable of bearing a child.

'I don't know . . . You think you will ever have a son?' he asked.

'I is not God,' she said.

'In we religion a man who din have a son could have more than one wife. You know that. If a man ain't have a son he going straight to hell. You know that too.'

She nodded to say yes. 'Is Daisy you talking about, ain't so?'

'Is Daisy I talking about,' he said, 'and I glad you know it. What about she? She ain't bad. What you saying, eh?'

Ratni rebelled, but her rebellion had nothing very volatile in it. She knew she was in the wrong. She knew she ought to bear sons; she knew she could bear no children. She had tried every device: she had secretly prayed to the Monkey God; secretly, too, she had fasted every Sunday for months, and offered ablutions of pure milk to the Sun God; not a *Shiva-Ratri* had gone by but she had gone to the temple of God Shiva and begged for the boon of a son. And not only she had acted on these devices, but Gurudeva himself had done so; and Gurudeva's mother, Jhulani, and her own mother, Phulmati. None of them had kept it a secret from her. But the boon had not been granted. All the gods had turned a deaf ear.

'When you bringing she?' she asked.

He said: 'I don't know. Any day.'

'Well,' she said, 'you can bring she. Is pack I going to pack; is me mooma and me poopa I going back to.'

He said: 'I ain't telling you to go; but if you *want* to go, I ain't stopping you either. All the same, leh me tell you – if you go you ain't coming back. Understand that. Don't say I din warn you. Orright.'

For reply Ratni began to pack her cardboard suitcase – the same suitcase that she had brought from her mother's on the morning following her marriage with Gurudeva. There wasn't much to pack, and when she was finished she spread some old jute sackings on the earth floor and went to sleep thereon, leaving the bed to Gurudeva alone.

In the morning Jaimungal, Jhulani, Mira and Dhira, Ramnath and Makhan, all stood round her, begging her not to go; but she only kept weeping and blowing her nose and wiping her tears with her *orhani* and saying, 'Is orright, Mai; is orright, Bap; let Daisy stay with him. I kian't live with him and another woman. Is either me or she.'

As for Gurudeva – he merely said, rather stiffly and indifferently, to the old man: 'Don't beg she, Bap. If she want to go, let she go. If she kian't live with me and Daisy, she can go back to she mooma. A man is not a man if he ain't got a son; and she – well, what I going do with she, Bap?'

The old man understood; had understood the situation all along; and, understanding, he knew he could not say nay.

'Well,' he said, 'it is not wrong for a man to have mor'an one wife, more so if he got no son. All the same, *beta*, people will laugh. It is –'

'Let them laugh, Bap,' said Gurudeva. 'I don't care. I not doing anything against me religion. I can prove it.'

But Ratni had gone.

Two days later Gurudeva brought in Daisy. The following week Pundit Sookhlal called up a panchayat against Gurudeva, for the latter's wrongfully putting away Ratni and, still more wrongfully, bringing in her place another wife.

17. *Gurudeva Becomes a Bachelor*

Gurudeva went to the panchayat armed with a copy of the *Ramayana*. He came in dhoti and *koortah*; and, in the fashion of priests (who must not touch leather with their hands lest those hands become unclean), in unlaced shoes. No socks. A peacock's feather adorned his silken yellow turban; and he wore resplendent caste-marks and no fewer than three rosaries.

The members of the panchayat were already in their place. They sat in Pundit Sookhlal's commodious *kuti*, and included Pundit Shivlochan, who had officiated at the nuptials of Gurudeva and Ratni, Sadhu Lalram, the temple-keeper; Mr Jagat Singh, the village provision shopkeeper; Jhagroo, the village barber; Gopisingh, a respected and respectful cane-farmer; Sardar Ramsaroop, foreman of labourers on the neighbouring sugar estate; Kuru Swami, the Madrasi palmist; Pundit Harikul, who was reputedly the best astrologer in the village.

Gurudeva 'ahemmed' as much as to say, 'I am here.'

He made an obeisance to the panch and an additional obeisance to Pundit Shivlochan. He hardly looked at Pundit Sookhlal and Pundit Sookhlal hardly looked at him. Pundit Shivlochan shifted nearer to Sadhu Lalram and beckoned Gurudeva to a seat.

At a word from her father Ratni came, her *orhani* drawn well down her face. Without looking at anybody she made straight for Gurudeva and stooped and touched his feet.

Gurudeva simply looked down at her, muttering in surprise, 'Eh! Eh!' Then, catching himself, he mumbled his benediction in the one word, 'Live!'

Ratni withdrew. In that act alone she had vindicated her honour as a wife; she had shown to the panch that she knew her wifely duty; that she was a wife indeed.

Pundit Sookhlal's yard was thronged with men and women, They stood around the *kuti*, waiting to hear what would happen, for the case was known to all.

Pundit Shivlochan was chief of the panch. That place had been given him by virtue of his rank – the foremost of the priests in the island, as well as the most learned. Pundit Shivlochan now passed two fingers over his thin, grey moustache and said:

'The hour is late; nearly three o'clock by the position of the sun. I take it those who should be present are present. Let us begin.'

Pundit Sookhlal called for Ratni again; she came, followed

by Phulmati, her mother, and her eldest sister, Roopani. She
was deliberately simply clothed, and it was difficult to say
whether she was shy or sad. She was probably both.

Except for some exclamatory remarks by Gurudeva the
proceedings were conducted wholly in Hindi.

The temple-keeper said: 'Let Pundit Sookhlal speak first.
It is he who has called the panchayat.'

Pundit Sookhlal stood up. He was in a dhoti and a merino.
'Most of you who are present this afternoon,' he began, 'were
also present when my Ratni was married to Gurudeva, a long,
long time ago.'

Some members of the panchayat nodded.

'He was a mere boy then, she a merer girl, a child. For all
these years there has been no complaint whatever against my
Ratni. She has been a model wife, a model daughter-in-law,
a model sister-in-law in the house of Jaimungal.'

'We know that,' said the shopkeeper, with an accusatory
look at Gurudeva.

'She has nobly put up with a lot,' continued Pundit
Sookhlal. 'A lot of beatings and other ill-treatment, mostly at
the hands of this Pundit Gurudeva –'

'A man,' said the shopkeeper, with another accusatory look
at Gurudeva, 'should not beat his wife.'

'Why,' asked Gurudeva, half rising, 'why you don' keep
you' dam mouth shut? Why you 'terrupting?'

Pundit Shivlochan raised both hands to heaven and said:
'No *Angrezi*, please! I do not understand *Angrezi*.'

'I tell you,' resumed Pundit Sookhlal, 'that once Gurudeva
thoroughly beat up my Ratni, yes; then he made her open the
palms of both hands, and when she had done that, he compelled her to spit on both hands, and she spat on both hands,
and he compelled her to lick the spittle, and she licked it. I
say it to his face; let him deny it if he can.'

Gurudeva gave Pundit Sookhlal a cutting look, but denied
nothing.

'But now – now, O members of the panch,' exclaimed Pundit Sookhlal, 'Pundit Gurudeva has seen fit to put my Ratni

away; he has seen fit to put her away in order to take unto him – would you believe it? – another woman.'

All the members of the panchayat looked at Gurudeva, as though they could not believe all this without looking at him.

Sardar Ramsaroop exclaimed: 'Ho! Ho!'

Sadhu Lalram said: 'That *is* bad.'

Kuru Swami put in: 'I will look at the girl's hands when all this is over!'

Mr Jagat Singh, the shopkeeper, said: 'The spit-and-lick story makes me feel to throw up.'

When these interruptions subsided, Pundit Sookhlal said: 'Thus far have you heard me, O Panch. I have called the panchayat in accordance with the *dharma*. Let Pundit Gurudeva show just cause why he should put away my Ratni.'

Pundit Shivlochan turned to Ratni. 'You have heard all that your father has said about your husband Pundit Gurudeva?'

Ratni nodded.

'Is everything that your father says true?'

She nodded again.

'He beats you a lot?'

'He used to.'

'He made you spit on your open hands and then lick it up?'

She nodded once more.

'That is bad,' said the shopkeeper, in English.

Gurudeva said, in English too: 'You ain't have no right to say that. You ain't she husband.'

Pundit Shivlochan said: 'No *Angrezi*. I do not understand it. I think it is time we heard Pundit Gurudeva. Is it true you have taken another woman?'

Gurudeva stood up.

'It is true,' he said. 'It is true and I want to see who can prove I have done wrong.'

The shopkeeper frowned. 'Let us hear you prove it,' he said, challengingly.

Gurudeva decided to adopt the Socratic method. He did

not know, of course, what the Socratic method was, but he had many times listened to police court proceedings at Chaguanas and knew how clever lawyers tripped and trapped witnesses on the witness stand just by a series of rapid questions and the answers they got thereto. He would put Pundit Sookhlal to shame and to owning defeat by a similar method of procedure.

'I will prove it,' he reiterated in his best Hindi. 'I crave the indulgence of the panch to permit me to ask a few questions. It is not necessary for me to make a speech, long or short.'

Pundit Shivlochan nodded assent.

Gurudeva held up the *Ramayana* in one hand.

'I suppose you all know what is this book I have here?'

Pundit Shivlochan peered closely and carefully; so did everybody else.

'Why,' said Pundit Shivlochan, 'as near as I can make out, it seems to be a copy of the *Ramayana*.'

Jhagroo, the barber, who did not know a letter in any language, echoed, '. . . a copy of the *Ramayana*.'

Mr Jagat Singh, the shopkeeper, said: 'I do not see what all this has to do with the complaint against Pundit Gurudeva.'

'Shut up!' exclaimed Gurudeva. 'If you do not have sense enough to see what I am driving at, why do you not just keep quiet?'

The shopkeeper said: 'I have not come here to keep quiet just to please you . . .'

Gurudeva ignored this last rejoinder of the shopkeeper's. 'You have guessed right,' he said to Pundit Shivlochan. 'Is it a good book or a bad book – this *Ramayana*?'

'He is just wasting everybody's time,' grumbled the shopkeeper.

'It is a holy book,' said Pundit Shivlochan. 'Everybody knows that. It is a book in which God Rama speaks.'

Gurudeva nodded as much as to say, 'Just go on answering like that till you admit just what I want you to admit.'

'It tells of King Dasaratha, does it not?'

'That it does,' replied Pundit Shivlochan.

'Was he a good man or a bad man?'

Pundit Shivlochan, staring into vacancy, considered the question; the shopkeeper slowly scratched his knee above his khaki trousers; the barber looked to Pundit Shivlochan.

'Assuredly King Dasaratha was a good man, a lover of the *dharma*, protector of his subjects, the father of God Rama.'

'Good! Good!' said Gurudeva; then asked: 'How many wives had he?'

'Three wives, of course.'

'All under one roof?'

'Yes, of course.'

'Why did he have as many as three wives?'

The shopkeeper looked cross.

Pundit Sookhlal appealed to Pundit Shivlochan. 'Surely we cannot have such questions asked in reference to King Dasaratha,' he said.

Pundit Shivlochan said: 'He has asked a question. He deserves an answer. I shall give him the answer: King Dasaratha had three wives because he had no son. If his first queen had given him a son, he probably would not have had other queens. He had three queens in the hope that one or the other might bear him a son.'

'*Shukriya*! Thank you!' said Gurudeva. 'You admit, then, that a man, being heirless, is justified in his having more than one wife?'

'He is justified,' said Pundit Shivlochan.

'He is justified,' mumbled the barber.

'Then, O Panch, I have done no wrong,' Gurudeva said. 'My position is exactly what was King Dasaratha's position. As you all know, Ratni bears me no son. She is not a child-bearing woman.'

Gurudeva was about to sit down, when the shopkeeper said:

'But, unlike you, King Dasaratha did not put away one wife every time he brought another. He kept all three. *You*, on the other hand, have put away Ratni.'

Gurudeva straightened up. 'You lie,' he shouted.

The shopkeeper stood up too. 'If you call me a liar, I will break your mouth,' he told Gurudeva. He began to roll up his shirt-sleeve.

Gurudeva went to roll his sleeve, too; then, realising it could not be done, since what he wore was a *koortah* with tight cuffs, he instead dashed off his turban.

Pundit Sookhlal said to Pundit Shivlochan: 'You see what kind of man this fellow is,' meaning Gurudeva. 'He utterly disrespects the panch.'

'Disrespects the panch,' echoed the barber.

Pundit Shivlochan said to Gurudeva and the shopkeeper: 'If you gentlemen insist on your beating up one another, the panchayat may as well be quashed. Sit down, Pundit Gurudeva! Sit down, Mr Jagat Singh!'

They sat down, breathing hard, clenching and unclenching their fists, each singeing the other with his hot look.

'What were you saying?' Pundit Shivlochan asked Gurudeva. 'What was the row about?'

'He as good as called me a liar. He said I had driven away Ratni.'

'And you did not?'

'I did *not*. She came away of her own accord She refused to live with another wife of mine.'

Pundit Shivlochan shook his head in a puzzled way. 'The affair takes on an altogether different complexion,' he said.

He called for Ratni. She came, her gaze on the ground.

'Is it true, O daughter, that Pundit Gurudeva did *not* drive you away?'

'He did not drive me away,' said Ratni.

'Did *you* leave him?'

'Yes, *Nana*,' said Ratni.

'Why?'

'He was bringing another woman.'

'It is your own fault, then,' said Pundit Shivlochan. 'You ought not to have left his care and protection. He was bringing, and in fact has since then brought, another wife. That was none of your business. Even if you had given him sons, that was none of your business. But you have borne him no son. You may go.'

Slowly, without a word, without raising her glance to any, Ratni turned and left the panch.

To his fellow-members of the panchayat Pundit Shivlochan said: 'A man may have more than one wife. In this case it is unfortunate, of course, but it is not wrong. This is my view.'

'My view,' said the barber.

The other members of the panch signified agreement.

Pundit Sookhlal stood up. He brought his hands together in a gesture of obeisance as well as of entreaty.

'I abide by the decision of the panch,' he said. 'The panch knows. But one thing more –'

The panch looked up. The shopkeeper cast a quick, suspicious glance at Gurudeva.

'I want to draw the attention of the panch to the fact that the woman that Pundit Gurudeva has taken as wife – she – she is a Christian.'

There was a murmur of surprise and disapproval.

'She wears hat,' added Pundit Sookhlal.

The murmur grew into a hum and commotion, as bees suddenly disturbed in a hive.

The barber passed his hand over his head as though to make sure *he* did not have a hat on.

'. . . and short, tight frocks, and high-heeled shoes,' said Pundit Sookhlal, still bowing and holding his hands together before the panch.

Pundit Shivlochan looked at Gurudeva as though he couldn't believe it was Gurudeva he was looking at. 'Is all this true?' he asked.

Gurudeva floundered for an answer. Nervously he began fingering his rosary. If he said yes he would be condemning himself; he could not say no: the facts about Daisy were too well known.

'Do not insult the panch by your silence,' shouted the shopkeeper. 'Answer the question.'

Still Gurudeva made no comment.

'Is it true that this woman eats cow's flesh and pig's flesh?' asked Pundit Shivlochan, his eyes opening bigger and his brows bunching together.

'Not since I took her as wife,' Gurudeva said. 'She no longer eats any kind of meat.'

'But she still wears *Angrezi* clothes and high-heeled shoes?' asked the shopkeeper. 'She still cuts her hair like a boy's and paints her cheeks and lips and –'

'Well – well, yes,' said Gurudeva; 'but not for long. I shall turn her into a Hindu. She will wear *chappals* instead of shoes; she will let her hair grow long once more. She will neither paint her cheeks nor go about bareheaded. She will wear *orhani*.'

Pundit Shivlochan looked at the other members of the panch as much as to say, 'Well, what do you say to this?'

The shopkeeper arched his brows and asked: 'But how can such a thing be done? How can a Christian become a Hindu? It is against the *dharma*.'

Gurudeva, once more forgetting he was not to talk in English, blurted out: 'You talking nonsense. You just showing spite because you want Daisy for yourself. I know. I know you was she boy friend. But she give you up. She ain't want you any more. She – besides, you don't know what you talking. You just don't know that these days a Christian can turn Hindu . . . Look at Mungroo. Ain't Mungroo was a Christian too? But ain't he come back a Hindu so as to teach in the Mahasabha school? If you don't know what you talking 'bout why don't you keep you' mouth shut? These days Christian can turn Hindu.'

'It is true,' said Pundit Shivlochan. 'I have seen it done.'

'It is true,' commented the barber.

The other members of the panch nodded. The proposition would be all right, providing –

'Providing,' put in the shopkeeper, 'that the woman forth-with gives up her *Angrezi* ways.'

Sadhu Lalram asked: 'But what if she does not carry out the wishes of the panch? In this country –'

The shopkeeper said: 'If the woman refuses to comply with the wishes of the panch – if she refuses, Pundit Gurudeva must disown her at once. If he does not disown her – if he does not put her out of his house – he may regard himself as being deemed a *ku-jat*, an outcaste, by the panch.'

Pundit Shivlochan asked Gurudeva:

'You have heard. What do you say to that?'

'It is good,' said Gurudeva, wiping his brows.

But it wasn't good. For when Gurudeva told Daisy what had happened at the panchayat – how, after winning the first round he had lost the second that came up, rather unexpec-tedly, because of the cunning of Pundit Sookhlal; and how the panch had ordered him to see that she discard her hat and take on *orhani*, and walk in *chappals* instead of shoes, and to let her hair grow long, and to wear long skirts, and to give up the use of rouge and lipstick – when he had told Daisy all this, Daisy took a deep breath, jammed her hands against her waist, flashed a contemptuous look at Gurudeva and said:

'Well! They must be nuts!'

Gurudeva looked pained and puzzled. Clearly, he had not expected Daisy would be so utterly uncompromising.

'Don't talk so, Dais,' he said cajolingly. 'If you don't do what they say, is trouble you going get me in ... I mean, they will make me *ku-jat*, put me out of the panch. You better think it over, Dais, and save me from all this trouble. Look, I give them me word that you will turn a Hindu.'

She turned another searching look on Gurudeva, and said, briefly and explicitly:

'You must be nuts too! You and the set of you!'

Gurudeva opened his eyes wide.

Daisy added: 'Me? Turn Hindu? Ha! Man, don't make me laugh. Me wear *ghungri* and *orhani* and *chappals* and long hair? Me give up rouge and lipstick? You can all go to hell.'

'I see,' said Gurudeva, vexed now, and thunderstruck. 'And if you kian't do as I say, you better go too.'

'Hell with you!' said Daisy.

And she went before the little mirror she had set up against the wall in Gurudeva's room – which was all the room she had – and began to fix her hair. Leaving Gurudeva outside, she banged the door shut; in ten minutes she had changed into fresh clothes; then went to work with powder, rouge and lipstick; then packed her suitcase and flew out of the room, to catch the late bus to Port of Spain.

Gurudeva, old Jaimungal and, in fact, all the other members of the household, stood against the veranda rail and watched her go – to all but Gurudeva, the embodiment of an evil thing leaving them at last.

Quietly and sadly Gurudeva said to the old man:

'So you see, Bap, once mo' I is a bachelor again.' He meditated a moment, then said, more to himself than to anyone else: 'Look to me I was born not to have a son.'

'Yes, *beta*,' said Jaimungal; then, catching himself, said quickly, 'No, *beta*.'

Jhulani said: 'Leh she go, *beta*; you goin' get plenty more.'

'Yes, Mai,' said Gurudeva.

They Named Him Mohun

Mohun's coming into this world of light was not an occasion of joy for anyone. There were reasons. In the first place, three months before his birth, Bipti, his mother, had left his father's home, as it turned out, never to return. With her two children – Sohani, aged four, and Krishna, a little over two years old – she had trudged seven miles to her mother's on a hot and dusty day. And ere Bipti had half told her tale of woe – how Durga had continued being tyrannically stingy, how one dared not pick a biscuit out of the biscuit tin without his finding out; the quarrelling that followed, and the words that often gave place to blows, with Bipti, and worse still, with Durga's own mother as the victims – ere Bipti had half told her tale of woe, Soomin, her mother, looking straight at the bigness of her, cried out, 'Shame!'

It was a two-way rebuke, aimed not only at Durga, who, she well knew, was a sinfully mean fellow; but the rebuke, hard as steel, had for its target the un-born Mohun as well. There and then the old woman gave out that the child – be it man or be it woman – was bound to be a creature of evil destiny. 'And what else can it be?' she asked, as though some one had contradicted her, 'seeing it has already initiated a tragedy while yet in its mother's belly!'

And then, some three months later, as though to confirm the awful prognostication, Boodhani, the dais, at the moment of Mohun's birth, gave out in a whispered scream that it was better that the child had not been conceived at all, or, having been conceived, it had breathed its last the moment it touched Mother Earth.

Disregarding the child's sharp cries that pierced the deep night silence in the hut, Boodhani said: 'It is a man-child, but alas! He will live and grow only to eat his mother and father, and who knows who else. Behold, the wretch took birth in the wrong way; and behold, it has come with six fingers on each hand! It is bound to eat its mother and father.'

A hush, an awful hush, descended into that hut then, and Soomin, who stood near by, stooped and looked at the infant, and then straightened up and sighed, and sighing, smote her forehead with both hands, and said: 'Alas! It is true. The child is *chha-angura* – six-fingered: an incarnation of evil, a most ill-starred child, if ever there was one. Born in the wrong way too!'

And from the adjoining room came the petulant, tottering voice of Bikram, Mohun's grandfather, who asked: 'And what is it this time? Is it a man-child? Tell me that only.' His voice held anxious beseechment, but Soomin made no answer, and the midwife obligingly answering for Soomin, said: 'A man-child, sure enough, but born in the wrong way, and born, too, with six fingers on each hand.'

Hearing this, the old man groaned and shifted in his *khatiah*, that creaked and groaned with him too, as if to share in his protests, for it was old and rickety like the old man himself, and the hempen lines were worn and torn in years of use.

So the gloom deepened in that hut in the rice-lands, and by the following day there was not a man or woman in the village who did not hold with Boodhani that an evil thing had happened in the house of Bikram, because a grandson born unto him was a *chha-angura* – a six-fingered infant; and as though to heighten the effect, born too in the wrong way, and on a Saturday, at the unseemly hour of midnight. Mohun was voted then to be the embodiment as well as the harbinger of all that would be inauspicious and crooked and ugly for all concerned, for all linked with him in blood, but especially for his mother and father.

In the still, grey dawn Soomin went out and cut lengths of the thorny cactus that grew for hedge on the roadside. And she cut the cactus into lengths of six inches or that long, and hung a piece over or against every aperture or cranny; and this she did to prevent the entry of evil spirits and malignant witches, for she would take no chances, seeing so much evil had already befallen.

Later that same day the priest was called, and he was known to be a good man and a holy one; and one, moreover, who could read the *patra*, the astrological almanac, and cast a horoscope and tell in a minute the luck or ill-luck of a child; what it should guard against as it grew up and the name it should have in consonance with its horoscope. Against his coming Soomin took away the *khatiah* almost from under old Bikram, and told him half sarcastically to walk a bit for exercise. Then, grumbling because of the hard lot he thought he was meeting in his old age, the old man wobbled and creaked out of the *khatiah* that had ever been bed, table and chair for him.

And Soomin, asking no one's help, dragged the *khatiah* out to the gallery and spread on it her best-washed sheet of flour-sacks, and on top of the white sheet she put three white pillows stuffed with the flowers of sugar-cane.

And when the pundit arrived, Soomin forthwith brought him water in a *lotah* or brass jug, as was the custom. And he took it and washed his hands with just a palmful under the low-hanging grass eaves, and with another palmful performed a gargle, a loud gargle. Then he turned towards the hut and very ceremoniously sprinkled a few drops over himself and a few drops over Soomin and some before and around him, as though to make everybody and everything clean and holy.

Then he sat down upon the *khatiah*, which became suddenly complainingly vocal; but the pundit, ignoring its complaint, said: 'Peace be on this house and on all who dwell herein. Rama! Rama!'

Then Soomin went down on her haunches against the wall, facing the pundit, and respectfully adjusted her *orhani* and clasped her palms and said: 'Punditji, a man-child was born unto my Bipti, at about midnight, and the child came the wrong way, with six fingers on each hand.'

The pundit groaned and became significantly quiet. Then he shrugged his shoulders and said with sudden determination, 'Oh, it is bad; for it is written of such that he will bring evil upon his mother and father and will be an evil influence even unto himself. But grieve not, for I will tell you to do that which, if done, will dispel the evil, and good will come out of bad. Yes, good will come out of bad.'

And he dipped his hand in the capacious pocket of his *koortah* and brought out his *patra*, rolled and wrapped in red cloth with strings at either end. He undid the strings and unrolled the book, broad and wobbly upon his thighs, and began to read mumblingly to himself. And he turned the pages and read again, and turned a page or two more and read further, his finger on the line, as though the words would not stay otherwise.

Then he said: 'Well, the first syllable of the child's name is indicated to be *Mo*, and you may add any suffix to it.'

And Soomin mumbled a word or two, to hit upon a seemly suffix, but grew confused and begged for help.

'But, Punditji,' she said, 'it were better you suggested the termination to the syllable *Mo*, for I can think of no other than *hun*.'

And the pundit brightened up and clapped his hands and said: 'But that is good! That is very good! *Mo-hun* shall he be called, and a prettier and more meaningful name a child could not possibly have; for *Mohun* means the Beloved, and it is the name the cow-maids gave to the Lord Krishna himself.'

And the pundit shut the book triumphantly.

But Soomin saw that the pundit had forgotten to tell her what would be the child's luck and what it should guard against as it grew up, and also what was it that had to be done in order to dispel the ill-omens that characterized its coming. So she quickly and apologetically reminded him of all this; and he brought out from his cloth-parcel another book, and mumbling, 'Mo, Mo, Mo,' opened the book and found a page and read and said: 'The child was born under the planet Mool – a bad planet. He will have broad frontal teeth, with spaces between. A bad sign: he will be a *randi-baj* and a *phakkar* – a ladies' man and a spendthrift. He must guard against water: never go near well, river, pond or sea; must not climb trees, nor look up while standing or sitting under a tree. He will have an inauspicious sneeze. That is all.'

'But what about removing the ill-omens, Punditji? Of his taking birth the wrong way, of his being six-fingered, of his being born in Mool, and on a Saturday?'

'As to all these ugly signs, and especially of his being born in Mool,' said the pundit, 'do thou this: for twenty-one days, from the hour and day of his birth, let not the infant see its father's face, nor the father the infant's. Then let the father see the infant in a reflection of mustard oil contained in a brass platter. Let the brass platter be clean and gleaming. That is all.'

'Well,' said Soomin, 'that I will do, though for my part I would not wish to see that Durga again, the cruelly mingy man that he is. But for Bipti's sake . . .' And Soomin undid the knot that she always kept at a corner of her *orhani*, and got out a florin and gave it to the pundit, saying she was sorry she was so poor, otherwise she could have given him more. And the pundit, wrapping the *patra*, smiled and said she was not to worry on that score and that she had done well enough, according to her means.

On the appointed day Soomin called Durga, and had him see Mohun in a reflection of mustard oil, and then told him, rather bluntly, that she wished to see him no more. And Durga, taking instant umbrage – as who should not? – walked away in a huff.

But Soomin felt safe, and she felt so far safe that, despite protests from the old man, who grumbled on the folly of incurring expenses on the birth of the son of a mere daughter, she resolved to hold a *barahi*, a twelfth-day celebration on the birth of a man-child.

2

Soomin decided that the *barahi* must turn out a grand affair. She took care that every householder in the rice-lands was invited. Of writing invitations she was altogether ignorant. The printed card that so many of the villagers were nowadays using she deemed but a recent innovation. It was pretty, to be sure, but was it more impressive? Was it as Indian as the traditional saffron-dyed rice? No, with the printed card she had no affinity.

She reached up to the small shelf in old Bikram's room and took from it the tiny wooden cabinet in which, four decades or so ago, Bikram had brought her the vermilion powder for their nuptial ceremony; and from this *dibbi* she took out the stub of pencil that Bikram had kept therein for years, for he could read and write a little. Then she fetched a paper bag from the lean-to kitchen – the bag that had contained last fortnight's flour – and she carefully flattened the paper against her stomach so as to rid it of the multitude of creases, and gave it to the old man, together with the pencil, saying, 'Write now. Write the names I call; for I propose to invite every man and every woman to this *barahi*, come what may. I have attended every *barahi* and every wedding and every ceremony of whatever kind for these years past; and it is time I got back some of what I have given in gifts and presents, now that I am bringing off this thing. Write.'

So Bikram gave forth a throat sound that was partly a groan, partly a protest, and partly a cough. And he sat up slowly on the *khatiah*, and took from Soomin the paper and pencil, ready to write, without comment, on his lap.

He was none too pleased that this *barahi* should be brought off, seeing he stood in need of medicine and better nourishment, which he thought he was hardly getting.

And Soomin noticed the sour taciturnity of the old man and said again: 'Now write; write whether you like it or not.'

Therefore Bikram set pencil to paper, and the names that Soomin called grew into two long, black columns that seemed to exhaust the old man in the writing, so much so that no sooner the last name was written than he threw away the pencil and paper and went flat on his back and closed his eyes and said he was done for.

And Soomin took up the pencil and paper and said, with a very displeased look at Bikram, that that was all right as far as she was concerned; and he could take to his *khatiah* once more, and keep there, living like a snake, for that was all he was good at.

For answer Bikram covered himself up with his coverlet from head to toe.

And Soomin took a handful of rice and dyed it with saffron and gave it to Jhagroo, the village barber, who took the rice in his cotton cloth. Then Soomin handed the barber the list of names and begged him to see that every person listed on the paper bag had his five grains or more of the invitation rice, so that none could say he or she was not invited.

Came the *barahi*; and indeed it turned out a grand affair – a carouse to speak of and remember. Bitpi was almost unrecognizable. Not for years had she been so gaudily dressed. She was all new clothes. And beside her in the *khatiah* in which she reclined with Mohun at her side, there were still more clothes – stack upon stack of new clothes; and dozens of silver bracelets and silver anklets for Mohun, and bonnets and booties; and stringed black beads to go round his little wrists and neck, to keep off *nazar*, otherwise the evil eye, for he was so pretty.

The more old-fashioned brought presents in the shape of parcels of flour and Irish potatoes and some salt; but these were few. For, in spite of the stern conservatism of Soomin and other folks such as Soomin, modernism had spread its tentacles in the village, though many still pretended that that could not be. So, many brought no clothes or food-gifts at all but handed Soomin a two-dollar or a one-dollar banknote, a florin or a shilling; but none dared give less, for the very shame of it.

And of course there was a great feasting. But what made the *barahi* a carouse was rum. Even Soomin, who seldom drank, drank that night, screening her cup with her *orhani* for shame's sake and for manners; and old Bikram also had what he called 'a shot or two'.

The women ate and drank within the hut, for it was not proper that they should do so in the presence of men-folk, who sat or stood around in Bikram's long cow-pen, watching old Ghoorahoo dance the Shiva dance, all smeared in ashes and wearing nothing but a loincloth, just as the ascetic god, Shiva, is popularly supposed to be.

The women, sitting, squatting, or being simply down on their haunches, all round Bipti, sang nativity songs, addressed not to Mohun but to the infant Rama and the infant Krishna, the incarnations of the four-armed Vishnu. And as the night wore on, and more and more rum was taken, the nativity songs gave place to other songs, and still later to a medley of songs. Jasmin, the grass-cutter's daughter, the prettiest girl in the village, ventured with a mongrel composition – that is, the words were mostly English, but the tune wholly Indian, the refrain being:

> *Every time I passing, girl,*
> *You grinding massala.*

It was, everybody agreed, a hot 'leh-go'.

Then, just to show that she too was no novice at composing, Rohini, the star singer in the rice-lands, quickly retaliated with:

> *Marajin must be powder up*
> *And waiting for me!*

Then, to show that she could go one better, Rohini stood up and began to dance. And Mungari joined Rohini in the dancing, amid a crescendo of singing and drumming and clapping.

Suddenly Rohini took hold of Soomin and forced her, too, to dance, though she was so old. And Soomin, though begging to be excused, was bound to comply, for she was the hostess, and, more than being the hostess, she was the proud grandmother of a man-child. The whole hut resounded with the merry-making, and the rhythmic thunder of drums and cymbals could be heard a mile away.

Then, quite unexpectedly, Durga, Mohun's father, walked into the long pen. He wore a pair of dark trousers and a *koortah*, and on his head he carried an old felt hat. He walked right up to the assembly, and addressing no one in particular, yet addressing everybody, he threw his head back and folded his hands, and asked:

'And what can be the meaning of all this? I want to know!'

Old Ghoorahoo stopped dancing and the drummer stopped drumming, and everybody looked up at Durga in wonder, for it was known he was not wanted there.

'Is it written in the ancient books,' asked Durga, 'that at a jubilation on the birth of a son the whole village should be invited, except the father? Is it written . . .'

And Soomin, hearing Durga's loud voice, came out quickly to the cow-pen, and jammed her hands against her waist – a thing she ought not to have done – and looked Durga straight in the eye, and asked:

'And is it written that a man should put away his wife every time she is made heavy-footed, so that the expenses consequent on child-bearing should be borne by others? It is shame you have not got, Durga, that you should dare to show yourself before this assembly without blackening your face with pot's black!'

This occurred deep in the night; and some said Durga was quite wrong to come, and others that Soomin ought not to have insulted him as she did, seeing he *was* her son-in-law, one whose feet she had washed in a marriage tent in token of the fact.

And Soomin, sensing what the people thought, said she did not care who thought what; but that *she* knew Durga was no good as a husband, nor yet as a father, and that it was for want of shame that he had dared to show his face at all, and . . .

But just then the pundit – he who had named Mohun – came out to Soomin and touched her gently on the shoulder and beckoned her aside. And when he thought he was sufficiently far away from the people, he said to her:

'Look, daughter. Do not allow yourself to say in a moment of anger what you would not say in your soberer senses. With all his faults Durga remains unquestionably Bipti's husband. Nothing can undo that. So say the holy books. A gift you made of Bipti to Durga, invoking the gods as witnesses. A gift once given cannot be reclaimed; still less can it be given to another. That is the law. Therefore I say for your good and for the good of Bipti and in recognition of the law that you should say nothing that should cause these two to part for ever.'

And Soomin bowed her head and said: '*Hanh*, Punditji. Yes, Punditji.'

Then she returned to the cow-pen and cast a brief look at Durga, and said simply, 'You may stay.'

My Uncle Dalloo

My Uncle Dalloo was, without doubt, the cutest as well as the cleverest man in our village. He was held to be the light not only of my grandfather Gangaram's household, but he was regarded as the light of the whole village. The qualities that raised him to this pinnacle were multiple. He was perspicacious, conniving, and versatile. He was, for instance, the only person in the village who could read and write. And my Uncle Dalloo could read and write not only Hindi – and some Sanskrit – which alone would have been sufficient to raise him high above the rest of our microscopic community, but he could read and write English too. And it was this *Angrezi* qualification of his, to begin with, that quite dazzled and benumbed the villagers. Many I knew who literally prostrated themselves before him in those days, pleading Babaji this, Babaji that.

But his being bilingual was not all the magic. More potent than his being bilingual was the fact that my Uncle Dalloo was a Brahmin of the first water – a most uncompromising member of the priestly caste, tenaciously, inexorably, fantastically and fanatically orthodox. Catch him eating so much as a grain of *channa* with his boots on! Or let him catch *you* calling yourself a Brahmin, or a Maharaj, or a Singh, and not keeping the *churki* – the tuft of hair, long, knotted, and conspicuous – on the crown of the head! Literally and otherwise, Uncle Dalloo would make you *ku-jat* or outcaste on the spot. He was like that.

If by some chance you could hit upon the truth, that my Uncle Dalloo's brand of English was no better than that of a baboo's, you would take good care not to let him know what you thought of it, or of him; otherwise you would soon discover that existence could be a devilishly hazardous business; or, as young Dookhoo the grass-cutter put it, 'Living would become water more than flour for you'. But no fear; in our cul-de-sac of a village there appeared to be none with either so much sense or so much rashness. So Uncle Dalloo reigned unchallenged – a kind of an intellectual superman, Babaji and Maharaj of all he surveyed. His word was law.

For all this Uncle Dalloo was neither very formidable-looking nor a very prepossessing person. He was just cute, about thirty-five when I knew him; small and spare, cherubic and tender. He was singularly and pathetically bald-pated; indeed, he gave you the impression that he was born that way. How else could you explain that tight, shiny scalp of his, with just a straggling fringe of hair above the ears, fine and anaemic things, like sun-starved grass around a gleaming pond?

He never worked with his hands. Certainly I had never seen him grace a cutlass or a hoe. He said he was not born for that kind of life. He said he was a Brahmin. No one could quarrel with him for that – least of all my Aunt Leela. Her he kept in place by a variety of Brahminic subtleties, such as, if she did not obey him in this or that matter she was sure to be reborn into a beetle or into a snake or even into a scorpion. And my Aunt Leela, being herself a Brahmini, albeit Trinidad-born, and having heard nothing to the contrary all her life, quite believed all this. So she obeyed.

I can well guess what kind of life Uncle Dalloo must have led in India. It was plain he came from an impoverished middle-class family who had fallen on hard times in the wake of the Mutiny. I have a strong suspicion that even at the age of eighteen or twenty he must have led a rather grim sort of life; possibly he was well on the way to living on his wits. Uncle Dalloo prided himself on his being Cawnpore-born and bred, and the grand way in which he expatiated on the exploits of the Cawnpore-*wallahs* made all other human beings outside Cawnpore seem insipid and third-rate.

He had attended a government school where, in addition to Hindi, the sirdar also taught the boys some English. In his gay moods he often recited with great feeling and in that peculiar Indian English of his the whole of 'Rule, Britannia'. It was the only poem he ever recited in English. I doubt whether he knew another; but with it he at once charmed and confounded the villagers. They listened open-mouthed, in dumb amazement, not understanding a word of it. But Uncle Dalloo took this as a great compliment. He knew he had established himself in their opinion as a brilliant *Angrezi* scholar.

How a *pukka shaharia* – a rank city man – like my Uncle Dalloo came to dwell in a bowl of a place like Chandernagore was for a long time a wonder to me. When I came to know him better it was clear that that was just the move *he* would be very likely to make in the circumstances. You see, my grandfather Gangaram was not a poor man. A third of the length and breadth of Chandernagore was his; a lovely patch of cocoa plantation on the other side of the settlement was his too; his long pen was never without at least a dozen head of cattle; and, though he himself was chary of admitting the fact, it was somehow known that he had money in the Post Office savings bank up in Chaguanas, the market town, three miles away. Add to this the fact that my Aunt Leela, hard on marriageable age, slight and small like Uncle Dalloo himself, with long black hair and limpid dark eyes, was uncomplainingly attractive. What wonder, then, that soon enough Uncle Dalloo had not only married my Aunt Leela, but, as much as my grandfather himself, became adviser and man in authority.

Most surviving India-born Indians in Trinidad recount tall tales how they were fooled by wily recruiters into coming to the *tapu* to work on sugar and cocoa plantations. But Uncle Dalloo had no such tales to recount of himself. *He* was not fooled into his being recruited by anybody. He was himself a recruiter. Scores of the thousand and one men and women who found themselves on board the good ship *Mutla* bound for Trinidad *tapu* were recruited by him, he claimed. In virtue of this he was automatically made a sirdar over his fellow-emigrants the very day he set foot on board the ship. In virtue of the same fact he continued being a sirdar on Tortuga Estate, to which he was indentured. Thereafter, his indentureship period over, he kept being a sirdar on one plantation or another till he moved in with my grandfather Gangaram to become house son-in-law. And this explains why, in typical sirdar fashion, he habitually clad himself in khaki trousers and tunic, never ventured out unless he was well-booted, and never handled a cutlass or a hoe. Once a sirdar always a sirdar, seemed to be *his* way.

This, his being neatly clad in khaki from neck to ankle, and his going about in boots, made my Uncle Dalloo appear quite a phenomenon to the villagers. They respected him all the more for it. The fact is nobody else in Chandernagore wore boots, and few wore trousers. They couldn't. Chandernagore was not a town. Far, far from it. Chandernagore was a lagoon – for half the year at any rate. It contained, among other animate and inanimate phenomena, about a dozen huts, mostly primitive grass-thatched habitations, planted anywhere and anyhow in the lowlands.

From a quarter of a mile these huts made you think of some gargantuan, prehistoric monsters that had rambled in the slime and slush of the lagoon and then, no longer able to carry themselves, had died, greyed, become fossilized, and remained rooted and inert for ever. For six months of the year the place abounded in flood and mud; often enough the mud reached to the very doors of the huts; floods inundated the earthen floors. The villagers did not mind all this. They were in their element. Mud and they were kin. They welcomed rain, they delighted in floods. These things, they gleefully told one another, were a godsend for the paddy crops. Outsiders looked upon the Chandernagorean as a kind of amphibian; the Chandernagoreans on their part looked upon outsiders as extraordinary people, in that they wore far too much clothes.

Therefore was my Uncle Dalloo looked upon as an extra-ordinary man. He was so unlike the Chandernagoreans. In that watery, paddy-begetting expanse who but he would want to be in khaki trousers and tunic! And who but he would want to wear boots! Not trousers but mostly short dhotis were what the other men-folk wore. As for boots . . . some of the more fastidious villagers, like my grandfather Gangaram, permitted themselves the luxury of a pair of sabots – not when there was mud though, but when there was little or no mud at all.

Uncle Dalloo was a kind of Dr Know-All too. There was no problem he could not solve, no enigma he could not un-ravel, no ailment he could not get rid of. Hardly a day passed but a villager or two would come to him, wanting to know this and to know that. Nothing was too big for him to tackle; nothing was too little.

Except when he was voluntarily made a gift of a shilling or two, he did not as a rule exact payments for his services. He could not make himself so obviously mean. But indirectly he benefited enormously. In the rice-planting season, for example, he got acre upon acre of my grandfather Ganga-ram's part of the lagoon planted in rice without paying a cent for labour. At reaping time, too, he got all the paddy reaped, threshed, bagged and toted much in the same gratis kind of way.

He was seldom refused a loan; none dared refuse him a favour. If one did he was likely to find, not long after, all his young rice seedlings mysteriously eaten up at the top by cattle or nipped off under water by crabs. Nobody would know whose cattle ate the seedlings nor how crabs came into the rice patch. It would surprise no one if the sufferer came to Uncle Dalloo and begged him to solve yet another enigma.

Uncle Dalloo had a way with him when put to these tasks. First he would ask some questions. Then he would squat upon his heels, jam his elbows upon his knees, prop his chin upon his hands. As though his brain could not function well enough otherwise. Then he would meditate. He would meditate in a hard, gruelling sort of stare, forehead creased, gaze on ground. If anybody, not knowing he was far gone in thought, interrupted him, he would snap out, 'Shut up!' and none would dare break into his thoughts a second time. If his questions, the answers thereto, and the meditations that followed, did not fetch him a ready solution, he would call for his *Yotish*, which is a kind of Indian *Napoleon's Book of Fate*, but with a deal of religious tang about it; or he would call for his Bible, an ancient, musty, mutilated copy of the Authorized Version which he had kept for years, though I doubt whether he really appreciated or understood the contents of that great book.

One short incident, and I shall be through with this sketch of my Uncle Dalloo.

One evening old Ramdat came to him. This Ramdat was a gnarled, bow-backed, swarthy fellow of about forty or forty-five. Always you saw him in a short cotton dhoti and in a merino, or shirt of some sort, mostly made out of a flour-sack. The grey house against which fluttered from tall bamboo staffs half a dozen red flags put up to Hanuman, the Monkey God, was his.

'Babaji!' moaned Ramdat, slouching down on his heels, for he would not dare to squat on a level with my Uncle Dalloo, who at the moment was reclining on his stringed bed in the gallery. 'Babaji,' repeated Ramdat, 'I find myself in a great trouble. I come to you in a great distress ... She ... she has run away.'

Uncle Dalloo sat up. 'She who?'

'My Joogni ... the last daughter. She is gone!'

Uncle Dalloo went on his heels now, put his hands around his knees so as to brace his posture. 'Gone where?' he asked.

'That is what I want *you* to tell me, Babaji.'

'Hm!' exclaimed Uncle Dalloo; and you could sense there was plenty in that 'hm'. 'How old is the girl?' he asked.

'Going fifteen this year, Babaji.'

Uncle Dalloo was suddenly visibly annoyed. 'You are a fool of a man,' he said. 'You are a slack fellow. You ought to

have had the girl married at least a year ago. It is the law. All
the Shastras say so. You could be punished for your slack-
ness.'

Old Ramdat trembled. 'I know; I do not deny it, Babaji. I
would have had the child married last marriage season; it
was not easy to find a suitable match for her.'

Uncle Dalloo waved aside the excuse. 'There are suitable
people right in this village. One match is enough; two would
be one too many ... Where and when was the girl last
seen?'

'At about nine yesterday morning. She pushed her clothes
in a bucket and went to wash at Chirkut's pond.'

Uncle Dalloo called for his Bible, key and string. The
moment I heard him call for these things, I knew he had
already had his answer. I knew he had solved the mystery of
Joogni's disappearance. If he had not, he would have called
for his *Yotish*; for then, whatever the answer, right or
wrong, it would be the *Yotish* to praise or blame, not Uncle
Dalloo.

My Aunt Leela brought the Bible, the long key and the
string. Then, still squatting on his stringed bed, Uncle
Dalloo went to work. He opened the book in the middle,
placed the key perpendicularly between the pages, with the
knob-end sticking out. Then he shut the book and bound it
tightly with the string, so that the knob-end of the key kept
sticking out.

'Come now,' he said, meaning me.

I knew what he wanted me to do. The Bible would hang on
the key; the key would hang from the tip of Uncle Dalloo's
forefinger on the one side, and from the tip of my own forefinger on the other side. We would squat facing each other,
with the Bible suspended precariously between us.

We did this.

It was a dramatic moment. On whoever's name the Bible
turned, that person would be the man who had made away
with Joogni. Everybody's eyes were on that Bible. There
were my Aunt Leela and my Cousin Rampat looking on too.

Old Ramdat watched the Bible as though his life depended on it.

'Steady now!' said Uncle Dalloo. Then he began: 'By Saint Peter, by Saint Paul, *Ramu* has run away with Joogni.'

I said my end of the formula: 'By Saint Peter, by Saint Paul, Ramu *ain't* run away with Joogni.'

The Bible remained steady.

'By Saint Peter, by Saint Paul,' recited Uncle Dalloo, '*Arjun* has run away with Joogni.'

It was my turn now. 'By Saint Peter, by Saint Paul, Arjun *ain't* run away with Joogni.'

Still the Bible remained steady.

'By Saint Peter, by Saint Paul . . .'

Within five minutes Uncle Dalloo and I had repeated the lullaby on the names of almost every youngster in the village – married and unmarried. The book didn't spin. Uncle Dalloo pondered, tried to recall the names of other young gallants. We all had our eyes glued, so to speak, on the Bible. Who could be the culprit? It wasn't Ramu, it wasn't Arjun, it wasn't –

'Perhaps,' cut in my Aunt Leela, 'perhaps the girl hasn't run away at all. Perhaps she is drowned in Chirkut's pond. Perhaps . . .'

'Shut up!' snapped Uncle Dalloo. 'Let me think.'

We kept mum.

'Ah!' exclaimed Uncle Dalloo. 'Steady now! By Saint Peter, by Saint Paul, *Jagna* has run away with Joogni.'

'By Saint Peter, by . . .'

Suddenly old Ramdat drew a long breath . . . The Bible was turning; I am dead sure I didn't see Uncle Dalloo's finger shake; nor did mine. But the Bible *was* turning. It described almost a circle, the key slipped from Uncle Dalloo's finger; the book fell with a thud.

'There!' exclaimed Uncle Dalloo triumphantly. 'There's your answer. It is Jagna who has run away with Joogni.'

Old Ramdat, dumb with rage and shame, groaned and gnashed his teeth, but said nothing.

When he was gone, my Aunt Leela said to my Uncle Dalloo: 'But how did you hit so unerringly on Jagna? Is it true?'

Uncle Dalloo said: 'It is very true. All parties to a row or an argument in this village come to me for advice. If you had been home earlier today, you would have seen when Jagna's father came to me. *His* son, too, is not at home since yesterday.'

'Where is he, then?'

'Hiding with Joogni in Nanaan's hut in the next village,' said Uncle Dalloo.

The Wedding Came

Sitting on the *dainki* – the eight-foot long wooden machine for pounding paddy – and seeing old Jokhoo, the match-maker, and Lalta, her father, talking in the open turf-thatched hut, Leela began to feel certain that the wedding would come. It seemed one of those things that nobody could stop: there was something elemental about it – like the coming of rain, or night.

To her this wedding symbolized night, for it held in it a vague threat, a thing fraught with the mystery of the unknown. But the worst of it was that she would be taken away from Ganpat.

That thought gave her a thump at the pit of her stomach and brought on a lump in her throat. Had not Ganpat himself vowed that no one could take her away from him?

She stood up from the *dainki* and went out in the metallic glare of the midday sun. The air was heavy with the warm scent of freshly cut rice, and the heat haze shimmered in the distance. Shading her eyes from the glare with one hand, Leela scanned the scattered groups of men and women gathering the rice harvest in the flat lands. There he was! A quarter of a mile away, bathed in the haze and shimmer of the hard light; but she could make him out easily. He was different.

She could hear the heavy thud of the paddy-laden stalks as the men beat them by the handfuls on to the wooden *matchan* – a slatted table of round wood.

Ganpat was the best beater of the lot. She could see that. He threshed with a sustained rhythmical swing of his arms, never pausing for rest.

('Ganpat, Ganpat! Have you forgotten? That day, out in the grass-lands, where we sat close together under the mango tree, you vowed that you would allow no one to take me away from you. Nestling closer, I asked, "How?" and the tiny stem of grass in your mouth moved from side to side. "I do not know yet," you said, "but be sure never will I allow anyone to take you away from me. That I swear to, Leela!" And now the wedding is coming, Ganpat. Here are old Jokhoo and my father talking about it – perhaps fixing the very day. Ganpat! Ganpat!')

Not once did he look her way, and she sighed and turned into the adjoining tapia hut, and took up a *cocoye* broom that lay on the ground like a neglected thing and set to sweeping away the freshly risen dust from the earthen floor.

He used to come to the hut at midday to eat his food; others came too; for out in the rice-lands the water in the *cocal* was hot and rancid under the broiling sun, and here Lalta gladly gave them water drawn from the recently installed water tap on the roadside; and the grass hut afforded them an hour of truly welcome relief from the heat and sweat of the paddy-fields. But he had not come to the hut since that last meeting in the grass-lands, and she wondered why.

Leela liked him the very first time he came to the hut. He was tall and dark and lithe, and he had a merry good nature. He was not a bit like the husbands of so many of the newly married girls in the village: crude, glum fellows, who went through life as though it were a sin to be merry: who were so awfully domineering with their wives.

She finished the sweeping and came back on the *dainki*. Striving for nonchalance, she was yet eager to hear what Jokhoo had to say.

Jokhoo was a queer old fellow who eschewed all work that required manual effort. The only time he had ever worked with his hands was when he was bound for five years on the sugar plantation to which he had come from India five-and-twenty years ago. After that he had given himself, as it were, a lifelong holiday. If he had ever given a thought to becoming a family man, he had rid himself of the idea soon enough. He was tramp, story-teller, and raiser of false alarms. The young fellows of the village, when they would see him coming, would point to him and laugh and say, 'Larmer coming, boy!' Larmer was short for Alarmer – a nickname bestowed on him in recognition of the alarms he so often raised.

Once, late in the night, he woke up the whole village by shouting out that Seemungal's house in the next village, two miles away, was burning down. It was not true, of course. Yet he was a harmless enough fellow. He had no house of his own, but he never lacked shelter. People liked him and gladly gave him lodging – and food too – because of the wonderful stories he told – stories that had to do with ancient kings such as Dasaratha and Janak and Vikramaditya and Asoka and who not; and he cracked huge jokes, so that it was difficult to say what the people liked more – the jokes, or the stories. Certainly he brought laughter in a drab world.

He knew everybody's affairs and everybody knew his; yet he would often try to make one believe that he was holding a lot back. Because of his bohemianism he had inevitably found himself as a matchmaker. He knew by name all the unmarried and marriageable youths twenty miles around; he knew their history, genealogy, their vices and their virtues. He had brought about a number of successful marriages and to these he pointed with pride. He liked the job. It was easy, it fitted in nicely with his trampings, and it brought him money as well as clothing.

The richer people did not trust him with such important matters, however. A mere tramp! Some even called him a charlatan. He shrugged his shoulders and treated such remarks with indifference. But even Lalta had taken him with misgivings.

Squatting with Lalta now on the sugar-bag spread on the ground, Jokhoo spread his lanky hands in a gesture of disgust.

'Everything has gone wrong again,' he announced. 'It

seems as though the girl will have to go without a husband for yet another year.'

'What is the matter now?' Lalta asked hotly. 'Is not my Leela good enough for that son of Raghoo's? The girl can cook and wash and keep a clean hut; even gather fodder for cows. Add to this the fact that the child is doubtlessly good-looking; slim, yet plump of body, dark-eyed, with a complexion that is verily of the colour of honey. What more can any man desire in a wife?'

Lalta was a staunch, self-respecting Hindu, and in a staunch, self-respecting way it was none of Leela's affair that she was about to be married. He was nearing the sixty-year span and the grey hair on his head had thinned down – and oh, how thinned down! He had few teeth left. If you looked at him well, you thought of a sucked orange. But a sucked orange that had lain in the sun for a whole day. Not all the salt seas between India and Trinidad, nor his thirty years' residence in the melting-pot of the island, had done much to tone down the stern conservatism of him. In more ways than one he was a rock.

At thirty he had married, in the middle of his indenture-ship on the plantation to which he had come, a Trinidad-born Hindu girl. She died when Leela, the only child, was aged six. Not wishing to inflict a stepmother on the child, he had not married a second time. He had taken good care of Leela and she had not disappointed him. At seventeen he was sure she was all that any Hindu girl should be. In keeping with the prevailing custom, not one day had he sent her to the Canadian Mission school in the village. His conservatism re-belled against sending girl-children to school. He was sure they came to no good. In the first place, they learned to write love-letters, then again, they wore knee-length frocks, and – the most shameful thing of all – many of them chose their own husbands! Irrespective of caste too!

He was glad and proud he had saved Leela from all this.

Yet he was not a happy man. He passed sleepless nights; for, after her tenth year – so said the marriage manual – every day that passed leaving Leela unwed meant – apart from the opprobrium of the village – that the caverns of hell had opened so much the wider, ready to engulf in their gaping void his defaulting soul. He had read the Ancients and he knew. Knew and trembled.

'Tell me,' he asked again, 'is not my Leela good enough for that son of Raghoo's?'

Jokhoo leaned forward on his thin, sparsely clad legs that were bent under him like those of a cricket. 'It is not a question of the girl not being good enough, O Lalta. But thou pridest thyself on belonging to the priestly caste, and really there seems to be perennially a dearth of such youths. Especially for one such as thee, who art too poor.'

He paused to note the effect of his words; then he dropped the hammer. 'Ten pounds in hard cash is the dowry for the son of Raghoo. Can you afford that much?'

Lalta wilted at the demand. With trembling fingers he undid the mildewy length of cotton from around his head and with it dried the perspiration that had come upon his face.

'Ten pounds!' he groaned. 'Why, in all my life I have not even seen so much ready wealth, much less to own it. Only a milch-cow I have, a heifer and a few goats. But I have no money. And money is what you are after. Money and cattle.' Lalta trembled with rage.

Jokhoo gave an asthmatic cough and shifted his position on the sugar-bag. The cough was full of meaning. It said: 'You may go on eating yourself, but you have no idea what I have up my sleeve.'

Lalta did not catch the hint. His gaze was on the ground. He was in a reflective mood.

'Long have the elders of the village looked at me askance,' he said. 'As though I have killed a cow. For long I have not dared to go to functions in the village. Such humiliation! And all this just because of this one fault – keeping in my house a daughter seventeen years old and unmarried!'

He relapsed into moody silence. Neither of them spoke, but a glad gleam of mischief shone in Jokhoo's eyes. Then angrily

Lalta turned to him with: 'Many a man have I engaged to find a husband for the girl, but after their peregrinations, lasting a month, sometimes two months or more, always they have returned – like you – looking sour, apologetic, full of regrets. Always the humbug has lain in my not affording the dowry money.'

Jokhoo rubbed his palms together, coughed and said: 'And yet, thanks to me O Lalta, out of this same difficulty there is to emerge a great good.'

'What can you mean?' Lalta asked eagerly. 'Speak plainly.'

'Nay, I speak in no riddle. Yesterday in the house of Raghoo I had words with the man who is determined to out-bid you. He is Ganpat, wealthy son of Ramachandra . . .'

'The same who refused the hand of my Leela for his son two years ago?'

'The very same.'

'May the man rot in the belly of hell!'

'Nay! Nay! Thou hast not heard all, or else thou wouldst not speak so rashly,' Jokhoo warned. 'Since his father's death – for Ramachandra is dead, as thou knowest – the youth has been left with a sister to marry off. To the son of Raghoo he is marrying her, ever willing to pay a higher dowry than any man.'

'May he perish with his wealth!' said Lalta.

'Curb thy anger,' said Jokhoo; 'for yesterday in the heat of anger I insulted Raghoo. "Wicked is the age," I said, "when men sell their sons to the highest bidders." He was hot with anger and made to strike me down. Then Ganpat stepped between, and begged my pardon. With clasped palms – as befits a well-mannered youth – he said: "I am deeply grieved, O Jokhoo, over the wrong that I have done. But if I have deprived a maiden of a prospective husband by taking him for my sister's spouse, is there no way in which I, as an unmarried fellow, may mend the harm?"'

'And?'

'And the wedding is fixed, O Lalta. Long has been the girl's karma in the blossoming, but great when it blossomed.

For, more than having a good husband, she will have neither mother-in-law nor father-in-law to torment her.'

Tears welled up in Lalta's eyes, and when he spoke there was a tremor in his voice. '*Wha-wha*, Jokhoo!' he exclaimed. 'Thou art a great matchmaker. The others were fools . . . But the dowry – how much is the dowry?'

'Oh, that!' Jokhoo answered carelessly. 'Only ten shillings! A mere formality.'

Leela stood up from the *dainki* and took up the bucket and went out to the water tap. The thumping at the pit of her stomach remained, and the lump in her throat, too; but now they were tokens of a throbbing, deep-felt joy . . . 'Ganpat, Ganpat . . .!' A lament transformed into a song.

Dookhani and Mungal

They said that she was rude and crude, that she had no manners and little shame. Sumintra, her mother-in-law, said it; once or twice even Radha and Rookmin, her sisters-in-law, had said it when they came to spend a day or two away from their husbands. But what hurt Dookhani more than any of these imputations were her mother-in-law's too frequent taunts that she, Dookhani, was as worthless as a barren cow. That, at any rate, thought Dookhani, was true. Twenty years old she was now and married five years; yet she remained childless.

Such stark sterility solidified and symbolized a rebuke, flung at her, as it were, by the gods.

Dookhani wept. Today she wept more poignantly perhaps than she had ever done before. For today Sumintra had not only likened her to a barren cow, but in a paroxysm of savage rage and contempt had also spat upon her face; and as Dookhani, shocked and hurt almost beyond words, cried out, 'Ah, Mai! You have spat upon me, and I am no leper,' Sumintra turned swiftly, like a snarling cat, and took up the fire-tongs that was still hot with the heat of the cooking-place, and struck her with it resoundingly on the shoulder.

'*Bahila!*' she had snapped.

Perhaps it was well for all concerned that Mungal was not in the house when this thing happened. Quiet though he was by temperament, he might have reacted badly against this sort of thing when Dookhani was concerned. For, without knowing it perhaps, he had come to love Dookhani in his own reserved, one might say dumb, fashion. Only the old man, squatting on his heels at the end of the gallery, had seen what had happened. He had protested, to be sure – a series of spasmodic throat noises that seemed to suffocate him ere they came out – but to Sumintra, twice stronger and tauter than he, his protest was altogether ineffectual. He too was a good-for-nothing, hardly able to fetch or carry his own brass jug.

When Mungal came from the sugar-fields at dusk, Dookhani was still in the kitchen. Looking at her it was hard for him to say whether she was asleep or sick, or whether she was crying. She had finished the cooking – dahl, *bharth*, mango chutney – and had washed the wares and swept the house with the broom of palm leaves that Mungal had cut for her the Sunday before and which she had made with her own hands. Then she lighted the two tin lamps in the two rooms of the house, and the one in the kitchen. Then she slumped down on the mud floor with her back against the wall, and wept and dried her tears at intervals and wept again. A leaden weariness of soul and body stole upon her and she put her hands around her upturned knees and bowed her head into them as tightly as in a vice.

Seeing her thus, he murmured, 'Hm!'

She did not look up.

He stuck, first the cutlass, then the crookstick, between a rafter and the low grass covering; then he turned and looked at her again and asked, in a vaguely curious voice:

'Now, what has happened to you?'

Still she did not answer, did not raise her head. He looked down at her more intently. 'But what is the matter? Why are you like this? Tell me.'

A sob shook her – shook her whole body. Then she jerked her head up and looked at him portentously, almost viciously. 'Go and ask your mother,' she said.

And suddenly he knew. So his mother had again likened her to a barren cow? Sudden anger reddened his eyes almost as much as hers were red with weeping.

'All right,' he said, with sudden masculine decision, 'go and pack your clothes.'

He began to roll up his dirt-spattered trousers with an energy that was equally sudden; and she got up and moved away to bring him water in a bucket.

It pleased her to hear him say what he had said. He was on *her* side. It meant in effect that he would send her away to her mother's hut. Well, he had said that not because he was displeased with her, but because he was displeased with his own mother. Though he had seldom carried it out, it was not the first time that he had made this threat. It was his method of protest. He could not actually question his mother. If he did everybody in the village would hear about it, and the thing would be grossly exaggerated and invested with all the horror of a tragedy, with all the horror of rank filial ingratitude; and the whole village – but more so the elders – would shake their heads tragically and say in a knowing way that it was indeed the *Kali-Yuga* – the Black Age – come upon the world. It was *Kali-Yuga*, to be sure, when a son took his own mother to task because of the greater love he bore his wife. And stanzas would be quoted and fables told to show that the Ancients knew what they wrote when they prophesied the misdeeds of these times.

And though Mungal had seen many a fellow recklessly run the risk of being thus quoted and commented upon for loving their wives too much and above the affection they showed their mothers, he himself shrank from taking any such risks – except in his own quiet way – which was to keep glum.

Dookhani felt pleased. From the water tap she cast him a brief backward glance full of affection and pride. This husband of hers was good to her. What did it matter that his mother was such a termagant? He understood her . . . and he was not bad-looking either . . . Strong and compact, fairly tall, straight and dark as a bamboo . . .

She brought him the water along with the calabash dipper, setting the bucket under the grass eaves, against the half-wall that ran the length of the kitchen.

She said: 'Now, do not mind that. What has happened has happened. Wash yourself and come and eat.' In her voice was the gentleness of a woman reasoning with a wayward child.

He mumbled something and, stooping, began to wash his foot.

She turned into the kitchen, making towards the *chulha*, the cooking-place, near which upon a box that had once contained tinned salmon were the pots with food. From the *matchan* immediately above she took down a shining *thali*, a brass plate, and started to spoon out rice in it. She did it neatly, gracefully, as though performing a ritual, leaving half the *thali* bare for the dahl. On top of the rice she put a lump of chutney. Then she doubled a sugar-sack and spread it on the mud floor, against the wall, away from the *chulha*. And this done, she placed the food-laden *thali* before the bag. Fetching a brass jug, she filled it with water and put the vessel beside the *thali*. She brought the tin lamp nearer, contracting her nostrils at the thick pungent smoke it gave out. Then with a glad breath of relief she came out to the gallery and, bending over the short wall, said to him kindly and quietly: 'Come now and eat.'

He finished rinsing his ears, and straightened up. 'I am not hungry. I want no food. You go and pack your things.'

She pouted her lips cajolingly and came out and held him gently by the hand. 'Well, Man' – that was what she called him; that, in fact, was her name of endearment for him; and anyway it was not proper that she should call his name – 'Well, Man, it is *me* she beat . . .' There! It was out. She bit her lip at the mistake. She had not meant to tell him that his mother had actually beaten her; not at any rate that she had struck her with the *simta*.

His jaw stiffened. 'What! She hit you? What for?'

Suddenly Dookhani was quite frightened. She hesitated.

'Oh, well, she just touched me. It was not anything. It was my fault. I put too much water in the dahl, and she did not like it . . . But it is all right. I do not want any row about it, Man. What has happened has happened. She has not killed me. Come and eat.'

He shook off her hand. 'No. I want to know everything. What did she hit you for?'

She achieved a smile and gave a short laugh. 'In a way,' she said, 'it was a joke – a big joke.'

'Joke? How?'

'Well, you see, I was in the yard sweeping; and Mai – she was right here, in the kitchen. I had given her food and I thought she was eating. Then I heard her bawling – calling me as though something or somebody was about to kill her; as though her life depended on how quickly I reached to her rescue. I ran to her. The food before her was untouched. She seemed taut with anger; she was crazy, hysterical. I could not say what had happened and knew not what to do. "You bitch!" she snarled. "Do not stand there and gape! Save me! Hold me by the hair and pull me up! I am drowning!"

'I could not understand. I thought she had suddenly gone mad; but I held her by the hair and tried with all my strength to lift her. I could not. I began to cry. Then she dashed away my hands and stood up and gnashed her teeth at me and said, "You fat, barren bitch, cannot you see that you have put too much water in the dahl – enough to drown an elephant?"

'I was dumb with shame, I felt an utter fool. Then when I tried to explain that there was not enough dahl in the house and that I threw in a little more water than I usually do, so that the dahl could reach everybody, she said I was being rude. She spat on my face; then she struck me . . .'

'With what?'

'With . . . with – well, with the *simta* . . . here.' Dookhani bared one shoulder and showed him a purple spot.

He bounded for the house, to find his mother, but quickly she clung on to him. 'No,' she pleaded, 'no! Do not make a row tonight. Come . . . come, Man, and eat your food.'

He suffered himself to be led to his food, and piloting him upon the bag-spread, she pressed him gently. 'Sit down, Man. Sit down and eat. You are not vexed with your food, are you?'

He grunted and began to eat, eating with his bare hand,
eating – well, not ravenously, but with relish and gusto –
head down, minding nobody and nothing but his food. His
long, strong fingers ploughed through the rice, took in dahl,
mixed in chutney. He ate and ate. And Dookhani sat against
the wall, facing him, hands clasped against one up-turned
knee, watching him, waiting on him for whatever he might
want in the way of a second or third serving.

He would not have to call. She had developed a sixth
sense that told her exactly when he wanted more rice, more
dahl or more of anything or everything that was to be had.

The rice heap dwindled, the dahl lessened, the chutney
vanished. He belched. Then he straightened up and stayed
his hand and mouth a while for rest. He took up the brass
jug with the hand hitherto unemployed, and drank in large,
telling gulps ... glut-glut-gluck, glut-glut-gluck, glut-glut-
gluck. Like that. And he set down the jug and belched again
– the full, free belch of repletion. Overcome for the moment
by the sheer process of eating and drinking, as it were, he
rested his head against the wall, his hand on his lap and his
eyes on Dookhani's face. Then he began to eat once more,
slowly now, almost leisurely.

She watched his *thali* and brought him more rice. He
stayed his hand to let her empty the spoon into the *thali*.
More dahl, more chutney. She refilled the brass jug, then
went back to wait upon him.

He belched and with that straightened his back once
more. He drank more water, and belched again.

Dookhani asked, 'More *bharth*?'

He set down the brass jug. Languid with repletion, he
looked at her and did not answer. Then slowly he passed his
hand – the hand with which he was not eating – under his
shirt, and fondled his belly ... Lazy, sleepy, drunk with
satiety, he said, 'No. No more. I am filled ... God, I am
sleepy! Sleepy and tired. You go and make the bed.'

Late in the night Dookhani dug one finger against his ribs

and said: 'Man, ai Man!' In the dark her voice was a half whisper.

He started, rubbing the sleep out of his eyes, and said excitedly, 'Yes!'

'You know . . .' She raised herself on one elbow and whispered in his ear.

'Chut!' he said. 'Is it for that you woke me up?' Abruptly he turned his face away and covered himself from head to toes. 'You are talking nonsense.' His voice, heavy with sleep, came from under the coverlet.

'But it is true – this time,' she said.

'All right, then. But shut your mouth now and sleep.'

They slept.

In the morning when they awoke Mungal had a good look at Dookhani. She was passing into the kitchen and, seeing him looking at herself like that, she stopped and let him.

She too was looking at him – slyly, sweetly, with a smile that caressed even while it rebuked him for his lack of faith and slowness of comprehension.

He found himself looking at the middle of her. Well, she did not seem any different. Nothing at all seemed to have happened to her. She certainly did not seem any bigger.

'You sure?' he asked incredulously.

The sly, quiet smile on Dookhani's face deepened.

'Mhm!' she said.

'How do you know?'

'I know. I was not certain all the time, but I am sure now.'

Well, he felt suddenly tremendously proud. He felt, in fact, lifted out of himself. He moved to the bucket and taking the calabash began to wash his face; then he felt he could dash away the calabash and run to her and caress her, and jump and shout because of the sudden access of joy which he felt . . . But such things were simply not done.

'Oh, God!' he begged. 'Let it be a man-child.'

Panchayat

Puzzled and not knowing which alternative to adopt – whether to put Dilraj before the magistrate, or to call up a panchayat against him – Subhadra, Moonia's widowed mother, decided to consult Babu Dinabandhu, kindly and patriarchal in his flowing silver beard and long white dhoti. Babuji's gurgling sandpaper voice, heavy and mellow with the wisdom of the Ancients, carried the weight of authority. The wealthiest cane-farmer in the village he was too, and a man who commanded obedience by the simple process of a smile or a frown.

'Babuji,' Subhadra said, 'what to do? Courthouse or panchayat?'

Babuji knew what the widow was talking about. Subhadra's complaint was an old one – an annually recurring bother.

Babuji thoughtfully stroked his beard; then he hummed a couplet from the *Ramayana* and topped it with a stanza from Kabir. 'There you have your answer,' he said. 'Call up a panchayat.'

So a panchayat was called, and today, a Sunday, was the day for it – four-thirty o'clock in the afternoon. And everybody knew about it and everybody was interested; for in these amazingly modern times a panchayat was a rare event. The machinery of the simple village tribunal, which had in the past removed so many domestic cleavages as well as settled or imposed punishments for religious or social anomalies, had become rusty or obsolete.

People preferred the law courts nowadays, because there the magistrate often imposed a heavy penalty upon the delinquent in terms of dollars and cents, and sometimes even sent him straight to jail; but here at the panchayat the heaviest penalty was ostracism, or alternatively a community feast that hardly cost the guilty party anything above a half bag of flour, some rice, ghee, and a few pounds of Irish potatoes. And sometimes the defaulter simply stamped his foot and walked away from the panchayat with impunity.

After all, one did not have to serve a prison term for disobeying a panchayat decision. There was the penalty of social boycott of course, which proscribed the rebel from being invited to religious and social functions. But again, who cared over such ostracism in these amazingly democratic times – especially in this polyglot island of many races and many creeds? Trinidad was not India.

So, mainly because of the novelty of it, the panchayat was causing quite a stir – thanks to Jhagroo, the village barber, who had broadcast the news a week in advance, in the course of his Sunday rounds. Half an hour before the time, Subhadra's yard, hot and dusty under the March sun, was thronged with men, women and children. On benches and boxes, and a few chairs borrowed from obliging and more 'westernized' neighbours, sat the members of the panchayat. They sat in one long line under Subhadra's spreading mango tree. They numbered twelve men in all. Babuji, more patriarchal than ever in milk-white dhoti and *koortah* and turban, was the acknowledged head of the tribunal. Lending colour and prestige to the occasion was Pundit Ramananda who, twelve years ago, had performed the nuptials that had made Moonia and Dilraj man and wife. Present also were the lesser lights: the village grocer, the itinerant sadhu, the barber, the small money-lender.

Babuji twiddled his fingers between his beard and looked at the sun to ascertain the time of the day. A bird twittered on the mango branches. Babuji said: 'Let those who are concerned in this come forward.'

Out of the throng emerged Dilraj. He was of middle height, clear-complexioned, and looked all right in trousers and shirt. He was about thirty years old and a son of the Punjab. He bowed to the panch and stood before the assembly with his hat in his hands.

Next came Subhadra, her *orhani* pulled well down her forehead.

Beside Subhadra Moonia took her stand.

'Speak, daughter,' urged Babuji. 'What is thy plaint?'

But suddenly Moonia was very shy. Thin and pathetically nervous, she stood before the assembly that Sunday afternoon with bowed head, her large, dark eyes cast on the ground. As dull as her mien were her clothes – flimsy things that had once been white and red.

And when the patriarchal gentleman coughed and once more bade her speak, she opened her mouth, but no words came; only tears filled her eyes.

'Babuji,' she ventured at length with a tremor in her voice, 'three times he tricked me. Let him not trick me a fourth time. Let him swear before the panch that he will not desert me again. Let him swear by the Ganga.'

'Does that mean you will return to him again, foolish woman?' Subhadra's voice was pungent with contempt.

'I will swear,' put in Dilraj, ignoring the interruption. 'I will take up the Ganga. Just get me a *lotah*-ful of river water.'

'His word has no value,' snapped Subhadra. Her dark eyes flashed anger. 'Listen, Babuji,' she said. 'Let me speak.'

Babuji nodded assent.

Sixteen years old was Moonia, Subhadra said, when in the presence of a vast assembly she gave her in marriage to Dilraj. He was a good-looking fellow, the son of a Punjabi; and she had taken it for granted that he was as good as he looked. Woman never made a greater mistake. He was a bad man, a *chandahl*, a rogue.

'Thrice he has deserted Moonia,' she told the panch. 'And each time she has come to my house, given birth to her child, and then – behold! ere the child is three months old, back she has gone to the man again. Am I to be made a fool every time?'

Subhadra paused for breath. A gleam of satisfaction lit Babuji's eyes.

'Today,' Subhadra said, 'let it be decided for the last time whether it is not but just that Dilraj be deprived of Moonia altogether. Whether she should not be free to take unto her another husband.'

Stern disapproval spread over Babuji's wrinkled face. 'Let Dilraj speak now,' he said.

And Dilraj spoke. 'Only two questions, Babuji,' he pleaded. 'People keep brass vessels and often in the moving and re-moving of them the vessels clash and give forth sounds. May it not be so too with people who live together?'

Babuji nodded. 'That is true. A little quarrel, a little laughter, and a little tear are at once the salt and sweet of life. Without them we have not lived.'

'One more question, Babuji,' argued Dilraj. 'You are a man who has had children?'

'To be sure! To be sure!' Babuji exclaimed reminiscently. 'There was my Raghoonandan . . . a chubby little fellow . . .'

'Good!' said Dilraj, with evident satisfaction. 'And once or twice, when the child was a babe, you might have taken him upon your lap and he may have soiled your dhoti?'

'Many times he did that,' smiled Babuji. 'Raghoonandan had the ugly knack of wetting me through and through almost every time I took him up . . . Raghoonandan!'

'Ah-ha!' exclaimed Dilraj. 'But you did not cut off your leg because of that? You did not throw away the child in the gutter?'

'No,' said Babuji. 'No.'

'Babuji,' Dilraj said, 'you are wise; I am as foolish as a child. It is the greatness of the wise to forgive the erring. So I have heard it said.'

'Just talk,' said Subhadra. 'Talk and nothing more.'

'Let Moonia speak now,' said Babuji. 'Speak, daughter; do you want to return to your husband?'

'Babuji,' Moonia said, very quietly, 'he is, as you have just said, my husband.'

'Then the panchayat is over. Let the good woman return to her husband.'

Babuji's voice held finality.

Obeah

I never did know whether to believe or not to believe in obeah; and even after this thing happened to me friend Dinnoo, I still don't know what to say. You see, it was like this—

For the last three days me friend Dinnoo didn't turn out to work. It was crop time, and he and me was carting canes from the estate cane-fields to the factory. Dinnoo was a first-class carter. He could manage the stubbornest mule or bison or ox, and after he had done with them they would each be as tame as anything and have a new name. He had nice names to give these animals. He would call one Hitler, another Mussolini, or Haile Selassie, or Punjabi – and once he even named an old ox Mahatma Gandhi. He didn't know much about these people, but he knew Mussolini was a kind of bully who had beaten Haile Selassie, who was a king in Africa; that Mahatma Gandhi, a holy man, was always doing things that got him into jail in India, and that Hitler was a kind of human octopus who was the cause of the whole war. That is the sort of fellow Dinnoo was; popular with everybody, and knowing.

After he had finished packing a cart it was a pleasure to look at the handiwork. The canes was twice longer than the cart and tortuous and bent like bisons' horns. Troublesome. People who didn't know the art of loading loaded the canes pell-mell on the carts. But not Dinnoo. In front and behind Dinnoo made a packed cart look like the smooth, measured parting of me sister-in-law's hair when she is all dressed up for Sunday. But that is not the story . . .

The fact is we was short of hands, and the driver says to

me, sarcastic like: 'Find out what's wrong wit' dat fellow Dinnoo. Tell 'im 'e better don' preten' belly-ache. Tell 'im if 'e don' come out tomorrow 'e will find calculating money on Saturday can be a puzzlin' kine of arit'metic. Tell 'im dat for me.'

I know what that means. Yes. The driver is a man who doesn't make joke. No. So, after dinner that evening, I take a stroll to Dinnoo's house in me own village. I meet Dinnoo's mooma sweeping the cane-trash and things in the yard in front her house. A hen with three chicks is busy scratching in a dung-heap, and a cart with one wheel is leaning against a post in the pen. Dinnoo's mooma looks sullen and dull, and though she knows I am there she doesn't look at me.

'Dinnoo Mooma,' I says, 'where is Dinnoo?'

Dinnoo's mooma just raises her head and looks at me once, still sweeping. 'He ain't home,' she says after a time. 'He playin' sweet-man these days. He puttin' handkerchief rong 'e neck and shoes in 'e foot, and 'e partin' 'e hair and goin' out for walk. You will fine 'im sittin' on the culvert by the river. Move from befo' me, bwai, or the dus' will go in you' eye.'

Dinnoo is doleful when I meets him on the culvert. True enough, he has his hair parted and shining with coconut oil, and there is a maroon-coloured handkerchief round his neck and shining shoes in his foot. That is a strange thing, to be sure. For I have never known Dinnoo to part his hair before and to put on handkerchief for style; and the only time I ever see him wearing shoes is once or twice when he goes to a wedding.

Dinnoo is kicking his heels against the concrete, and his chin is resting on the palm of his hand. He looks up at me and smiles in a sad kind of way, as though all his family is dead and he left an orphan.

'Come and sit dong, Gobin boy,' Dinnoo says to me, in a heavy, dull voice. 'Is trouble Ah fine meself in. Come and Ah will tell you.' And when I does so, he puts his hand across me shoulder like one friend leaning on another for courage and sympathy. 'Ha!' he says with a sigh. 'A helluva thing happen to me, Gobin boy. Ah kian't eat, Ah kian't sleep, and Ah kian't wo'k.' And he sighs again and leans the heavier on me.

I grow frighten for Dinnoo. He is not a boy to talk like that. I have always known him to be a happy-go-lucky fellow. But now his voice sounds thick and break up, as though he has a plum or something like that sticking down his throat. I can't get the heart to give him the driver's message after this, so I says, 'True, Dinnoo boy?'

'True,' says Dinnoo. 'True, true!'

'What it is that happen, Dinnoo boy? What happen to you?'

Dinnoo puckers up his brows. 'You know that fellow Joogna, up Golconda?' he asks.

I shake my head to say yes; for I know Joogna. I know Joogna got married a fortnight ago.

'Well, it is 'e wife,' says Dinnoo. 'Ah see she de odder day, Gobin boy. An' from de time Ah see she, Ah t'inkin' of she. She pretty, pretty! She was comin' wid she bucket for water by de water pipe on the road; an' Ah look at she an' she, too, look at me; an' Ah smile an' she smile back. Talk about pretty – well, *she* pretty!'

Dinnoo stops for wind, then suddenly he says:

'Put you' han' on me heart here, Gobin boy, an' hear how it goin' *dhaka-dhak, dhaka-dhak* – like Mr Mohun's rice-mill when de engine playin' de fool.'

And sure enough, Dinnoo's heart is beating fast.

'Well,' he says, 'every time Ah t'ink 'bout she, dis is what does happen. An' it ain' got a time when Ah don' t'ink 'bout that giol. It is de struth.'

'Who doubting you?' I says; 'but mind,' I warns him, 'you will get sick if you go on like this.'

'An' all de time,' says Dinnoo, 'Ah ain' even know who daughter she is. Only she name Ah know. Inari. What to do, Gobin boy. What to do to get she?'

Well, I really don't know what to say to Dinnoo. I want

to laugh, and then I feel sorry for him, too, and I don't want to hurt his feelings. Dinnoo is me friend – me best friend – and just for that I would really like to see him get this girl. But how? The girl is already married, and I know Dinnoo is heading for trouble.

'Look here,' I says, 'you is me friend – me best friend – Dinnoo boy. I would give me right hand for you, and you know it. But let me tell you this: it is a wrong thing you doing. I don't know where this girl come from, but I hear she is a pretty thing and . . .'

'Is dat you sayin' so easy?' says Dinnoo, with heat. 'She is – well, boy, Gobin, Ah ain' see anodder giol like she. Like de dolly me grandmooma buy for me lil sister last Christmas. Like . . .'

'I know that,' I says. 'But it is a wrong thing you doing all the same. The girl got she husband already, and if you look to take she away from she man, it will mean trouble. Them fellows up in Golconda don' make fun. You trouble one man and you trouble the whole bunch. They will sharpen up their cutlasses and do for you. Take me foolish advice, Dinnoo boy, and forget the woman.'

'Never!' says Dinnoo. 'Dat kian't happen. Ah love de giol an' – by hook or by crook – Ah goin' get she.'

'It will be no use,' I says. 'They goin' take she back from you.'

'Over me dead body!' says Dinnoo. 'Look, Gobin,' he says in a softer voice and with a look in his eyes as if he seeing things, 'look, Ah seein' she now. She comin' wid she bucket in she han', an' she walkin' like she got spring in she wais'. She pretty, pretty! Like de dolly me grandmooma buy for me lil sister . . . Put you' han' on me heart there . . .'

I know how it is. It is no use trying to reason with Dinnoo. I was in the mess meself once or twice, and I know it is a thing that makes you do things you wouldn't do in your proper sense. All the same I meself begin to worry. Fact is I don't want Dinnoo to shine up his hair with coconut oil and tie handkerchief round his neck and go up Golconda with his hands in his pockets and stand up on the road before Joogna's house and whistle love songs. That will sure mean trouble for him.

Then suddenly Dinnoo brightens up and gives me a hunch on the ribs. 'Eh-heh!' he says, excited. 'Ah know what Ah goin' to do. Is obeah for she!'

Well, you could have knocked me down with a feather, as they say. I never knew Dinnoo believed in obeah.

'Obeah!' I says. 'And who will do the obeah for you? You?'

'Is not me,' says Dinnoo. 'Is Mohungoo for she!'

I suppose I must have looked as a man who doesn't know anything. So Dinnoo says to me, 'But you mean to say you don' know de man dey call Mohungoo? You mus' be dead! Well, leh me tell you, it ain't got anyt'ing he kian't do. Orright. You remember Boodhia? You remember she had a case in de court de odder day for t'rowing water in she milk?'

I nod my head.

'Orright. And you remember de magistrate dismiss de case?'

I nod my head again.

'Well,' says Dinnoo, 'dat was obeah. And you remember old Beharry had two foot and now 'e only got one?'

I nod my head.

'Orright den; is obeah take away de odder foot. An' you remember dat pretty, pretty giol Topee bring away for 'e wife – ever see she yet, Gobin boy?'

'Yes,' I says, 'I see she a'ready.'

'Orright den; is Mohungoo get she for 'im . . . Ah tell you what, Gobin boy. Leh we go to dis man, Mohungoo, to-morrow – no, leh we go now. God! Ah kian't forget dat giol.'

It is no use telling Dinnoo no; so we jumps on our bi-cycles – I going back for mine at home – and rides up to the place of this man, Mohungoo, and meets him in his little grass house, up in Chickland in the bush.

It is not dark yet – just about lamp-lighting time – and Mohungoo is sitting on a cross-bar in his cow-pen behind his house, with the cow just behind him. This Mohungoo is a meagre kind of a man, and tall and thin; and he is wearing only a short dhoti and a cheap, thin merino that makes all his bones show up. The man looks like a spirit, but he seems brisk all the same, with smart, shining eyes. See he see us, he jumps down from the cross-bar, brisk as a game-cock. He smiles and bows to me and to Dinnoo in a welcoming sort of way, all the time rubbing the thin palms of his hands together, like if he wants to get them warm.

'Ah know all-you was coming,' he says. 'Ah know de moment all-you been talking 'bout me powers.'

He fetches an old soap-box that is lying in the yard, and beats the dust off its sides and puts it in the pen for us very ceremoniously. 'You can sit dong,' he says, 'an' make you'self comfortable.' He returns to his perch on the cross-bar.

Dinnoo grows very eager. 'Look,' he says to Mohungoo, 'I ain' goin' beat about de bush. Is a giol Ah fall in love wid.'

'Don' tell me,' says Mohungoo. 'Ah know dat a'ready. Ah know it from de time Ah look in you' eye. Is Mohungoo you is talking to.'

Dinnoo hunches me hard and sly in the ribs. 'What Ah tell you?' he whispers proudly. 'Is a wonder how de man know!'

'Dey tell me,' Dinnoo says, 'dat you can do anyt'ing. You t'ink you can get dis giol for me?'

'Hm!' says Mohungoo, and this 'hm!' is full of meaning. He looks up at a Jack-Spaniard nest hanging down from a rafter above his head, and begins to think. Then he looks at Dinnoo.

'Get she for you?' he says. 'She will worship de dust of you' foot, she will follow you like a dog followin' 'e master, she will want you as fish want water, she will . . .'

'Orright,' says Dinnoo, very glad; 'dat will do; Ah b'lieve you. Ho' much?'

The obeahman looks up at the Jack-Spaniard nest once more and slowly scratches his chin. Then he looks down at Dinnoo, straight in his eye. 'Ten dollars in advance,' he says, 'an' ten dollars after you get de giol. Dat is cheap. Is material Ah have to buy. De essence of *dilbahar*, which de giol will have to smell on you' handkerchief in de name of me *devi*, will alone cos' five dollars. An' den me *devi* will want she goat, she clothes, an' she nose-ring. Twenty dollars alto-gedder.'

'Orright,' says Dinnoo, 'but do it quick. Make she want me like fish want water.'

'But you talk to she a'ready?' asks Mohungoo.

'Not exactly,' says Dinnoo. 'But Ah look at she and smile, an' she look at me an' smile back. Dat is all.'

'Dat is 'nough,' says Mohungoo. 'Come inside de house.'

So we goes into the house, and Mohungoo leaves us for a while and goes out to a water barrel under the grass eaves and dips water with a calabash dipper, and washes his hands and face and foot very carefully. Then he performs a loud gargle with some water, and that done, he sprinkles some water over him, as though to make himself holy, muttering meanwhile I know not what. Then he comes in and calls out, 'Ei!' and a woman answers from the other side of the mud-wall parti-tion and says, 'Oi!'

'Come out,' says the obeahman, 'an' sit dong for me. Is wo'k Ah have to wo'k on you.'

Well, I begin to wonder what the woman has got to do with it, and while I am still wondering, she comes in from the next room, quiet and obedient, and sits down flat on the mud floor, like a good child, carefully crossing her legs beneath her skirt. She is about thirty-five or forty years old, short and fat, colour of dry cashew-nut, but not pretty.

'She is me wife,' says the obeahman. 'Is on she Ah does call me *devi*.'

'What Ah tell you?' says Dinnoo to me on the sly.

Then Mohungoo reaches for a brass plate and a small wooden box and a tin cup from on top of a shelf; and takes a box of matches and sits down on his foot, *chookoo-mookoo* before his wife. Quickly the woman looses out her long black hair and lets it fall over her shoulders and face and ears, crazy like, till her face is all behind her hair. Then Mohungoo sets down the brass plate on the ground between him and the woman, and opens the tin cup very carefully and takes out a lump of camphor from it; and from the box he takes out a phial with something like molasses in it. All the time the woman is sitting very quiet, bending forward, all hair and no face.

Then Mohungoo places five cloves in line before the woman, and puts the camphor in the middle of the brass plate and lights it with a match. Now he shuts his eyes and presses his palms flat together, prayful like, and begins to mutter under his breath, like he is praying hard before the woman. He mutters and mutters, and then he begins to sweat. Then this Mohungoo, still sweating, opens his eyes and takes up the brass plate with the lighted camphor in it and stoops over the woman and makes a few passes over her head.

She begins to vibrate, slow at first, then hard, then harder; then her teeth begins to chatter as though she is seized with ague.

'It is de *devi* comin' on she now,' says Dinnoo to me in a whisper.

'I have come already,' says the woman in a new voice, and for the first time in Hindi. 'I am ready to do my duty. Tell me what you want.'

'It is this boy here – (what is your name?)'

'Dinnoo,' says Dinnoo, quickly.

'It is this boy here – Dinnoo. He has fallen in love with a girl. What are you saying?' Mohungoo, too, is carrying on the dialogue in Hindi now. 'Speak!' says he. 'Can he have her?'

'I want my goat,' says the woman.

'You will get your goat,' says Mohungoo, 'and it will be a big ram.'

'I want my clothes,' says the woman. 'It is a long time you have not given me clothes.'

'You will get your clothes,' says Mohungoo, 'and they will be silk and satin.'

'I want my jewel,' says the woman.

'Well, you will get your jewel too,' says Mohungoo, with a wink at Dinnoo; 'and it will be a gold ring for your nose. Now, what do you say?'

'He can have her,' says the *devi*.

'How?' asks Mohungoo.

'Let her but breathe the essence of *dilbahar* in my name, mixed with the sweat of Dinnoo's armpit. She will fly into his arms.'

'Anything more?' asks Mohungoo.

'Yes,' says the *devi* from behind her curtain of hair. 'Let him also take a sip of honey in my name, flavoured with the cloves you have just offered me. Let him talk to her while his mouth is still sweet. She will listen to his words as though she is listening to music ... But her name? I must know her name to turn her mind Dinnoo-wards.'

'Inari,' says Dinnoo, quickly.

The woman takes a quick, deep breath, like she got a blow in her belly; and she jerks up her head and gets up quickly as lightning and dashes apart the long hair from before her face, and grinds her teeth and gives Dinnoo such a look, that I think if looks could kill, Dinnoo would be a dead man.

'Is dis giol a married person?' cuts in Mohungoo, switching to the English language.

'She is,' says Dinnoo. 'An' is a wonder how –'

'Never mine dat,' says Mohungoo, very vexed now. 'An' she got a mole on she lef' cheek? An' she married to a fellow named Joogna up in Golconda?'

'*Dat* is de giol,' says Dinnoo, 'an' it is a ...'

But before I could say 'Aip!' Mohungoo grabs me friend Dinnoo by the throat and begins to choke him hard against the wall until Dinnoo begins to stifle for life. And then the woman falls upon him, too, wild as a wild cat, and scratches up his face. 'No mo' pretty face fo' you,' she says, hissing like a snake.

I move to rescue me friend. 'I cannot understand the

meaning of this roughness,' I says. 'You will kill the boy. He ain' do you anything.'

'He ain' do me anyt'ing!' says Mohungoo, his eyes red with rage. 'You know who 'e want for wife – you know?'

'No,' I says. 'I donno.'

Mohungoo relaxes his hold on Dinnoo's throat. 'Well,' he says, 'leh me tell you. She is me own daughter!'

In the Village

She sat in the dingy hammock in the gallery of the turf-thatched hut. Her bare feet rested on the bare earth; for earth was the floor of the hut and of earth also were the walls. Some two yards off, level with the ground was the earth *chulha* or cooking-place. Jussodra, the eldest child of the house, a girl aged nineteen, sat on a *peerha*, some three inches off the ground. Jussodra was glum.

I had been making a survey of social conditions in the peasant Indian village with the romantic name of El Dorado. The name means 'The Golden One', but in this village all that looked yellow was mostly dirt, and all that looked green was mostly bush. I had been there the day before, but then she was at work in the sugar-fields. Neighbours, I gathered, had told her that I had called and that I would be calling again, and had given her a hint as to what I was after.

'You come, then?' she asked, as though she had always known me. 'Come in,' she said, 'siddong,' and she shoved towards me an empty soap-box. As I was shortly to learn, it was the only article of furniture in the hut. And it was a gift from the local provision shopkeeper.

I embarked on the usual routine explanation, but as though to save me from so much bother, she hurriedly but politely cut me short. 'Yes, yes,' she said; 'Ah know. Me neighbour tell me.' She paused thoughtfully. 'So you want to know how we po' labourers live? Who want to know? De gov'ment?'

I said yes.

'But Ah wonder why,' she said. 'T'ink dey care?' And she gave a quiet chuckle, pregnant with doubt. 'All the same,'

she said, still doubtful, 'Ah ain't have not'ing, so Ah don'
have anyt'ing to hide. Ah mean, Ah so po' it would be stupid
to mek meself look poorer. You kian see fo' you'self.'

The hut inside was almost empty. A few sugar-sacks were
dumped in a corner; some faded, nondescript garments hung
on a line that was stretched from one wall to another; a pair of
work trousers hung from a nail on the wall; from another
nail hung a felt hat that had seen better days; a bucket in
the gallery; some cups and pots and pans near the *chulha*;
two cutlasses, a hoe and a crookstick leaning against the
wall, and – to cap the ensemble – a baby, some one year old,
asleep on a bag – spread on the mud floor.

Everything in that hut seemed to be competing for a prize
in drabness.

'It is me luck,' said the woman in the hammock, spreading
her hands in emphasis.

Her name, she said, was Mangarie. It was not her real
name; but it was the name most people knew her by. It
meant Tuesday, bcecause she might have been born on a
Tuesday. She was thirty-eight years old, she said, and she
was a Hindu. They were all Hindus; but beyond a few of
Hinduism's more popular forms, such as *Shiva-Ratri* and
Rama-Leela and pujas and *Suraj-Purana* recitations, she
knew little else of Hinduism. Her main claim to being a
Hindu was that she was born in a Hindu home. That was
enough for her, as that had been enough for her father, who
was India-born, who knew just a little Hindi, barely enough
to enable him to plod through the *Ramayana* or the *Prem
Sagar* or the *Hanuman Ashtak* or the *Dahn-Leela*; but not at
all enough to enable him even to attempt to read the *Bhagavad Gita* or a *Purana* or an *Upanishad*, which were in
Sanskrit. He did not even know there were such books as
the *Upanishads*.

Was she sorry that she wasn't a Christian?

'Sorry for what?' There was defiance in Mangarie's voice,
and fire in her eye. 'Dat won' help. Ah would still have to
sweat lak a beast in de cane-field for nex' to not'ing. Ah don'

mine sweatin', you know. We *mus'* sweat. But to sweat and still to starve. Dat is what is hard – livin' from han' to mout'. But look at me neighbour. Ain' she is a Christian too? Well, she does have to wo'k jus' like me. She kian't even go to church now, because she have to put on clean clothes. Wey she goin' get dem?' And she laughed again.

Most of the answers that Mangarie gave to my questions were given fairly easily and quickly. But when I asked her what she thought could be the annual rental value of her one-room hut she laughed outright once more.

'Dis?' she said. 'Who will want to rent a t'ing like dis! You better ask anodder question.' And even Jussodra, who hitherto sat, a fixture of immobility, relaxed in a smile.

'Seventeen years now dis house standin' here,' Mangarie added. 'Fus' an' only house we buil' wid we own han' after we get married – me and me husband. Kian't take a new frame now.' She meant the top structure that served for roof. 'Many times people come to repair, but dey look at de walls an' shake dey head an' say no. De walls crack; an' de posts and dem standin' only by de grace of God. Kian't take a new frame, dey say.'

But even if Mangarie's hut could stand repairs and thus be restored to a semblance of its former respectability, she could not do so without breaking the Buildings Regulations. 'Eider you put up a bran' new house,' she explained, 'wid concrete pillars – concrete, mind you – and boa'd floor, an' galvanize cover, or you don' put up any house at all. Dat is de law. But po' me. Wey Ah goin' get cement and stone an' san' an' boa'd an' galvanize; an' real carpenters, an' dis an' dat an' de odder? No. Look like we people mus' go to live in de bush – if we mus' live at all.'

Married at sixteen, Mangarie is the mother of nine children – 'all born in dis same lil house', the mother explained – 'an' all boys, 'cept de girl!'

I hinted that she must regard herself lucky having as many as eight sons.

'Lucky me eye!' she said. 'No help. Take de big boys: one

shame to wo'k in de field, because he can read an' write; de odder lookin' for wo'k and kian't get any.'

Mangarie began to think. 'Eight or nine dollars a fort-night – dat is all,' she said. 'An' eleven mout' to feed and eleven body to clothes. Lucky for we dat de Syrian does come, so we get clothes on trust.'

Mangarie said the big girl is too big to go to work, the two bigger boys too ashamed to work in field or garden; and the others must go to school.

'So mostly it is me an' me husband who does wo'k at all; but he sick wid back pain, an' me wid fever. It is a wonder we does mek out at all,' she said.

'Nine dollars and some cents; dat is all,' said Mangarie. 'An' de girl to married, an' de house to build. Dat is me trouble.'

The Engagement

Romesh stood at the roadside before his house, idly looking up the road and leisurely fondling his belly. He was shirtless, and his belly – the most noticeable feature of the man – rose high, wide and heavy in front of him. He had a short and rotund aspect. His trousers – mud-spattered – were rolled up to the knees; which indicated the depth of the water and mud through which he had waded that day in the lagoon. Romesh planted rice in the lagoon. At forty-six, except for some sparse hair around the base of the head, he was quite bald.

It was almost dusk, and the earth lay cool and lush after the intermittent showers of the day. The two cows and the heifer had been brought in from the lastro near by, and Hardai, Romesh's wife, was putting the fire under the heap of half-dried grass in the pen back of the house, to make the smoke to keep away the mosquitoes that had already begun their ominous chant.

Romesh looked up and down the road, looking for no one in particular, and nodding to passing acquaintances.

Then he saw Baigan. Romesh knew Baigan. He knew him, first, as the man from Golconda – the man who kept two wives under one roof and had lots of daughters, had been giving away one, sometimes two of them, in marriage every year, and seemed never at an end of giving them away. And then, too, Romesh knew Baigan as a big cane-farmer, a landowner, not perhaps very plentifully supplied with ready money, but a man of substance nevertheless; a respectful and respectable man.

'*Sita-Rama*!' said Baigan. Bringing his palms together, he

carried the salutation chest high and bent down a little. Seldom did anyone make obeisance to Romesh in this very ceremonious way. He was surprised, touched and flattered. He gave an enormous smile that made pouches under his eyes and sudden hillocks in the region of the cheek-bones, as, equally ceremoniously, he returned the salutation.

'To tell you the truth,' Baigan said, 'it is you I have come to see. I very much want to see you.'

Romesh's hand paused thoughtfully on his belly, as he looked Baigan quizzically in the eye. 'Yes, brother,' he said; 'you are welcome. Do come and be seated.' And he led the visitor under the house – which stood on six-foot hardwood pillars – and he put a bench for the visitor and he himself sat down on a soap-box.

'Say then, brother,' coaxed Romesh, respectfully handing Baigan a cigarette. 'What can this very important matter be?' He struck a match and held it to Baigan's cigarette. 'Speak,' he urged. 'I am all ears.'

Baigan looked at Romesh, and after a puff or two said, slowly and methodically, as though the thought was too sweet and sacred for hurried utterance:

'You know, I have yet another daughter – my Kamli – a pretty child – just going in her fifteenth year; the youngest and the last. *You* have a son. Same caste. A good match. A very good match! What do you say?'

Romesh did not answer at once. He bowed his head and kept looking at his mud-spattered feet. The smoke from the grass-heap in the pen rose in a thick cloud that penetrated his nostrils and smarted the eyes.

'A good match!' Baigan said again, looking at Romesh as though he wanted to hypnotize him.

Romesh, raising his head after what seemed a long meditation, said: 'A good match. I do not deny it. But I am in no position to have my Kanhaia married just yet. True, the boy has grown unusually well for his age – already he is tall and straight like a young bamboo; but he is only seventeen. Boys are seldom married at sixteen or seventeen nowadays.

Times have changed. No doubt the youngster can safely go without a wife for another two or three years. But just now ... just now my place is not fixed for receiving a daughter-in-law. I have first to extend the house; provide one or two things; then I can see to getting the boy married. But not yet. Not yet, brother. No room!'

Baigan laughed – a quiet, soothing, reassuring laugh it was. He said to Romesh: 'Look, you are worrying over trifles. Room! What more room is needed? A *kothri* – a mere closet.' And Baigan paused to wag a forefinger to lend emphasis to what he was saying. 'I am not one of those who bring up their daughters in the grand way. I know better than that. A daughter is not for ever a member of her father's household. She belongs to her husband. And who can say what kind of a home her karma will lead her to? None can know that. So from the outset I have brought up my Kamli to suit. She is accustomed to hard work; and, however hard her lot, she will neither grumble nor complain. Now, what do you say?'

'I am still wondering,' Romesh said.

'About what?' Baigan asked.

'Well, for one thing, wedding means money. I have no money. I am not a rich man. Only this old house I have – and it leaks; a cow or two, a couple of old donkeys; and some canes. That is all. But money – I have no . . .'

'As to that,' Baigan put in quickly, 'I shall give the boy a good *teeluck* – a good dowry; say, two hundred dollars. Now what do you say?'

Baigan leaned forward, anxious for an answer.

Romesh pondered. Slowly, very slowly, he fondled his belly. Then, looking up, wanting to say no, he heard himself saying, 'All right. I think it will be all right. I shall let you know – say Sunday.'

And Baigan knew he was being dismissed, and he stood up, saying everything was very gratifying; and he humbly joined his hands and bent his head slightly to Romesh, who stood up too, and said, with great concern and regret: 'Well, brother, surely you are not leaving without eating? Please eat. Food is ready.' But Romesh knew Baigan would not eat, for no good Hindu eats at his son-in-law's or would-be son-in-law's.

'Forgive me, brother,' said Baigan. 'You are very kind, but really I have no appetite . . . *Achha, Sita-Rama*! Well, God be with you!'

And Romesh's hand fussed on his belly and he said: 'Well, brother, if you cannot you cannot. *Achha, Sita-Rama*! Good, then; God be with you!'

And Baigan left.

That night Romesh tossed in his bed till late; for, much as he wanted to sleep, no sleep would come. His thoughts could not stop dwelling on Kanhaia and on the contemplated marriage of Kanhaia. He did not want to make himself a fool. The advent of a daughter-in-law was sooner or later so often climaxed by the walk-out of the son – especially these days. One half of him was glad, even anxious, to get the boy married; for there was the ever-present danger of his falling in with a Negress; the other half of Romesh was distrustful and afraid. To have a daughter-in-law who was modest, even as his own wife, Hardai, had been modest in her time; who would wear her skirt so long that its hem would go right down to the ankles, and whose *orhani* would never be off her head; who, moreover, would one day bring forth a son; who would look after his seven smaller children with real sisterly care and devotion; yet who in all things would acknowledge Hardai, the children's mother, as mistress and final authority in the house – why, to have such a girl for daughter-in-law would be a blessing and a joy for ever.

But suppose . . . Suppose the girl, despite Baigan's boasts, turned out the brazen sort, the kind who would think nothing of coming before him, or before any stranger, man or woman, without her *orhani*, giggling and talking freely and as shamelessly as any boy; who would not even know enough Hindi to call him *Baba*, and who would wear ridiculously short, tight skirts that clean showed up the shape of her body . . . suppose . . . Well, most daughters-in-law were like that these days. Romesh had heard of some of these newly married girls in the village. People sneakingly referred to them as 'high-fliers'. He knew what that meant, and he knew the type. They wore a scanty length of lace or something like lace for *orhani*, that hardly covered the head, and their plump young breasts under their thin bodice not at all. They had no shame and they refused to be managed by their mothers-in-law. They did not want to be managed. Some of them refused to be managed even by their husbands . . . Let a fellow but so much as give her a slap – leave alone a beating – and at once she runs to the police, and from the police to the magistrate, in court. Suppose . . .

He nudged his wife. 'Ai!' he said. There was no answer. 'You hearin'?' Snores. 'You ain't hearin'?'

She woke up. 'You calling me, man?'

'Yes,' he said. 'I kian't sleep. Kian't sleep for hell. 'Bout this Kanhaia business . . . I don't know. Think it will be orright?'

They were speaking in English now, and their English was as mutilated as any language can possibly be mutilated.

Hardai said: 'It depend. It depend on the girl. Don't get fool wid good looks. Let Kanhaia see the girl too. No cat in bag, man. That sort of thing don't do these days. But leh we sleep.'

So Romesh sent a message to Baigan the very next day, saying that he and Kanhaia, with three or four of their nearest relations, would be coming on the forthcoming Sunday, to see the child, which is what all brides-to-be, no matter what their ages, are conventionally called. And Baigan sent back word saying he was glad – very glad – and that Romesh and his relations would be most welcome and that he was pleased and proud to know that the boy was coming too, for he would have an opportunity of seeing the girl with his own eyes, and not rely on hearsay, and make up his mind whether he found her pretty or not, so that he could not, a month or a year after their marriage, say he wanted her no more.

Then Romesh sent for his elder brothers-in-law, Dhanuk and Kumar, and for his nephew Gopal, who all lived in the

next village, and told them what was afoot, and invited them
to make the party with him to go to Baigan of Golconda on
Sunday, to see the child. And Dhanuk and Kumar and Gopal
came on the appointed day, each in his best trousers and
koortah, ready to go to Golconda.

Then Romesh got into his best clothes too; but when they
were all set, Kanhaia still sat in his dirty clothes on the
donkey-cart in the yard, his chin on his hand, moping.

'Come on, boy,' Romesh called, with a father's authority.
'Go change your clothes.'

'What!' said Dhanuk.

'What!' said Kumar.

'Eh! Eh!' said Gopal.

'Come, come, Kanhaia,' Dhanuk coaxed. 'Look sharp,
hurry up, boy!'

'Hurry up for what? I ain't going nowhere. I ain't marrie-
ding,' Kanhaia said.

'What!' said Kumar.

'You bound to go,' said Gopal.

Then Hardai came, and patting Kanhaia, spoke softly and
placatingly to him. 'Come, son. Don' do like this. Don' make
you' poopa and you' mooma shame. Go change your clothes.'

And then Dhanuk and Kumar and Gopal all came and
petted Kanhaia and begged him to get up; but Kanhaia still
sat unmoved and petulant.

Then in an awful, menacing tone Romesh let everybody
know that he was really getting damned vexed, and that if
they did not look sharp he was just the man to put his hand
on Kanhaia, and take off his (Romesh's) clothes, and never
go anywhere and let the whole damned thing go to hell.

'You see that!' Dhanuk told Kanhaia. 'You get you' poopa
vex.'

Then everybody left Kanhaia and came to Romesh and
begged *him* not to get vexed; and, evidently seeing thngs
were taking a very ugly turn, Kanhaia suddenly got up and
said:

'Orright then; I will go. Tell Bap not to get vex.' And he

went into the house and was soon ready in new trousers and shirt, but just to show that he did not care a bit what the Baigan household should think of him, he refused to wear a necktie and a jacket, and very nearly went without his shoes.

The Romesh party arrived at their destination in a taxi. The house stood a stone's throw away from the narrow country road, and Baigan, hearing the honk of the car, came out to meet the visitors. He received them with great civility.

It was a large house with a spacious yard, and it stood in open grounds. It was without doubt a rich man's house, thought Romesh. Baigan had a chair for each guest in his long front veranda, in addition to a charpoy or string-bed at one end, for whoever might want to recline on that.

Baigan's women-folk kept strictly indoors. No one talked of Kamli. That would have been unconventional. Instead they talked of the cane crop and the weather. Baigan related to his guests the story of Mahatma Gandhi's tragic death. From the Gandhi incident he went on to the whys and wherefores of the froghopper pest that was ruining the sugar-fields. Half an hour went by. Then Baigan gave the word for Kamli to come.

And Kamli came, a small girl with bare feet, in quite plain clothes, without a single item of adornment. In both hands she bore a brass jug containing water. Her head and bosom were *orhani*-covered, but her face was left open, for all to see. She might have been fifteen: she was thin, tall enough for her age, with a complexion that was of the colour of a polished cacao bean.

She advanced slowly, head bowed, but not so bowed as to make it difficult for others to see her face below the edge of her *orhani*. She advanced looking at no one, uttering no word. She might have been in a trance – in a trance of utter shyness.

So might she have approached the image of Shiva in the temple in her village on the holy night of *Shiva-Ratri*, to breathe a prayer or, had she been older, to ask a boon of the god.

Slowly, humbly, almost tremblingly, Kamli made straight for Romesh; for none other had a right to receive this first jugful of water from her, for none else was the father of Kanhaia, her husband-to-be.

Romesh stood up. He was not bound to; the privilege of remaining sitting was his. But the spectacle was a little too much for him. He was too pleased, too moved, too humbled at so much respect and such reverence from so small a person.

He took the *lotah*, saying gently in Hindi: 'Very good, daughter! God bless you! Live long!' It was of course the stereotype formula of benediction, but Romesh meant every word of it. Then he sat down and put the *lotah* on the floor at his feet. He did not want water. He knew, as everybody there knew, that Kamli had brought water for him not because he might be thirsty, but because her doing so made a decent and pretty excuse for her to appear before him and before Kanhaia and Kanhaia's male relations, so that they could see her, so that they could inspect her. To have appeared before them empty-handed, just to show herself, would have been too crude.

Kanhaia cast one brief glance at Kamli the moment she came; then he was too shy to look at her again. He did not want the elders to catch him looking at her. Dhanuk and Kumar and Gopal looked at her long and well. But Kamli looked at no one. As far as *her* seeing the visitors was concerned, they might as well have not been there.

Yet there was no insolence in her, no tinge of disrespect to any; only a leaden shyness that was like a physical pain. And this was her shield.

Kamli turned to go.

Romesh said: 'Wait, daughter!' He pushed his hand into his trouser-pocket and brought out a two-dollar banknote, and said to Kamli: 'Take this, *beti*; buy cake.'

But Kamli appeared to hesitate, not knowing whether it was right or wrong to take the money; so Romesh, not wanting to embarrass her further, passed the banknote to Baigan, saying, in English now:

'Here, brother, give this to the child from me.' And Baigan took the note and gave it to Kamli, saying in Hindi:

'This is from the father of your husband-to-be. Take it. There is no shame in that, and no harm. Now, *beti*, go.'

Kamli withdrew.

Baigan said to Romesh: 'Well, brother, you have seen the child. I hope you are satisfied.'

Romesh said: 'I see no fault.'

'Well, then,' Baigan added, 'it is for Kanhaia to talk now. Let him say what he has to say or hold his peace for ever.'

Kanhaia said: 'I ain't have nothing to say. Everything depend on Bap.'

Baigan said: 'The boy must be shy. Well, let him go out in the yard with his cousin Gopal and talk it over. Let him be sure in his own mind.'

So Kanhaia and Gopal went out in the yard, where none in the gallery could hear them. And they talked in hurried whispers for a minute or two and forthwith returned to the house.

'Is orright,' announced Gopal. 'Kanhaia like the child.'

'Yes, I like she,' said Kanhaia, surprised at the vigour of his own voice.

It was as it should be. Kamli was all right. So thought Romesh. So thought everybody. Only a fast girl would have watched visitors unabashed in the face; or, worse still, dared to use her tongue in talk. But Kamli was meek, unobtrusive, pretty too.

That evening when Hardai asked Romesh what he thought of the girl, he said in a glad voice: 'Ah, she is a *gow*.' A cow. Romesh might have said Kamli was a lamb; yet he could not by that have paid the girl a greater compliment, nor given her a better recommendation; for he had ever regarded the cow, even as countless generations of his ancestors had regarded the cow, as at once the symbol and embodiment of true goodness – gentle, long-suffering, the giver of plenty.

'T'ank God!' said Hardai, greatly relieved, greatly pleased.

The Gratuity

Sanyasi wanted his gratuity. The last few weeks he had been thinking of it more and more; and these last few days he could hardly think of anything else. The thing, in fact, invaded his mind with a strange persistence; it gathered a force and momentum over which he lost all control.

Sanyasi was a road-mender. It was not that he felt too tired from age, or could not carry on because of ill-health. He could hardly have been more than fifty-five; and though he often boasted he was sixty-five (or more!) it was only to show how strong and capable he was in spite of his age. No, Sanyasi felt neither ill nor weary. It was simply that he had convinced himself that he had qualified. 'Qualified' was a word that he often used these days.

He would say he had qualified for a gratuity from the government and he would maintain that it was just right and lawful that he should get it. And he was eager to show a good many people in the road-gang itself that he could and would get the gratuity. He wanted it established that he was no fool; that he knew the ropes, while others merely talked.

But he hoped, too, that the gratuity would put an end to his many difficulties. For one thing, he would pay off Sam Lookin, the Chinese provision shopkeeper and retail spirit-dealer, who was becoming distressingly insistent; for another, he would knock down the crude and crooked grass-and-tapia hut that had been housing him, his wife and their two small sons for the last twelve years, and put up a new house – raised off the ground this time – with neat tapia walls and with a roof of galvanized iron. No more grass!

Sanyasi coughed. He sat on a rickety settee in the gallery, thoughtfully smoking a cigarette, and the smoke suddenly rasped his throat. So he coughed, and the cough sent him into a short convulsion, which communicated itself to the settee, which creaked and leaned awry against the half-wall.

Sanyasi, steadying himself, muttered, 'You bitch!' But whether the expletive was directed to the cough, or to the settee, or to the cigarette, no one will know.

He uncrossed his legs (he had been sitting yogi-manner), broke off the burning end of the cigarette, blew on his thumb and forefinger, blew on the salvaged piece of cigarette itself, then carefully put the butt with the matches in the match-box. 'You stay dey,' he said, addressing the half-smoked cigarette.

Then Sanyasi brought both heels right up on the settee, so that his knees nearly touched his chin; leant back against the wall and, encircling his knees with his hands, fixed a meditative gaze on a single blade of grass that hung loose from the thatch.

Then he began to talk – talking not to Dharnee, who sat near by, nipping *bhaji* in a tin basin – but talking to the hanging blade of grass.

'Must get it,' he said. 'Bound to get it. Don' tell me I kian't!' He paused in his soliloquy, and then added: 'Some one t'ousand dollars. Kiant' be less ... Set meself up in business. Mule and cart. Trafficking. Ground provision, banana, breadfuit. Be me own boss. Hm!'

On a sudden Dharnee shoved the tin basin from in front of her. 'Eh, eh!' she exclaimed. 'But what happen? You going crazy or what? Talking to you'self?'

He said: 'Crazy? Who crazy? I ain't crazy. This gratuity business now ...'

'Oh, that!' Dharnee was suddenly full of contempt. 'You will get what you lookin' for,' she said, and did not give

Sanyasi another look. She tried to appear as though she had clean forgotten Sanyasi and his talk of the gratuity, but in truth she could not. She had heard him talk of the gratuity too often, but she had never liked it.

'All the same,' Sanyasi said, disregarding his wife's pessimism, 't'ink I will send in me application.'

He stood up and cast his eye on the thatch, spotted the grass-knife sticking in the grass and took it. 'Goin' for me grass now,' he said to Dharnee. 'You bring in the cow.'

He limped away.

Sanyasi was a joke in the village. Because he was tall and limped badly in one foot, children and even grown-ups teasingly called him Lang Tam Crab-Ketcher; because he had a thick black-and-grey moustache that went up in loops at the ends, many people, but more so the youngsters, facetiously called him *Moach*. As though the man was all moustache and nothing else. But even Dharnee – when she was annoyed at Sanyasi (which was often) – found the moustache quite aggravated her annoyance. The thing seemed to her to embody all the man's pomposity. It certainly imparted to Sanyasi a look of an aggressive quality, that in contrast made the other fellows in the village look tame.

When Sanyasi was not in the company of the elders, say on occasions such as weddings or panchayats, he did not much mind being called Moach or Lang Tam Crab-Ketcher. In fact, he sometimes enjoyed the fun with the hecklers. But when he happened to be with the elders – and he was an elder himself – he took serious umbrage at the bestowers of these epithets. His personality was hurt.

And once or twice he had even been known to hurl stones and bottles as well as abuse – unprintable abuse – at his tormentors.

And his tormentors would simply guffaw and jump about in mad delight.

And Sanyasi would leave the elders and take after the boys, and when he was sure the elders could not hear him, he would say to the youngsters: 'You dogs! You sons of bitches! Who is Moach? Who is Lang Tam? Who is Crab-Ketcher?' And with every question he would shoot a missile, asking: 'Moach is your mother man? Lang Tam is your mother man? Crab-Ketcher is your mother man?'

And the boys would once more jump about in a boisterous harlequinade, keeping at a safe distance from Sanyasi, expertly dodging his missiles – lengths of wood, bottles, stones.

Discomfited, all his missiles going wide of their targets, Sanyasi, shining with sweat and breathing hard, would return to the elders in the cow-pen or in the thatched open hut, or under the mango tree, and would say – the words coming out in pieces – he didn't know what the world was coming to; that the young people were going to the dogs, utterly without respect for their elders.

And the elders would shake their heads to agree with Sanyasi, and one of the company would observe it was all due to lack of training and to *kusanghat* – bad companionship – and all the others would say, yes, it was all due to *kusanghat*.

How or why Sanyasi came to be called Sanyasi, probably he himself could not say. For a *sanyasi* was a holy man, a sadhu, one who eschewed fish and flesh food and intoxicating drinks of all kinds; one, moreover, who usually wore under his *koortah* or merino a bead of the sacred *tulsi* wood. Sanyasi wore no bead of the sacred *tulsi*. He wouldn't think of it. And, far from eschewing flesh and fish, he would make a long and noisy row with Dharnee if a pay-day passed without at least crab or cascadura as part of the evening meal. On the other hand, not only was Sanyasi no teetotaller, but he took more rum than was good for him. If, at the same pay-day meal, Dharnee should hint to Sanyasi that he had already had enough rum for one man, Sanyasi would stop eating and glare at Dharnee and ask what the hell she meant by suggesting that he should have just dry hash. And there would almost always be a long and noisy row; when, to end it, Dharnee would push her things into the old and sagging cardboard box and, weeping copiously, would say she was going –

going anywhere – rather than stay with a disgusting sot like Sanyasi.

And Sanyasi, without a look at her, would emit a sonorous *choops* and say: 'To hell wid you. Tom drunk, but Tom ain' no fool!'

Sometimes the row would take place because Sanyasi would come home quite late after pay, hardly able to walk or talk straight, a cloth bundle hanging from one hand, weighting him down, the bundle containing cascadura or crab or fish among other items of the fortnightly ration – everything hopelessly mixed up: cascadura with flour, sugar with salt; kerosene in everything.

Seeing Sanyasi's top-heavy state, seeing most of the foodstuff irreclaimably spoilt, Dharnee for the first minute or two would be dumb with chagrin. Then she would erupt on Sanyasi: 'But look at this puncheon! Look at this ol' soak, this sponge, this . . .'

Sanyasi's defence would be he couldn't help it. He couldn't have made himself less than a man. The fellows at the rum-shop had stood one another drinks. If he didn't stand his hand when his turn came, he would have been called a nail. It was true he had got himself a little sweet, but it was only because he had to keep his self-respect.

And so it remains a mystery to this day why Sanyasi came to be called Sanyasi. His real name was Jagat-Guru, which meant World Teacher. But only the elders addressed him by it.

And the application for the gratuity was written; and it was Motee, the lawyer's clerk, who was looked upon verily as a lawyer in the village, who wrote it, charging Sanyasi five shillings to do it.

And truly, just as Motee had guaranteed, within a fortnight Sanyasi received a long envelope. It bore on one side the words: *On His Majesty's Service*. Sanyasi, who could read a little, read the superscription and knew at once the communication was for him from the Colonial Secretary. The letter in the long envelope told him that his application for a gratuity had been received and that the matter was under consideration.

Sanyasi jumped with delight.

Another fortnight passed and another letter came to Sanyasi, and this requested him to present himself to the District Medical Officer for a medical examination and report. Sanyasi complied. Amid heavy groans and sighs he told the D.M.O. that he was done for; his back ached so much . . . his belly . . . his . . .

'All right,' said the D.M.O., indicating a cubicle. 'Go in there and take off your shirt.'

A couple of weeks later Sanyasi got a third communication. This requested him to call at Head Office in Port of Spain, in order to receive his gratuity. The letter contained no hint as to the sum involved.

'See!' Sanyasi told Dharnee. 'What I tell you? They callin' me for me gratuity. No mo' hard work, thank God.'

Dharnee made no comment.

The whole village knew Sanyasi was getting a gratuity. Sanyasi had seen to that. He had been going about with the letters sticking conspicuously out of his shirt pocket, so that everybody should see that he was no ordinary fellow. Yes! And the Colonial Secretary addressed him as 'Sir' and signed himself as his – Sanyasi's – 'obedient servant'.

'You don' believe it?' he would say, even though nobody was doubting him. 'Look! See for you'self!' And he would promptly open one or more of the letters, and begin to read.

And the people – young and old – began to show him respect. And Sanyasi wanted them to respect him. It appeared to him that even some of the wicked youngsters had stopped calling him names. At last he was proving it to everybody that he was not one to be trifled with.

Sanyasi went to town.

A Mr Butter took him to the Treasury. Sanyasi was seeing

the buildings for the first time, and he was awed. This was a thing to talk about when he returned to his village.

Only at the counter did Sanyasi learn that the gratuity amounted to exactly one hundred and thirty-seven dollars.

'Sign here,' said Mr Butter, placing the voucher open before Sanyasi and pointing to the dotted line.

Suddenly Sanyasi was quite mortified, quite nonplussed, quite shattered. 'B-but, Mr Butter . . .'

'Shut up, man,' counselled Mr Butter. 'Don't make a fuss.'

'B-but I work mor'an fifteen years.'

'Yes,' said Mr Butter. 'But mostly tasks. Task is contract. Contract doesn't count . . .'

'But Mr Motee say . . . And besides, this kian't buy a mule. Is trafficking I plan to do. Bananas, ground prov . . .'

'All right,' said Mr Butter. 'Take it or leave it.'

'I goin' take it,' said Sanyasi, not knowing how to back out. 'But mind,' he warned, 'I going back to work – and I going write the Governor.'

That afternoon Sanyasi travelled in three stages, patronizing a rumshop at each stop. In the first place, he drank in Port of Spain, stopping at 'The Standard'. Then he hopped off the bus at San Juan. Then, not minding how or when he reached home, he gaily broke off journey at Curepe. He thought he was particularly lucky, for he met friends and acquaintances everywhere he stopped. Most of them he had neither seen nor remembered for years; and on any other day Sanyasi would probably have gone his way without noticing any of them, or at most with no more than a shake of the head or a wave of the hand, to acknowledge mere recognition and to show sense of manners. But that day was no ordinary day. It was indeed a red-letter day. The world seemed to diffuse a wondrous enchantment in which everybody lived, moved and had his being. It was a world that radiated sweet fellowship and unalloyed happiness. And he, Sanyasi, was the centre and source of that happiness, so that everybody he met became hail-fellow-well-met.

He treated them all at the rumshops; called for a quart at the least hint and, pulling out banknotes from all his pockets, repeatedly let everybody know that 'money was no object', and that if Tom was drunk, Tom was still not a fool.

If anyone thought he was a *makhichus* – a miser – he would show him he was not. If anyone thought that his finances were controlled by his wife he would show him he was wrong . . . Sanyasi trod on air; he felt he could almost fly . . . such was his frenzy.

Reaching home at last, he continued the spree far into the night. And the next day, after an hour or two of respite, he called his friends and started the spree afresh. Money? He would sway and stagger and thrust his hands into his pockets . . . He had money. Observing that rum went better 'with a feed', he killed many head of the precious poultry that Dharnee reared; had chicken fried and chicken in curry; paratha, dahl-puri – and rum.

Dharnee sweated at the *chulha*. She was compelled to. The two boys ran to and from the rumshop, bringing and going back for more rum.

No sooner had Dharnee finished the cooking than the men began to eat.

Motee ate sitting on a soap-box. Sanyasi sat on his hams on the bare earthen floor, legs drawn up, back to wall. Nanda and Gokool, Sanyasi's road-gang mates, sat astride at either end of a bench, their plates between them. Juman, the village barber, squatted on his heels.

In the middle of the eaters, within arm's reach, stood the rum bottle; and about the bottle, glasses.

They ate fast and ate with relish; ate with heads down; ate with bare hands; until the hot food broke sweat on their faces.

Sanyasi said, '*Chuts*!' and slackened his belt. Gokool did likewise. Motee belched. Nanda threw back his head and blew through his lips till they rolled like drum-sticks on a drum. 'Kian't eat no mo',' he said, truthfully.

'Open you's belt, man,' said Sanyasi. 'Do like me. Make room for more.'

'Don't leh the glass get cold, man!'

'That's right, man!'

'Good rum, man!'

'Goin' down like oil, man!'

By midday bottles littered the mud floor. The small boy at length gathered them and put them in a corner, saying he would sell them to Lookin and with the money they fetched he would buy a packet of starlights for Christmas.

The eaters praised their host. They praised him in loud, fulsome talk, punctuated with bursts of rum-sodden, tuneless and crooked songs. Sanyasi had indeed qualities of generosity that few equalled. They had always known Sanyasi was a man like that, though they had never said it before. Sanyasi was this, Sanyasi was that. Sanyasi was 'a damn good man'.

And Sanyasi made Nanda and Gokool promise that they would never again call him Moach or Crab-Ketcher or Lang Tam. And Nanda and Gokool struck their chests and said not only would they never call him Moach but they vowed they would do for the man – whoever he might be – who dared to call Sanyasi Moach or Crab-Ketcher or Lang Tam.

And for the moment it seemed they meant every word, and no doubt they did. And because they seemed so earnest, Sanyasi gave them more rum, more chicken, more dahl-puri; said they were good boys, after all.

On the third day of the spree Dharnee fled.

'Let 'er go,' said Sanyasi. 'Tom drunk, but Tom ain' no fool.'

A week later Sanyasi returned to the work gang. He had scarcely been spreading asphalt for three minutes when a messenger from the chief overseer informed him he was not to work.

'What!' exclaimed Sanyasi. Then: 'Why not?'

''Cause you get gratuity,' said the messenger. 'And 'cause you medically unfit.'

'But Mr Motee . . . Mr Motee say . . .'

Disgust spread on the messenger's face. 'Work then, but work without pay.'

Sanyasi tossed away the raker.

'Orright then,' he said, 'but I will write the Governor.'

2

Everybody in the village knew that Sanyasi had got a gratuity and that he had gone and spent a lot of the money on sprees. They knew, too, that when he returned to the road-gang the overseer informed him he could no longer be employed: he had retired on a gratuity on grounds of ill-health. Sanyasi, returning home, told his wife that he was so 'cut-up' that he just had to drown his worries in more rum. Which he did.

By evening he was prostrate. He lay flat on the earthen floor, writhing as in the agony of death. He said he was sure he was dying, and asked everybody's forgiveness for whatever wrongs he might have done, knowingly or unknowingly. He beckoned his two small sons, Rekha and Lekha, and when they came he gave them his blessings with a frothing mouth and counselled them to take care of Dharnee when he was gone.

A lot of people gathered round Sanyasi. One of them began to fan him with a felt hat. Another quickly fetched a green lime, cut it in two and briskly began rubbing one half of the lime on Sanyasi's soles. Dharnee fetched the small bottle that contained *achar* and begged Sanyasi to chew and swallow a piece of the hot mango stuff.

'Open your mouth, man,' she urged. 'Only one piece . . . It is *achar*; it will cut away the rum.'

Sanyasi flung a drunken hand at her.

'Orright, you bitch,' said Dharnee, 'remain there and dead.'

But Sanyasi didn't die. Next morning he staggered up for the tin can on the small shelf against the wall in his room.

The tin can, which once contained condensed milk, was Sanyasi's bank. Whether he had money in it or no, a cowrie always reposed at the bottom of the can. The cowrie was for luck; it was also a symbol for cash.

Squatting on his heels, Sanyasi emptied the contents of the can on the floor – some crumpled banknotes, some silver pieces, some coppers. Slowly, almost painfully, he began to count. He counted the money once, he counted it a second time, repeated the process a third time. Each time he made the total a different amount. His head ached and swirled, and when he belched he still belched rum.

Dharnee, seeing him counting and re-counting the money, said: 'Eh, eh! But you still drunk, nuh?'

'Drunk? I done with that,' he said. 'No mo' rum.' He shoved the money to her. 'Heh,' he said. 'You count it. Me head swimmin'.'

Dharnee quailed. This was no easy matter for her. She had never handled so much money and, even more handicapping, she could count only from one to twenty. Beyond twenty she used grains of corn, or paddy, or peas, or match sticks, whichever were nearest to hand. But counting banknotes was not in her line. Counting banknotes was not the same thing as counting five-cent heaps of mangoes or ochroes or melongenes. You didn't have to know the value of mangoes or ochroes or melongenes by their colour. But it was just this mystery with banknotes. You had to know their colour, and certain marks, to know what they were worth.

A five-dollar banknote was greenish. Sanyasi sometimes brought one or two of these on a pay-day – if he didn't go and get drunk first. There was a figure on it that resembled her grass-knife. Sanyasi had told her that that was a five. A two-dollar banknote was blue, with a mark that had a curl in it like Sanyasi's moustache. A pink paper was one dollar. Sanyasi brought more of these than any of the others. They were the easiest to recognize: they carried a mark that was like the mile-pole before Jankee's house side of the Main Road.

But just how a five-dollar note was different from a twenty-dollar one, Dharnee couldn't say. Sanyasi had spoken of those but had never brought one for her . . . Suppose he had one or two of these today . . .

She backed away from the money. 'Not me, papa!' she said. 'Is how you expect me to count so much money all by meself? Them pink notes now . . . with the mark like you' . . .'

Sanyasi called for a drink of water, and when it was brought him drank a cupful – to steady himself; then he moistened his thumb and forefinger, just as he had seen the paymaster do when paying on pay-days. Then he set to re-checking the money in a most determined way. He counted it twice.

'Sixty-t'ree dollars and one cent,' he said. 'That is all.'

'The balance gone in spree,' said Dharnee. 'Is a hundred and thirty-seven dollars you did get for your gratuity . . . Fifteen years' work. Now what you goin' do? Sit down and scratch?'

Sanyasi's forehead creased in thought. 'Well,' he said, 'I kian't buy a mule, and I kian't buy a horse. Well, is a donkey I have to buy. Is traffickin' I have to do . . . Bananas, ground provision . . . Besides,' he broke off, 'I must show something for me gratuity . . . Oh, me head! I giddy, giddy!'

'Sure!' said Dharnee, sarcastically.

And a donkey Sanyasi did buy. Away in Tobago he went to get it. The creature was at large in a field of scrubby needle-grass. Sanyasi saw it from a distance and at first mistook it for a goat. The owner, a rugged Barbadian, who seemed to have been born with a mellow clay pipe sticking out of a corner of his mouth, didn't seem keen on selling the animal.

'Wot? Sell? Hwoy, I doan't care to sell um,' he said. 'Too young. It ain't finish growing.'

Sanyasi said that it was precisely a young donkey that he wanted. Sanyasi grew persuasive and at length the Barbadian parted with the donkey. He made it clear, though, that he had done Sanyasi an uncommon favour.

'T"ank you!' said Sanyasi, and led away the donkey by one ear till he reached the first shop and bought a length of rope.

One afternoon as Sanyasi stood on the roadside watching the donkey crop the green grass, Motee the law clerk (Sanyasi's best friend), came along. He stopped and leaned on the handlebar of his bicycle and gave the donkey a quick, quizzical look.

'So this is the donkey?'

Motee's question sounded as though he was not sure that that was the donkey. Indeed, he sounded as though he was not sure that that was a donkey at all.

'Yes,' said Sanyasi, smiling. 'This is the donkey. Come from way up in Tobago.'

Motee half closed one eye and gave the animal a searching, thoughtful look. 'Too small,' he commented, 'and half starved.'

Indeed the creature was small. A midget of a donkey it was – only slightly bigger than a big goat. It was in truth the smallest donkey one had ever seen in the village. And not only small, but pathetically and ridiculously emaciated. It stood on spindly legs that looked like props. Its mouse-grey belly bulged and hung earthward, as though gravitation was too much for it. The animal's long, broad ears seemed much too long and broad for the rest of its body. Altogether, its ascetic emaciation, bulging belly, spindly legs and enormous ears made it look like a caricature come alive. It looked a freak that had somehow survived.

'What you going to do with it?' Motee asked.

'Traffickin' . . . Be me own boss,' Sanyasi said.

'How much?' asked Motee, jerking his chin towards the donkey. It was as though he expected Sanyasi to say he had paid ten cents for the animal.

'Forty dollars,' said Sanyasi.

Motee clucked his tongue.

This defied interpretation, so Sanyasi asked:

'What you mean?'

'Too old,' Motee said.

'Not old,' countered Sanyasi. 'Young. He young-young!'

Sanyasi gave a low chuckle, as much as to say it was fun how some people, such as Motee, though otherwise quite intelligent, could not tell a young donkey from an old one.

'Come and see,' he said. 'He front teeth still have to come.' And Sanyasi went to the jackass and promptly forced open its mouth with both hands. 'See,' he said, keeping the creature's mouth agape.

Motee put down the bicycle and went and peeped into the donkey's cavernous mouth. He had a satisfying look; then straightened up and wiped his face and neck with a broad handkerchief.

'It ain't that the donkey so young that all of his teeth ain't grow,' Motee said. 'The fact is, the donkey so old that some of his teeth drop a'ready.' Motee gave Sanyasi a pathetic look and asked, 'Where you buy him?'

Sanyasi said: 'I tell you a'ready – in Tobago. Way up in a place call Canaan. Man who sell it said he was young.'

'What you call it?'

Sanyasi was taken aback. Having never given this aspect of the business a thought, he was suddenly quite puzzled, almost ashamed.

'Oh, nothing,' he said. 'Just Donkey. We call it Donkey.'

'Call 'im Canaan,' suggested Motee, and rode off.

So Sanyasi, patting the donkey on the vertebrae, gurgled, 'Canaan, Canaan, Canaan,' as though murmuring a mantram or incantation, and played his tongue about his lips, as though to get the full taste of the name, and evidently liking it, led the jackass home and told his wife and sons that henceforth they must call the donkey Canaan.

Dharnee thought the name had reference to sugar-cane, but Sanyasi told her she was too stupid, and that the donkey was named Canaan because it had come from a place way up in Tobago called Canaan.

'Oho, *achha*!' said Dharnee, in conciliatory mood, and returned to her *chulha*, mumbling, 'Canaan, Canaan,' so as to get accustomed to the strange name.

Sanyasi had neither a cart nor a single item of harness, but he was eager to try out Canaan. So he borrowed his neighbour Ramu's cart and harness. Of course everything was twice over-size for Canaan, so that the little donkey seemed overburdened with just the harness, leave alone the cart.

'*Jooi*!' shouted Sanyasi, standing in the middle of the cart, reins in hand, a whip slung from one shoulder. 'Hi, you!' But the donkey seemed rooted to the earth, its legs planted well apart. It seemed determined not to move.

Then, recollecting that the donkey's name was Canaan, Sanyasi gave a jerk to the reins and cried with great gusto, 'Hi, Canaan! Canaan, you bitch!' As the donkey still didn't move, Sanyasi yelled, 'Canaan, you mother-ass!'

Canaan went forward a step or two, then stopped.

Sanyasi had given much time to the making of the whip – a whip which carried a handle of poui wood. Now he slashed Canaan with it.

'Get on, Canaan! Hi, Canaan!'

The donkey broke into a surprisingly brisk walk for about six yards, then put on brakes, then stopped.

'*Ha-ya-yai*!' groaned Sanyasi, sweating profusely, shaking his head from left to right and then from right to left, as much as to say that he was damned – that he didn't know what to say or what to do.

It being a 'try-out', half the village had turned out to witness the event. Sanyasi felt quite disgraced by Canaan. He had expected the animal to show some mettle. Instead . . .

'Hi, Canaan!'

Four fellows jumped upon the cart. Sanyasi cast a sour look at them, but much as he wanted to tell them to get to hell, he was secretly afraid to do so, lest they tell him to his face what they thought of the donkey.

'Hi, boy!'

But now the donkey positively could not or would not move. Sanyasi began to belabour Canaan with the stout end of the whip-stick. The creature came very much to life and broke into a pretty trot; but the moment Sanyasi stopped beating him, that moment he slowed down, staggered and stopped.

'Hi, Canaan!'

Suddenly to Sanyasi's cry of 'Hi, Canaan!' someone shouted, 'Hi, Grats!'

Sanyasi quailed. He knew 'Grats' was short for gratuity. He knew some wit was poking fun at him because the donkey represented the gratuity he had received. Now, not daring to call out, 'Hi, Canaan!' he simply wiped the sweat off his face, jerked the reins and shouted, 'Hi, Donkey!'

Half a dozen fellows shouted back, 'Hi, Grats!'

The fellows who had jumped on the cart jumped out and began to shout 'Hi, Grats!' too.

Sanyasi got off the cart, took hold of one of the shafts, and turned donkey-and-cart homeward.

On the way he met Motee.

'Well, and how is Canaan doin'?' asked Motee.

Sanyasi let go the shaft and the donkey came to a dead stop. Gasping for breath, his face and neck shining with sweat, Sanyasi said: 'Canaan? Who Canaan? Is not Canaan. Is me pullin'. Canaan me eye!'